I0614484

Revenge Hit

by

B Davis Kroon

The Ben Leit Series

This is a work of fiction. Names, characters, places, and incidents are either the product of the author's imagination or are used fictitiously, and any resemblance to actual persons living or dead, business establishments, events, or locales, is entirely coincidental.

Revenge Hit

COPYRIGHT © 2023 by Barbara Davis Kroon

All rights reserved. No part of this book may be used or reproduced in any manner whatsoever without written permission of the author or The Wild Rose Press, Inc. except in the case of brief quotations embodied in critical articles or reviews.
Contact Information: info@thewildrosepress.com

Cover Art by *The Wild Rose Press, Inc.*

The Wild Rose Press, Inc.
PO Box 708
Adams Basin, NY 14410-0708
Visit us at www.thewildrosepress.com

Publishing History
First Edition, 2023
Trade Paperback ISBN 978-1-5092-4956-5
Digital ISBN 978-1-5092-4957-2

The Ben Leit Series
Published in the United States of America

The EMTs unloaded a stretcher cart and wheeled it over. It seemed to take hours to stabilize the kid's head and neck. Finally, they slipped a green backboard under the kid, strapped him down, and lifted him onto the cart. To a smattering of applause, they wheeled the kid across the field to the ambulance.

Beeker laid his binoculars aside. He was pouring sweat. It felt like he'd taken that blow right to his middle. No way was he gonna stick around while the crowd amped up and the game got going as if this travesty had never happened. This kid would never be the same, not with that kind of a head injury. He'd be crazy, or mean; he'd wreck the rest of his life doing drugs. That's how it had been with Deek after that SEC game. That damned official should've stopped it. Could have stopped it.

By the time Beeker made it to his Navigator, his chest hurt so much, he ended up just sitting behind the wheel. He tilted his seat back, closed his eyes, and wheezed: one breath, then another.

In that SEC game, when Deek got hurt, it'd been a back judge. This time it was a side judge. And the hit on this kid was even worse than the ones Deek had taken. Those damned officials. No training, that's what it was. Fiascos like this one were their fault.

He needed to get home.

Praise for B Davis Kroon

"Somebody is killing college football officials. As the bodies of the worst of the worst pile up, Ben Leit is called in to help. Will he be able to stop the killer? Or will the needle for Ben find its target? Only one way to find out, read *Revenge Hit*. You'll be glad you did."
~ *Susan Clayton-Goldner, author of the Winston Radhauser mystery series*

B Davis Kroon has deftly blended a very serious and topical subject - violence in football and its lasting effects on its players - with a page-turning mystery. Not easy to do, but Kroon has done it! With its surprisingly human and relatable villain, *Revenge Hit* will take you places you didn't expect. What's more, we are re-introduced to Ben Leit, a hero deserving of many more books. You won't be disappointed.
~William Kenower, author of *Fearless Writing* and *Everyone Has What It Takes.*

"Too many missed penalty calls by a college football ref results in the player's death, and sets off a chain of murdered referees. *Revenge Hit* is a well-told psychological thriller about the hunt for who's killing the refs, and why. Davis Kroon delivers a story that will break your heart. What a great read!"
~ *Lily Gardner, author of the Lennox Cooper mystery series*

Dedication

For David, the boys in the band, and the memory of
CW

Acknowledgments

Trap Play would never have been completed without the support and encouragement of the Fat Friday (writers') group: Lily Gardner, Susan Whitcher, Carolyn Kurtz and Raina Croft. Thanks also to Ben Ly, MD and Miriam Resnick, for their advice and support. And, to the legal and domestic relations professionals I have had the pleasure of working with…no characters in this story were written in your image; rather, working with you helped me imagine Reggie Ford and his staff.

A sincere thank-you to my Wild Rose Press editor, Ally Robertson, for her sage advice and encouragement. Likewise, thanks to the artistic, promotional, and other talented and dedicated professionals at TWRP. Their networking, advice, and support have been invaluable.

Above all, my deep gratitude to my remarkable husband, David Kroon, for his patience, support, and willingness to listen to one more, and then one more, potential plot line.

Chapter 1

"Beeker" Beacham grabbed his binoculars, locked his Lincoln Navigator, and headed for Ohio Stadium. In spite of everything that had happened, he loved football. Loved it for how it could put a spin on an ordinary fall day and fill the air with shouts breaking across the old campus like the sycamore leaves that the grounds keepers would have to cart off during the week. Loved it for the nerve of the quarterback as he planted his feet and stood like a rock in that pocket behind the line, waiting to fire off the ball even as the opposing team's linebackers were rounding the corner to sack him. Loved it for the sweat, for the bruises and bad knees. He loved the smell of the stadium—the stale peanuts and garlic fries. Every home game, he was there, and his heart cracked for the guys (either old men or dead) who'd worn those hero jerseys that now hung like banners in the halls.

He shifted the strap on his binoculars and wound his way past the tailgaters and students. Past a handful of religious nuts angrily shouting their message at fans. Past the pep band and the statues where the younger alums took photos of their kids. Like always, the plaza was packed. The whole place was buzzing with rumors about a national championship.

Once security and the ticket taker cleared him, Beeker stepped into the shadowy underworld of the stadium with its maze of food vendors and sellers of game gear. Garlic fries in hand, he sailed on up to his seat in the Gus Papazian level, right on the 49-yard line. The whole way up, the loudspeakers' pregame reports bounced around the steel girders like pinballs.

Beeker nodded and smiled to the other guys in his box as he made his way to his seat. He reminded himself that once the game got going, he'd get dragged into his share of fist-bumps. He needed to be okay with that. It was what people did. So he went along. He wasn't friends with the guys, exactly. He didn't have friends exactly. He never did have friends, unless you counted chemistry. It didn't matter. The guys had football in common with him. Like Beeker, they had donated enough cash to keep the football program on the up-swing and they were damned proud of it.

They probably thought he'd played football. If they did, they were dead wrong. He'd never played, not even in the back yard. His big brother, Deek, had been a football star in high school. At University of Georgia, Deek had been a full-blown superstar; he'd played linebacker for Georgia in that SEC championship game against Alabama. People still talked about that game. Beeker had been nine years old back then. He'd already been to every high school game Deek had played, but that championship game… Being in the stands that day, it was like being inside a big drum with a hundred people banging on it.

Beeker stripped off his jacket, sat, and spent a few minutes going over the player list in his copy of the *Daily*. As he perused it, he worked that tight place in his shoulder. They'd said it was dislocated. They'd said he'd be fine. But sometimes it still bothered him.

He settled back into his seat just as the team ran off the field and the band lined up. Time for a pre-game serenade. Then the national anthem. The team thundered back onto the field. Then the coin toss. The kickoff.

Late in the first quarter, a visiting team linebacker took down a home team receiver running a wide-out. What the hell? What kind of a hit was that? And, wouldn't you know, the official missed the penalty call entirely. Beeker snatched up his game book, made a note of the time, the failed call, and from then on kept an eye on linebacker 37.

Mid-way through the second quarter, there it was again! Beeker almost dumped his fries as he went for his binoculars. His hand was shaking so bad it was hard to refocus them. But there was 37. Again, clocking another player with the top of his helmet. And still no call for Targeting. Were the officials blind? Seeing hits like that left him so woozy he could barely concentrate on the game.

At the start of the third quarter, the home team was ahead by ten. Four minutes in, the crack of another helmet-to-helmet hit resounded across the field and up into the stands. Loud and sudden. It cut through the roar of the 80,000 fans like a rifle shot. Players froze and stared downfield. The wide receiver and linebacker 37 had full-force collided and dropped to the Astroturf. Then 37 slowly stood, dragged off his helmet, took two steps, then sank to the ground. In an instant, his coaches muscled him off the field.

Beeker's right knee buckled and, for a second, he thought he might be sick. He fought the lurching in his stomach, he fought his damned knee, and breathed. The feel of the binoculars against his face helped him concentrate on the field. He focused on the kid in the red jersey who still lay prone and motionless where he'd fallen.

The kid's legs spread slightly as if he were still running. His left arm splayed away from his body, a perverse echo of the angle of his right arm. A few yards on, that side judge, the same one who missed the earlier hits, stood riveted to the 24-yard line.

A couple of coaches and the medical team were kneeling around the kid in the red jersey. A few feet away, three players hung back waiting for news they could give their teammates. An ambulance rolled partway onto the field. The EMTs unloaded a stretcher cart and wheeled it over. It seemed to take hours to stabilize the kid's head and neck. Finally, they slipped a green backboard under the kid, strapped him down, and lifted him onto the cart. To a smattering of applause, they wheeled the kid across the field to the ambulance.

Beeker laid his binoculars aside. He was pouring sweat. It felt like he'd taken that blow right to his middle. No way was he gonna stick around while the crowd amped up and the game got going as if this travesty had never happened. This kid would never be the same, not with that kind of a head injury. He'd be crazy, or mean; he'd wreck the rest of his life doing drugs. That's how it had been with Deek after that SEC game. That damned official should've stopped it. Could have stopped it.

By the time Beeker made it to his Navigator, his chest hurt so much, he ended up just sitting behind the wheel. He tilted his seat back, closed his eyes, and wheezed: one breath, then another.

In that SEC game, when Deek got hurt, it'd been a back judge. This time it was a side judge. And the hit on this kid was even worse than the ones Deek had taken. Those damned officials. No training, that's what it was. Fiascos like this one were their fault.

He needed to get home.

****

As he turned onto his driveway, Beeker glanced at the time. But that couldn't be right: six hours to make a two-hour drive? He didn't remember pulling off anywhere. Maybe he had. Seeing that kid had upset him. That was probably it. Or, he hadn't eaten. He would nuke a frozen dinner. He drove on into the garage, dumped his coat in the mudroom, and headed through the west wing of the house to the media room. He needed to check on that game.

Deek's photographs filled one long interior wall of the media room. Most of the black and whites were blow-ups from the Savannah Morning News: Deek as a high school freshman in his first game; Deek his sophomore year taking down some kid from Jenkins High—both of them mid-air, legs flying; Deek in his letterman's jacket; his junior year team picture. The ones from UGA were all so glossy and perfect, any of them could've been a cover for Sports Illustrated. In Beeker's favorite, Deek posed in a half-squat, his arms bent, as if he were going to catapult out of the picture frame and cross a scrimmage line that existed somewhere behind the photographer. A bright blue Georgia sky hung over Deek like a promise.

Beeker straightened the picture. "Jesus, Deek. It was your SEC game all over again."

He snagged his media wand off the recliner and turned on his DVR. Once he started the game's replay going, he fast-forwarded to the third quarter and braced his hands on his knees. The ball snapped, the offensive guard missed his block, and there was that sickening hit.

He'd thought he was prepared. But seeing it again, his body still roiled at the sound. He hit the mute button and ran the play again but in slow motion. The second the bodies collided, he hit *pause*.

A white towel lay on the Astroturf. A few feet away, five men squatted around the unconscious runner: one holding the boy's head, two others bracing his shoulders and hips. And standing on the sideline, maybe ten feet away, that damned official, with his mouth hanging open, his arms limp at his sides, and his face as blank as a potato.

Frame by frame, Beeker reversed the recording, then paused it. He walked up to the huge screen, close enough he could've touched it, and slow played what he'd just looked at to be sure what he'd seen.

That official was Deek's old drinking buddy. Pete Webber. Standing there like a stick.

Beeker scrubbed at his left eye.

How old had he been? Five? Or was it six when Deek brought Pete home from school like he'd found a stray dog. Could Pete stay for supper? Pete'd stayed all right. Those last two years when Deek was in high school, Pete had pretty much lived at their house; the two of them sneaking beers out of the refrigerator, smoking dope in the garage. Pete even followed Deek to UGA.

Their mom always said Pete hung around because being friends with Deek made him a *somebody*. But she was careful not to say it in front of Deek.

Beeker pulled a pen from his shirt pocket and tapped the image on his huge TV screen. It made him so mad he could've stabbed right through it.

"You see that, Deek? Pete Webber," he said. "Let's just see where your old buddy's hanging out."

Beeker marched down the hall to his office, parked himself in front of his computer, and jiggled the mouse. On his sixth search, he hit the Pete Webber Real Estate Ltd. website, complete with a smarmy photo of ol' Pete surrounded by a bunch of young women in short skirts.

Pete was living in Savannah. And it looked like he was dying his hair.

Deek would have sure had a laugh seeing that. And he'd have had plenty to say, too. Like, *Would ya look at that jackass working real estate? Hell, Pete's nothing but a waste of real estate.*

Beeker closed out the website and pulled up an e-edition of the Savannah Morning News—plenty of stories on a city hall restoration, a load of politics, a half-page about a local criminal trial they had going. For a nanosecond, he thought of telling his mother what he was looking at. But she was gone too. He knew that, but sometimes it seemed like she was still with him.

She'd loved Savannah. He hadn't been there in years. Nobody there would know him now. He'd been Beeker Sloane back then, skinny, with weird hair and coke bottle glasses, and people scared him so he sort of locked down. He'd just turned twelve when Deek wrecked everything for him. Everything for the family. For a lot of people. After Deek died, his mom had moved them to Ohio and changed their name to Beacham. He'd been Beeker Beacham ever since—Beeker mostly for his thing about chemistry.

But Savannah had been a good place to grow up. Awful at the end, but there'd been good years before. Probably he wouldn't recognize the old neighborhood.

He read through most all the local news, then went for the sports page.

"Football Player Dies from Ohio State Injury."

His chest felt like a hot knife was pushing through him. Like it would cut through to the other side. He wheezed; his elbows bored into the top of his computer desk. His left hand clamped over his mouth. His ears whooshed so loud it was like the ocean. He read the story through, then read it again. When he tried to speak, it felt like he'd been chopped right in the throat.

That kid, twenty years old, died from his head injuries.

Damn them. Damn all officials. They should be doing something to stop this.

Well, they're not, Beeker. So, why don't you?

"Sure! Do something!" Beeker bellowed. "Like what can I do?"

"Well, for a start… Pete coulda made a Targeting call on that first hit. Why not kill Pete?"

Beeker's eyes opened wide. He'd never forget that don't-give-a-shit voice. He glanced behind him. Nobody. But he'd heard what he'd heard.

"Deek?" he said.

Chapter 2

Labor Day Weekend at Husky Stadium in Seattle, and unlike most first games in the season, the U.W. Huskies had a packed house going for their long-time anticipated match with the Baird State (Minnesota) Ironmen. Loud stadium, louder crowd. It looked to be a great game. Who could've figured on that third play? The ball snapped, players exploded from their stance, and a bone-crushing thwack echoed up around the stadium.

A whistle blew the play dead, and the crowd went silent.

Up in the TV broadcast booth, Ben Leit felt that hit so hard he jerked back in his chair. Mack Gaston, Ben's partner for the telecast, motioned they needed to keep their conversation going. He asked Ben about the illegal hits with the crown of the helmet called Targeting. Ben swiped his hand across his mouth, then heard himself answer, "I dunno, Mack. That's one I gotta leave up to the officials."

The field crawled with non-players: five officials huddling, gesticulating; team staff kneeling beside the two fallen players. The Baird State linebacker pushed himself onto his hands and knees, stood, and slowly headed for the sideline. The Huskies' quarterback looked in worse shape. Sprawled on his back, knees bent. A pair of coaches knelt beside him. A man in a purple shirt was cupping a hand under the kid's neck, testing. A minute ticked by, then two. The injured quarterback sat up, his coaches helped him to his feet, and they walked off the field as if the hit was nothing at all.

The fact Ben had managed to form a complete sentence, let alone keep his cool, felt pretty much like a miracle. Because the minute those kids slammed into one another and dropped, it was like the last two years of his life had never happened and he was still lying flat on his back on the 40-yard line of MetLife Stadium. A team doctor had leaned over him. And later, somebody said it took ten minutes to bring him around.

That hit to his head knocked his NFL career clear into the crapper. And afterward, getting the official word about Chronic Traumatic Encephalopathy put him in a tail spin he didn't wake up from 'til he'd nearly killed a guy in a drunken street fight and ended up spending six months in mandatory rehab.

After today's mega-hit, the network cut to a commercial. Mack had been around football long enough, he'd heard all about Ben's concussions. He shot Ben a *you okay* look.

Ben wiped his hands on his jeans, gave Mack a thumbs up, and they were back on air. Anybody watching the game's broadcast would've said Ben did a great job, that he was destined for a big career with ESPN. Which was why, by the time the game wrapped up, he was feeling damned good about himself in spite of his stumble at the start of the game.

Game over, most of the fans flooded out of the big stadium and people either lined up for mass transit or headed for some post-game tailgating in the parking lots. On Lake Washington, the crowd of yachts and sport boats that had ferried fans to the stadium were moving out of their Union Bay moorage and heading either west through the narrow canal that connected Lake Washington and Lake Union, or east to the far shores of Lake Washington: Mercer Island, Bellevue, or points on south (as far as twelve miles on the water).

Ben headed down to the playing field to pick up a couple of interviews with the game's hot players; after that, he was done for the day. He shed the jacket and tie he'd worn for the TV camera, then set out for his house, less than twenty blocks away.

A closed street ran from the east end of Husky Stadium, past a half-dozen other sports facilities, all the way to the jammed parking lots. The whole place was alive with amateur athletes—mostly soccer and tennis players. As he reached the UW crew's Shell House, a herd of runners whooped past him. He'd forgotten that enthusiasm. The way kids jumped in and out of conversation groups. It was like watching flocks of birds swoop and dive.

A little plane towing a game-day message made one last pass over the tailgaters and headed south.

The last of the summer sun beat down on his shoulders as he took the cutoff path through the Union Bay Nature Area. The feathery heads of marsh grass shifted and circled in the late afternoon air. At the top of the marsh loop he stopped for a second just to take in the sparkling lake. It felt like he was the only man on the planet. But then, not ten yards away, a stream of kayakers paddled past.

Labor Day weekend and you could smell the end of summer in the air. The shift in the light, the little breeze, the last of the game fans on the far walkway. It was like a bell ringing inside him. Sure, he'd had a moment when the quarterback went down. Sure, it shook him, but in a couple of seconds he was chatting like old times. It was all good. He was back in football. Not on the field, but deep in the world of it. He could hardly wait for the game next Saturday.

Just after 6:00, he let himself into his house on Lake Washington. Mimi was sitting at the kitchen table, talking on the phone. She gave him an eye-roll—their signal she was on a family call. And who knew what was happening with that. He dumped his gym bag by the stairs, circled into the kitchen, and kissed the top of her head. Not interrupting, not eavesdropping, just he was on her side and wanted her to know. Once she smiled, he headed into the library that had been his dad's office.

There was a load of *saw you at the game* messages on the computer. Some Congresswoman had emailed; he couldn't think who she was. And his agent had forwarded his ESPN contract. *Yes!* He sent it to the printer, pulled out the bottom drawer to his desk, propped his feet up, and started reading his agent's comments.

He was texting his agent back when Mimi dragged a chair around to the side of his desk. She sat and tapped his shoe with her foot. "Me too, please," she said and put her feet up next to his.

She looked like one of those watercolor pictures of pixies, the kind you see in kids' books. But no way she was one.

She'd been a big deal honcho with her family's sports equipment company. In the long run, she might've been CEO. But between the corruption, her nutso family, and a corporate insider almost killing her… She dumped her career and flew into Seattle packing a Glock.

He leaned back in his chair and just looked at her. They'd been together almost a year and it still surprised him. He'd never felt easy with little women, and here she was, barely five feet tall, and she dazzled him. Okay, she was pretty. But what left him amazed was how strong she was. Strong mentally, physically, and strong like a warrior hero: courageous, loyal, dependable. He wasn't good enough for her. He'd never met a woman like her.

He sneaked a deep breath and met her brown-eyed gaze. How lucky could he get?

"How'd it go?" she said.

He pushed the contract pages he'd finished reading at her.

She fingered the first page around so she could see it, but then pulled her hand back and folded her arms. "You didn't say how the game went."

"Great. I was a little nervous going in, but once we got underway, it was great."

Her eyebrows had lifted. Meaning she had some doubts about the game or the contract or the phone call from her family. He focused on reassembling the contract's pages and putting them aside. If she didn't want to talk about the ESPN deal, they could do that later. But he wanted her take on it.

He shifted in his chair. "Something wrong?"

"Not wrong," she said. "I was just…" She had that little crease going between her eyebrows. She licked her lip. "You know, right at the beginning of the game? When they stopped everything to review that play?"

He said, "You watched the game?" How good was that? Finally watching, even without him.

"The one that knocked the quarterback down?" She

eyed him.

"Come on, Buddy. First game of the season, the kids make all kinds of mistakes. You saw it. The guys in the official review box took a look at the play. They're doing that a lot now. Just to send a message they're gonna look at anything close to Targeting this year. That's all."

She studied him. Finally, she said, "When those kids banged into each other, all I could think was how it must feel for you to see him go down like that."

"I'm fine." He shrugged. "Maybe one of us swore and network control cut us off. Dunno. But I'm fine."

"Good," she said and turned the contract around so she could see. But then pushed it away. "If you do this thing with ESPN, how many more hits like that will you see? I mean, what does that do to you?"

Without thinking, he cupped his hand over her knee. "I want you not to worry about me. Everybody was surprised at the hit. I mean, that early in the game. But, no big deal. Who was it on the phone?"

"Please don't."

"Don't what?" he said.

She eyed him a second. "I've seen you watch game film for the website. I've seen how tense you get. It seems like every time you see one of those hits… Don't you flash back to all the times that somebody planted you on the ground?"

"So, you're not okay with the ESPN gig?"

"Your sports website at least has the potential for doing something really good. This TV thing is selling yourself short, don't you think? You could be doing something really important with your life. Think of the impact your dad had."

But he wasn't his dad. And "doing something

important" meant making a commitment he couldn't step away from if it turned out he did have CTE. Why couldn't she see that?

Finally, she sighed. "It kills me thinking what it'll do to you, seeing these guys hurt."

"I see that," he said. And he should have dropped it right then. He'd said enough. But this was not the first time they'd had this discussion, not by a long shot, and he was sick of it.

"What do you want?" he said. "I'm no hero. And I'm sure as hell not the political man my dad became. You say the website eats my time. Why not? I have time. As for ESPN, do you think I'm so fragile I can't watch a football game without losing it?"

She'd been rubbing her hands together, staring at them. Eventually she licked her lips and made that popping sound she always made when she was cutting to the bottom line.

"You're not fragile. You know I don't think that." She put her feet down on the floor and sort of wiggled her shoes. "What I want is for us to be a team again. The way we were when we first met. God, it was like we were finishing one another's sentences back then."

"I thought we still were," he said.

"Yeah but... Anyway, what I want is that feeling, again."

"We can do that," he said.

But she went on as if she hadn't heard. "What I want...maybe it's always been about wanting. I want to fit in. Even before us. I didn't fit into my family. You know that. I didn't fit in as a corporate boss either. The truth is I don't see how I fit into your life now. Because...because I don't want to spend my life doing football."

So what do I do now? Football's my life.

Chapter 3

September 4. Beeker stared straight ahead, not really looking at his computer screen. He'd run out of excuses for not doing something himself. It was true, even if he couldn't fix everything about the officiating mess in college football, he could stop Pete Webber. And he should. Because stopping Pete Webber might save another kid's life.

How long would it take him to pull together enough game clips to convince Pete Webber to quit? A day at most if he used his notebooks. Another day, maybe two, to finalize the DVD. Should he send it as a DVD? Or would it be better to send a zip drive? He'd decide later. For now, he needed the Big10 notebooks.

He jammed himself out of his desk chair and consulted his records wall—one shelf for each of the major football conferences, the other two shelves plus the corners for the minor ones. Color coding the binders made it so simple keeping up. He was proud of his system. Right from the beginning he'd left space for future games.

He pulled the most recent three blue binders off the Big10 shelf and parked them on his computer chair while he set up a folding table. Now it was simply a matter of checking his notes for the game start—that would give him the officials' names. If Pete wasn't listed, he'd move on. Within a few minutes, he had a whole system going.

You're looking for Targeting.

Of course he was looking for Targeting. It was that head injury thirty years ago that made Deek go off the rails.

Pay attention. What about the late hits on the quarterback? You checking those too? They don't always look for a head injury there. And watch the quarterback's chin.

Beeker muttered and kept flagging entries in his binder where Pete Webber messed up. As he finished with the first notebook, he stared across the room. Something outside, on the street, he decided, or maybe a reflection in the glass. Was it Deek?

You forget about chop blocks? A lot of times the top guy ends up leading with his helmet and—

Beeker shut his eyes against the voice. He gripped his hands together and pressed until his fingers hurt. He was done with the voices. They gave him headaches. And after the voices, he knew, was sleepwalking, and who knew what else since there was nobody around to tell him. He was not going to go through it again. It was one thing when his mother died. It even made sense when he sold the company—he was alone, he hadn't built his home lab yet. But not now. Not again.

He took a deep breath and adjusted his binder so he could work at the computer and consult his notes. He shifted the data source on his computer over to the cpu he'd set up to hold Big10 games. He called up the first game, fast-forwarded to first quarter, game clock 7:23…and there was Pete Webber's blank mug.

He was in business.

By 2:00 a.m., Beeker had nineteen examples of Pete Webber not doing his job saved in video clips; eleven clearly showed at least one player limping off (or being carried off) the field. Except for writing the demand letter to Webber, and cloning the game clips onto a couple of DVDs, and shipping, he was done. Good job, Beeker! He'd earned a celebratory shower.

Before you break out your collection of loofas... You forget about that other Big10 official? John Brown?

Beeker's eyes slammed shut. He was not listening. Deek could go jump.

John Brown's just as bad. He worked some of the same games as Pete. You just been looking at him.

He was not going to think about John Brown. This was about getting Pete Webber off the field. His project was nearly complete. He was going to bed.

September 5. Beeker jammed on the clothes he'd worn the day before, microwaved a *Healthy Morning* breakfast and stuffed it down. Sausage was good, the rest was crap.

Back to his office.

The Big10 binders were right where he'd left them beside his computer. But…he'd used little red flags to mark the Pete Webber screw-ups. Now he was looking at yellow flags, seventeen of John Brown's screw-ups. He must've been sleep-walking.

Okay. He'd do John Brown, too. What could it hurt?

He fanned his way through his Big10 game notes and, clearly, John Brown was just as bad as Pete Webber. Two kids had been seriously concussed.

Beeker flicked the little yellow tags with a finger.

When he thought about it, getting rid of more than one man made sense. Making an example of two plainly incompetent officials would make it more obvious that his campaign was not personal. The issue was incompetency of the officials and that players were being wrecked. And it wasn't just the immediate damage. Some of those injuries would be permanent.

Would the idiots in charge of officiating realize that? He would make sure they did in his letter.

Again, he accessed his bank of Big10 games and followed the same process as the day before, this time focused on John Brown. By early afternoon, he had Brown nearly wrapped up.

In spite of how hungry he was, he finished downloading the Brown clips. Then made himself a sandwich. He was putting the turkey and mayo back in the fridge.

What about the Big12? You think they don't need to be taught a lesson?

Beeker closed the refrigerator door with a whomp.

You think the Big12 pays any attention to the Big10?

He was not going after another one.

Okay, fine. You don't care if some guy goes off the rails and shoots his family because his head's killing him. You don't care if he runs down some innocent jogger with his car. You don't care if—

Beeker whirled and glared around at the empty kitchen. Well, that was not true. He did care.

You care enough to walk out on a football game but not enough to do something about it. Oh, I get it.

Beeker stood in the center of the kitchen, huffing. He hated it when Deek got like this. He was not giving in. He was not... He was. "Who is it?" he said. "Who is it in the Big12? Who are you talking about?"

"Ooooo, I don't know. How about Lex Mincey? He'll blow your head off. Take a look. Big12 binders. They're orange in case you forgot. Bottom shelf."

Back in his office, Beeker set aside the all-but-complete compilations for Pete Webber and John Brown. He returned his Big10 binders to their proper shelf and retrieved the last three binders of Big12 games—not quite four years' worth, but close.

He set to work on the Lex Mincey games, flagging the notes that might relate to head injuries.

"If you're not impressed with Mincey, I could show you a guy in the Atlantic Coast Conference, or there's two in the SEC, or…there's a guy in the Pac12 that looks like he slept through an entire year, or…oh, there's a guy used to be in the SEC that moved to Arizona; he shows up in Mountain West games. But there's also—"

Beeker slapped a hand down on the binder he'd been reading. "Deek! Just hold it right there."

"Come on, Beeker. You been planning to do something like this for a long time. Why else set up these color-coded binders? Why else get a copy of most every college football game played? Why keep 'em on that big cpu in the corner? You think I didn't know about that? I bet you got more recorded football games stored on that thing than Fox Network and ESPN combined."

Beeker reached back and worked a kink out of his neck.

"How come you haven't done anything about it before now?" Deek said.

"I tried," Beeker said. "Last year after I sold the company, I spent months writing, emailing, calling, texting. I started with the NCAA but it turns out officiating is separate bunch called American Football Officiating. I never got anywhere with them."

"They need to get taught a lesson," Deek said. "You get that don't you? If we go after these conferences—"

"You know there are ten football conferences, right? You want to go after ten people? Twelve? Twenty? I don't think so. We are not going after that many people."

"You don't care what they're doing? You just want to be done with your project."

Beeker's throat convulsed. He couldn't get a decent breath. He worked his mouth like a trout, but couldn't get air. His eyes swam with tears—burning and washing down his face at the same time.

He did care. It destroyed him thinking what these kids went through. What their families went through watching their young men get wiped flat on the field.

He struggled a handkerchief out of his pants pocket and mopped his face. "You're wrong. I do care about these kids. But I know how you are, Deek. There will always be another."

Deek snorted. "Big10 and Big12. You think anybody from the East Coast or the South is gonna pay attention to them? Or West Coast for that matter?"

Beeker let go the breath he had latched onto. It was true, or at least likely, the other football conferences wouldn't see Webber, Brown, and Mincey as proof of a problem with all of college football. They sure wouldn't admit the officiating problem was their problem too.

"Okay." Beeker hated giving in, but Deek had a point. "Okay but just two more men. Two. I mean it. You pick which ones, and that's it. That's what I'm doing. Two. Old Pete, plus John Brown. I'm almost through with Lex Mincey, so him. Who else?"

"Five would be a good start. Let's see…West Coast: in the Pac12 the guy is named Matt Redweather."

"Okay. And the other one?" Beeker said. "Don't go rogue on me."

"Okay. The guy who used to be in the SEC that's with the Mountain West now. Chris Matsen."

Beeker's face was still burning. It hurt him, Deek saying he didn't care. Nothing was farther from the truth. It felt like the lives and safety of hundreds of kids were riding on him.

Once Deek shut up, Beeker finished downloading clips for Mincey, then wrapped up the games for the other two men. It was done in less than three days. He leaned back and stared at the list of game clips he'd pulled together.

For the last stage of his operation, Beeker used the computer in his lab. Which meant donning a hazmat suit, head gear, gloves, booties—the full regalia. He made peel-off labels for each of the packages. He prepared a separate letter to each of the officials using cheap white photocopy paper he'd purchased from a box store and hadn't opened until he was inside the lab. The Readers' Digest version of each letter: *Quit or retire. You'll regret it if you don't.*

He labeled each of his master discs with the official's name. He wiped down every label, page, and disc with tack cloth, then used a TCA cleaning cloth on every surface. Finally, he vacuum-sealed all five sets in a plastic and stored them in tomorrow's carry-on bag. Last step at home, he booked a flight to Atlanta—the U.S. airport with the busiest domestic traffic—and he booked two other flights to come home: Atlanta to JFK and LaGuardia to Cleveland.

The next morning, Beeker, traveling as Declan Sloane, flew into Hartsfield-Jackson International and cabbed to a downtown Atlanta mail service. The girl behind the counter was pretty in that cheerleader way, except she had a gap between her front teeth which Beeker couldn't stop looking at.

"You have nine-by-twelve envelopes?" Beeker said, doing his best to look helpless.

She did. How many would he like?

"Uh...my wife said...um...I'm supposed to have five packages go out. It's all in here," Beeker flopped his hermetically sealed plastic bag on the counter. And bless her heart, the girl sorted the packages and labeling out for him: Webber label on the envelope, Webber disc and letter inside, flap sealed, taped for security. And the same with the others. He hadn't even found it necessary to explain why he wasn't touching anything.

"And it'll go out today?" he said.

"Oh, yes sir. Just regular mail or...?"

"Regular's fine," Beeker said and paid cash. The postmark on all the packages was a mail drop in Atlanta. Who could say where they really came from? Exactly as it should be.

Deek might be seeing it as vengeance. But *he* didn't. This was about justice. And justice is way more powerful when it's anonymous.

He cabbed out to the Atlanta airport and Declan Sloane flew on to JFK. The cab ride from JFK to LaGuardia cost a bundle but worth it. Declan Sloane disappeared at JFK. Beeker flew home under his own name—no connection at all to Atlanta.

At home, first things first, he took that celebratory steam he had earned. He used an exfoliating mitt to scrub Webber, Brown, Mincey, and the other two out of his system. Then he shaved and waxed himself. Like he always did when he wrapped up a project.

It felt like he'd been reborn.

Chapter 4

Ben left his house on Lake Washington just after 10:00 a.m. and walked over to the University Village Starbucks.

Two days earlier, Skip Jackson (American Football Officiating's Security Liaison) had called asking for his help. And he had jumped at the idea of getting together with Jackson. Meeting with an AFO insider seemed like a golden opportunity to get a better handle on that side of the college game. Good for his website connections, good for his credibility as a TV commentator.

Of course, Mimi wouldn't be exactly celebrating if he agreed to handle an investigation. Which was what it sounded like they wanted him to do, investigate. But he could just call it a consult. She wouldn't worry about that.

From the phone call, he'd assumed Jackson was middle-aged, or even older—head of American Football Officiating's Security after all.

Obviously, he was wrong about that. Because the twenty-something putting in his coffee order was staring at Ben like *Be there in a minute*. And because, in Seattle, how many guys do you see wearing cowboy boots and a hubcap-sized belt buckle?

Ben snagged his usual coffee off the phone order counter, headed across the room, and grabbed a chair. A minute later, Jackson strolled over and stretched out his hand.

"Mr. Leit, I have to thank you for making the time to talk with me. I probably didn't make much sense on the phone. But we're hoping you can help."

"Let's hear what you got to say," Ben said.

Jackson angled his lanky frame into his chair. "Like I said on the phone, we have a man making threats to our officials. Serious threats. And we figure your website has to have heard from him, he's a football know-it-all and a complainer. And since your website covers all of college football—"

"We do our best," Ben said.

"Well, that's just it. You guys are coast-to-coast. Millions of subscribers. This guy has to be reading your stuff."

Ben sipped at his coffee. They had just over four million paid subscribers, but millions more people followed them on Twitter and LinkedIn.

"We think maybe he posts on one of the fan chat rooms in the Big10 conference."

"What makes you think Big10?"

Jackson shifted in his chair. "The first official he threatened works Big10 games. He has to be posting somewhere because... See, this guy is a complainer, but he really knows how to look at a football game and see what's wrong with it. He must be posting on one bulletin board or another. We're hoping you can come up with an email address, or if we're lucky, a name."

Ben put his cup down. "I assume you've already talked with the police."

"Uh... It's not that simple," Jackson said. "All I have is a few threats and one DVD. I brought a copy." He fished a zip drive out of a portfolio and laid it on the table.

It was written all over Jackson's suntanned face, he'd been for calling the cops. Somebody higher up the Officiating organization must've shot him down. Did that make sense to keep the police out of it? If AFO waited, and some official was attacked, the media would have a field day. On the other hand, if AFO brought in the police and the threats amounted to nothing, they would look like a bunch of fools.

Ben cleared his throat. Not his problem to solve.

"As far as the website goes," Ben said, "there are lot of football nuts out there. A lot of them use our chat rooms to blow off steam. I mean, it's thousands of comments a day during football season. So I'm not sure it makes sense to start looking at posts on our website in the hope you're going to find your man. And the truth is, I don't know how we'd even go about searching the website for your guy in all our chat rooms. Our administrator might know but... I think you're way better off talking to the police. Or FBI. Or, what about Homeland Security?"

Jackson's face pleaded for Ben to offer to help. "I shouldn't say this, but I'm afraid my bosses will just sweep it under the rug. I mean, this guy's not going to stop at telling some official *You'll regret it*. That's a threat even if he doesn't say what he's going to do. Check the files. Read his letters. He's screwy."

Jackson tapped the zip drive. "He sent a pair of three-hour DVDs to Pete Webber. The clips are from at least eighteen different football games, played over a five-year period, with a bunch of different schools."

"No consistency you can track in the games? Stadium? Cities?"

"Well, some. They're all Big10." Jackson shook his head. "You gotta think how many games this nutcase watched to put this thing together. How many times did he go over a play to get the clips that went into each DVD? Days? Weeks? A month? Who spends that kind of time if all he wants is to rattle somebody's cage? That's what worries me. He's not just blowing off steam. I get it, nothing has happened. But I don't want to wait until we have a shooting spree in some stadium, you know?"

Ben reached over and fiddled with the zip drive. He hadn't thought about a shooting spree. "How many officials has he sent these to?"

"Four men reported receiving them," Jackson said.

"Who?" Ben said and immediately wanted to kick himself. Asking was one more step into getting involved.

"There's two guys in the Big10: John Brown and Pete Webber. A Texas man, Lex Mincey, and a guy in Southern California, Matt Redweather. The DVDs I have are from Mr. Webber. But that's the trouble. It's only been a few weeks. There could be more guys that got this stuff. There may be more to come, we don't know. It's not like we can email every official, *Had any death threats lately?* Anyway, that's when I thought of you."

"You mean personally. Besides the website?"

"Well, yeah. We were kicking around what else we could do and I thought, Ben Leit's the perfect man to track this guy down. He hunted down a killer last year. He's not connected to the AFO, so…"

Getting involved personally was exactly the kind of a deal that would set Mimi's hair on fire. And she had a point: he'd made himself a target last year and nearly died in the process.

28

"Mr. Jackson, I think you have a wrong idea about me," Ben said. "I'm no detective."

"Call me Skip. Mr. Jackson's my dad. Could we at least get help from your website? I mean, if there was a way to check the bulletin boards your fans post on. Even just for the three football conferences we know he's been following."

"I would need to run it by the website board," Ben said. "You get that, right? It's not just a big website, it's a bunch of people involved."

Really, he needed the time to talk with Mimi. He hoped, once she saw there was no risk to him, she'd be okay.

"I'll try to get back to you by the end of the week, okay?"

He walked Jackson to the parking lot and waited until the car disappeared into traffic.

Back at the house, no Mimi. She'd left a note it was his turn to cook dinner.

Plenty of time for that. He headed into his office and downloaded the stuff on Jackson's zip drive. Which turned out to be a letter to the official named Webber and a media file. The letter didn't exactly make a death threat, but close enough. One thing stood out. The letter didn't have the usual misspellings, rants, or screwy wording like the stuff he'd seen posted in the website's chatrooms by the crackpot contingent.

The media file was comprised of clips from close to twenty games. He did a quick survey, and it seemed to him like every play should've had at least one penalty called, mostly for Targeting. But there were plenty of chop blocks and roughing the passer calls that probably should've been made, too. And there was always this one official standing around looking confused. Presumably Webber.

Ben flopped back in his desk chair and rubbed his eyes. This official, Webber, was completely incompetent. Why hadn't the guy received thousands of threats, that was the question.

Forty minutes later, he was putting the finishing touches on his memo to the website Board about Skip Jackson's request for help. Mimi backed her way through the front door and hefted two bulging bags onto the entryway floor. She had a look on her face like she'd just struck gold. "Bookstore," she said, peeled off her coat and draped it over the banister.

She swooped by his desk just long enough to wrap her arms around his shoulders and say, "Your Lincoln book still isn't in."

Before he could respond, she kissed him right below his ear and took off upstairs.

He could've asked her to stick around. He could have told her about his meeting with Jackson. But it didn't make sense to go down that road until he heard back from the board. Besides, she'd already made it halfway upstairs. He wrapped up his memo and pressed send.

Three hours later, he was dumping linguini and sauce into a pasta bowl and adding the sausages. That dish looked just like the picture in the magazine. Not bad if he said so himself. He grabbed a brick of Pecorino Romano out of the fridge and glanced across the foyer to the office where Mimi was still on the phone call she'd been on for the last hour.

Something hot was going on in Minnesota. He figured it was part of the federal investigation of her family's corporation. Her uncle, a manipulative jerk if ever there was one, had called at all kinds of unreasonable hours. And two thick envelopes had arrived for her from the U.S. Attorney's office. Most troubling: in the last few minutes of eavesdropping, he'd heard *Dad* way too many times.

"He did *what*?" She'd virtually yelled. And she never yelled. *And*, she had that little crease going between her eyebrows. She looked up and caught him staring.

He waggled the cheese at her and motioned at the table. The salad was waiting. The pasta was getting cold. Translation: he was starving. Truth: he needed to get her off that damned call before she exploded.

She nodded and said something into the phone. Whatever she said though, clearly didn't make any difference to the person on the other end of the line. She let go a long sigh and clapped a hand on the top of her head.

"Okay, okay." She hung up without saying goodbye. Then hustled into the kitchen and scooted onto her usual place on the kitchen banquette. She looked tired and owlish. Worse, she looked resigned.

To bypass the *who was it, what did they want* questions, he set man-size plates of pasta and sausage on their placemats and went to work grating more cheese. In seconds, the only sound in the kitchen was the clink of his silverware. Mimi had picked up her fork but it seemed like she was just rearranging her dinner. For sure, she wasn't eating.

"You all right?" he said.

She pushed her hair out of her eyes. "Uncle Ted says the feds are being reasonable but the plea deal keeps falling apart because of Terry and Larry Gilmore. They're still blaming Dad for everything. Everything. And that's just not fair." She glanced up at him and grimaced. "Anyway, I said I'd fly out tomorrow morning to help."

Tomorrow?

"How about I come with you?" he said. Not that he wanted to get involved in her family business. But he knew she was going to need an ally if she was dealing with both her dad and her uncle.

Her face shifted expressions about four times and settled on the resolved one with the stubborn chin. Pretty clearly, she hadn't thought he'd offer to go.

"Actually, this is one I need to handle myself," she said. "I'll be fine."

With a grin, she scooped her fork into her pasta, twirled it, and finally took a first bite.

Not worth it to push her about it. She'd already made her point: she needed a life.

But when a woman talks about needing a life… He couldn't help flashing back to when he was married. Kay had needed a life. She went to law school, and next thing he knew, they were headed for divorce court. Had he noticed anything wrong before he got the divorce papers? He had not. He'd been too swept up having his own life as a newbie in the NFL.

So, this time he was paying attention. "I'll miss you, you know," he said. "I get it, you need to go, but don't decide to move back there, okay?"

She stopped, another forkful midair, she looked at him for a second or two, then smiled. "Good job on the sauce. Thanks for doing dinner," she said.

He didn't trust her family, not after what had gone

on the year before. But she was tough. She'd be okay. And he could manage a while. By the time she got back, maybe Skip Jackson's problem would be in everybody's rear view mirror and she'd never need to know.

Watching her, though... Any fool could see something in the call shook her.

He pushed himself back from the table. "Why not hold off going for a day or two," he said. "Your dad can handle things. How about a getaway, just the two of us? We could take that place on Orcas Island you like so much."

"You're trying to make this about us. It's not about us," she said.

"I'm concerned about you," he said. "Where will you stay?" Not her dad. Please, God, not her uncle Ted.

She rolled her eyes. "My house, of course. Don't worry, I'm coming back. It's just...you know how Uncle Ted can be."

He did. Ted saw himself as The Hero because he blew the whistle on corruption inside the company. Had it ever occurred to Ted Halliday that bringing in the feds might put Mimi in danger? Apparently not. Ted had been right, and being right was all that mattered.

"You're sure you don't want me along? I hear I can be pretty good company."

She spent the rest of the evening packing. By the time they hit the sack, it felt like she'd already left for Minneapolis. The night sky ghosted their bedroom.

Just get through the night, get her on the plane and be Mr. Cheerful about it.

The shadow of her, the turn from her little waist... That was the thing, wasn't it? She always went to sleep curled against him. And tonight, she was hanging off the end of the earth with her back to him.

He reached up, behind him, and shifted the draperies so the light fell across their bed.

That hip… It made him hurt just watching her. And her skin so cool and soft…

He could've reached over to touch her. Sex might've helped. It sure would've done it for him. At least for the night. He rolled onto his back and tried making sense of the random-patterned ceiling.

Not sleeping. … Not sleeping. … Not sleeping.

He was going over what she'd said for the five hundredth time when the sheets rustled. And she curled against him.

Chapter 5

It didn't matter they were watching today's SEC game. Deek was still at it. "You see that tackle? You got to include this guy."

Beeker clamped a hand over his eyes and stretched back in his media room Barcalounger. Deek was right: they were looking at another kid somebody'd flattened—this time on the Astroturf at Mississippi State football stadium.

"That nickelback shoulda been called for Targeting right then."

Was this the way it was going to be from now on? Deek, bitching, insisting on adding more names? Always the voice from the next room over? Always in his life, but never really there?

"Five is enough!" Beeker said. Quietly, emphatically, using his no-argument voice. "Five is more than enough."

"You mean we just leave out the SEC?" Deek huffed.

Beeker shut the game off. He knew better than to yell. He also knew there was no point in confronting Deek. Because Deek wouldn't even be there. There'd just be the echo of Deek, and that chemical smell.

"Listen to me, Deek. Threatening another bunch of officials will just mean we don't know what we're doing. It implies we're just some nutty fan screeching about every other guy in a striped shirt."

"You don't get it—"

"Deek, I don't care how bad this SEC guy is. Maybe he just had a bad day today. You don't know. I'm telling you: No. More. Letters. Not to SEC officials or the Atlantic Coast Conference officials, or... Not to ANYBODY!"

"You *don't* even know what day it is," Deek brayed.

Beeker angled himself around, sat up, and pushed himself off the huge recliner. He needed air. He took off for the front porch. "It's Saturday," he snapped. "Okay? That's what day it is. Saturday."

Deek's Georgia drawl followed him down the hall— "Jesus, Beek... Hold on, Beek... Dammit, Beeker. A month ago, you crack up over this kid you saw go lights out and the Targeting call that shoulda been made. You spend the whole month staring at DVDs of Pete Webber's screw-ups. And now you can't remember what day it is?"

Beeker could feel Deek swirling around him.

He didn't care. And he hadn't spent a month working on those DVDs. It was a week, plus the travel for mailing. He stopped in the foyer, his hand gripping the front door handle. He would stay calm. Calm. He would not raise his voice. "Okay, what day is it?" he said.

"It's Pete Webber Day! Didn't you check the officiating list? Pete's still working for the Big10. He's out there today looking the wrong way, just like usual. I guess that's what he thinks of your threatening letter, huh?"

A blinding light hit behind Beeker's eyes. He grabbed for the bridge of his nose and pinched. He was bleeding. He made a dash into the kitchen, grabbed a towel, and jammed it against his face. Next stop, the refrigerator. He dragged out the bottom drawer and fumbled an icepack from the freezer. He checked the towel: still bleeding. He wrapped the blue slab in a fresh kitchen towel and headed for his bedroom.

Hours later, he woke up starving.

He made it to the kitchen, praise the Lord apparently without Deek's help, and pulled together some leftovers.

"I didn't mean to wind you up." Deek's voice, for once, sounded genuinely sorry.

Beeker laid the spoon he'd been using in the sink and, literally, counted to ten. He would not respond. He would not be angry. He would finish making his dinner.

"You still think about that kid? The one in the Ohio State game."

The microwave beeped and Beeker carried his leftover roast beef and mashed potatoes to the kitchen island. He arranged his plate and silverware the way he liked and sat. Yes, he thought about the kid. But he was not going to discuss it.

"He was a heck of a receiver, you know?" It sounded like Deek actually admired the boy who had died. "If you look at the first half of that game, before he got hit. He was really fast; you could see that. Must've done a 4.20. He could've played on Sunday, you know? Maybe even gone in the first round of the Draft. Just think what he missed. And mostly thanks to ol' Pete."

Beeker stuffed a mashed potato load into his mouth. It tasted like cardboard. He knew how it would be now, with Deek obsessed. The talk about that kid and the game and Pete Webber would go on until he found some way to shift Deek's attention.

Beeker kept his focus on his plate. Deek could talk

all he wanted; he wasn't going to answer.

"You gotta know, Pete Webber hasn't given that kid a thought. Not even now."

What made it so bad, every time he heard *that kid,* all he could see was that broken body sprawled on the grass and that little shrug Pete Webber gave as the ambulance drove off the field. Beeker forced himself to swallow. This was what his future would be. Smothered by that voice. He wasn't sure he could stand it.

But what if he didn't take Deek on at all? What if he refused to talk about the game or the kid who died, or Pete Webber? What if he went back to being the bored and boring scientist?

Would Deek go back to wherever he'd come from?

"Not the way it works, Beeker. You know that."

Beeker's fork slipped through his fingers and clattered to his plate. Could Deek hear inside his head?

"Come on, Be-e-e-eker. You know what needs to happen to ol' Pete. It'd be like putting a dog out of its misery. Pete never gave a damn about anybody but himself. He didn't even show up for my memorial service."

Beeker stirred at the brown goo on his plate. "We didn't have a memorial service."

"A lot you know."

"What do you mean, *a lot you know*?" Beeker said. "I know. I remember. I might've been a kid, but I was there."

Deek snorted. "I had friends, you know."

Beeker snatched up his plate, chucked what was left of the meat and potato in the garbage, then rinsed his dishes and loaded them in the dishwasher. Arguing with Deek was like arguing with God. Not that God was looking to kill a bunch of people.

Beeker stared around the immaculate kitchen, struggling to see something to distract his brain, something he should take care of. He'd never killed anything. Unless you counted going fishing. And he'd spent his life developing medicines that help people.

"Face it, Beek. Your best chance to get rid of me is to get rid of Pete Webber."

"Get rid?" Beeker spluttered. "How am I gonna get rid of Pete Webber? I don't have a gun. I wouldn't have the slightest idea how to kill Pete Webber."

"What about that stuff in your lab? You think I don't know about that? All those anesthetics you been working on? You could take out ten Pete Webbers and nobody would ever know what killed 'em."

Chapter 6

Ben slowed the treadmill from run…to jog…to stop. He turned off *Top Chef* and parked the remote on a shelf. Mimi'd been gone two and a half weeks. He missed her so much he ached. Funny how you could miss somebody so much when, a year ago, you didn't even know them.

He stretched his quads and stared around at the big party room they'd turned into a home gym. The house felt like an empty tomb and his workout had done nothing to shift that feeling. He turned back to the windows that opened out onto the lower deck.

It was a lousy day: a lowering sky, the rain-soaked terrace stretched out to the gray steps that led down to the dock on Lake Washington. Gray, gray, gray. You could feel the cold through the glass. And the chop on the water rolled out leaden and cruel until it disappeared into what looked like distant ghost shapes that he knew were the hills to the south.

It felt like everything was disappearing. He mopped the back of his neck with a towel.

Part of him had been thinking, once he signed a long-term contract with ESPN, once he got the okay from his doctor, maybe he'd talk with her about marriage. But was marrying her fair? What if they got married and three years down the road, he turned into vegetable thanks to CTE? But if he didn't develop CTE, and she got swallowed up in her family's business, where were they then?

For damned sure he wasn't gonna ask her to marry him in their nightly phone call. Maybe he'd call early. Just hear her voice.

She picked up on the second ring. "Are you okay?" It sounded like her mouth was full. "What's up?"

"Listen," he said. "I'm going nuts here missing you. What if I fly back to Minneapolis for a day or two?"

She was taking way too long to answer. He said, "I'm sorry, Buddy. If my coming back there makes it worse, I won't push you on it."

"It's not that."

"What if I said I'm gonna be in St. Louis anyway for a board meeting? You're on the way."

"I thought you guys were doing your meetings on Zoom."

"We were. But the guys are getting together at Jack Halprin's. You remember him. How about I swing by for a couple of days beforehand?"

She gave out one of those little grunts she made when she was frustrated. "It's just, there's never any time here. I'm up at five, I head into corporate headquarters, prep for the government team, they show up at seven, we work all day—"

"I'll pack you a lunch, how about that? We'll get together when you get home."

Silence. Then, he knew that sound, potato chips.

"I'll cook your favorite dinner."

"You know how to hurt a woman."

"How about if I throw in a back rub?" he said.

****

Seventeen hours later, she met him at the airport. She looked tired. Up close, of course, she managed a hug, a kiss; but took off for the car. *Overwork,* he decided. Because she talked the whole way to her car about the delay on the deal with the U.S. Attorney— distant cousins who'd never worked in the company had an ax to grind and they were taking this opportunity to deliver a whole bunch of whacks at her dad. She looked tired, but she sounded so strong—that much, at least, was good.

The real greeting came in the parking structure. He stopped her before she climbed into her car, kissed her the way he should have when he first got there, and held her. Held her long enough he felt her relax against him, felt her tuck her head under his chin and rest there. Felt her shiver when she took a deep breath and released it.

"So," he said. "What's going on?"

Most of her answer was more family story. Managing the family shareholders and former shareholders, it turned out, had been the assignment the company lawyers had given her.

She untangled herself from his arms, he assumed in order to wrap up her story. Instead, she said, "We're not doing dinner at home tonight. I'm sorry."

Well, that was disappointing. He'd had quite a menu in mind. "Not?"

Her Aunt Madge had organized a family dinner. Just Madge and Uncle Ted, and Mimi's dad.

Just? "No problem," he said. "I'll have dinner for you tomorrow. How's that?"

"You're sure? You're okay with a family dinner?" Her nose wrinkled like something smelled not right. "I know Ted's not your favorite person."

Dinner with that blowhard Ted would be like tiptoeing across a minefield. Adding Mimi's dad... That would be like doing the tiptoeing, but wearing clown shoes.

"I'm good," he said.

Bad enough Mimi's dad and uncle had an historic battle over who would be CEO of the family corporation. The great David Fitzroy won the fight by burying the hatchet in his brother-in-law Ted's back. And if that wasn't enough history to deal with, there was also the way Mimi's dad had treated her.

Word was, Fitzroy had turned narcissism into an art. The fact that he'd been stuck with a daughter, that her teachers said she was brilliant—Fitzroy wanted a kid who'd be useful, business-smart, somebody to make him look good. Not somebody brilliant.

When Mimi had first told him her family story, it had sounded like a soap opera. But an unauthorized biography of her dad came out the same week he announced his candidacy for the U.S. Senate. It came out the same week stories began to leak about corruption at Rex Sports. That bio not only scuttled Fitzroy's campaign, it also made it pretty clear that Mimi's family stories were right on the money.

History aside, the family dinner started out with everybody on their best behavior: Ted, not his usual bald-headed pushy self; and Fitzroy, engaging, courteous, interested, and it seemed like supportive. Still, like all *meet the boyfriend* dinners, there were too many stories about dead relatives and family holidays. Fitzroy had done his homework on Ben and had a couple of penetrating questions about the TV commentator world and how Ben had made the switch from NFL superstar to "retirement." The idea of retirement became its own topic. And Ben could see they were headed for trouble, given the possibility that Fitzroy might be "retiring" to a federal prison unless the company's (and Fitzroy's) lawyers could do a deal with the feds.

As if she'd suddenly thought of it and couldn't wait any longer, Mimi's Aunt Madge piped up with, "Mimi retired once. Did she tell you? She was a national champion gymnast. Well, junior division, but she was."

"She would've been a national champion if she'd stuck with it. Instead, she ran away from a little competition." Fitzroy might have thought he said it like he was teasing, but Ben couldn't see anything but disappointment. Twenty years, and the guy was still holding a grudge against his daughter.

Mimi was sitting way too straight and way too still. Whatever was next wasn't gonna be good.

Ben made a point of grinning at Fitzroy. "But she's a runner now. Every morning. She runs rings around me."

Madge managed to shift the talk to sports in Seattle, to Seattle weather, to fall color and what they were doing for Christmas, to ice fishing. An obvious soft ball aimed at Ted. Which he failed to catch, and the table went quiet.

At first, it seemed like Fitzroy was picking up the conversation when he lifted his wine glass and looked right at Ben. But then he said, "Good thing Mimi finally brought you. About time."

Was it a toast? Looked like one, didn't feel like one. Ben joined in with his iced tea—clink, clink around the table. Fitzroy's eyes seemed to tear up a little. He carefully set his glass down and shifted his focus to Mimi. "I gotta tell you, honey, you sure know how to pick 'em."

"Damned right," Uncle Ted put in.

Fitzroy glanced at Ted, then zeroed in on Ben again. "So, Ben…when's the big day?"

Mimi braced her hands on the edge of the table. "Dad? I said no."

Madge lurched to her feet. "Dessert? David, why don't *you* give me a hand?"

Ben glanced over at Mimi. Not the time to touch her. He took hold of the back of her chair instead and leaned close. "Whatever you want. Leave? Stay?"

Her answer, if she had one, was slow enough that Madge and Fitzroy reappeared with dessert plates and a Charlotte Russe. Suddenly, it was like the whole wedding idea had never been mentioned.

The dessert, part cake, part mousse and berries, looked pretty on their plates. But once he took a bite… Mostly it felt like a perfect metaphor for the whole dinner: lots of air and once in a while there was a raspberry.

Once they said their goodbyes and climbed into her car, it was blocks and blocks and blocks of silence. Eventually, at a stoplight, Mimi said, "You and Dad seemed pretty chummy."

"I wouldn't say chummy."

The light changed and she whipped a left turn onto a wide, sweeping street. "I had hoped you'd be a little more loyal, you know?" She had that tight chin going, which was never good.

Another abrupt turn.

"Loyal? Mimi, I—"

"He always does that," she said. "He charms his way around people, wheedles his way in. He uses that voice, pretends he's vulnerable…"

Another turn onto a street lined with turn-of-the-century houses.

She shook her head. "None of it's real. None of it." She muttered something more and went after a tissue in the box wedged between their seats.

"Let me do it." He wrestled a couple of whole tissues free and handed them to her.

Seeing her cry...Jesus.

Eventually she pulled into an alley; halfway down it, she braked, and her garage door glided open. It was dim inside. They rolled in and stopped. She was still gripping the wheel even after the door slid closed. She turned off the engine and sat slumped in the seat.

He stroked her shoulder and waited for as long as he could stand it.

"You know him, Buddy. I don't," he said. "But it seemed like he just wanted to get a read on whether you're gonna get hurt. I'm not gonna get taken in."

He watched her mostly-shadowed face. At least she was thinking about what he'd said. He licked his lip. "Trust me on this, Buddy. You can do that can't you?"

It took her a while. "I can do that, yes," she said.

"As far as what happened tonight..." He was sweating. "I know I should've talked to you about it before, but maybe your dad is right... The thing is... I don't know. But if you're up for a long engagement, maybe..."

"Oh, for heaven's sake!" She jammed her car door open, slammed it behind her, and headed into the house.

Chapter 7

Beeker was hoping that if he talked to Pete Webber face-to-face, Webber would see the light and quit. Holding onto that idea was what put him behind the wheel and kept him heading for Savannah on I-77. And the drive went pretty well down across Ohio and even through the Appalachian stretch of West Virginia, clear through North Carolina.

For one thing, Deek kept his trap shut. For another, traffic was mostly light.

There wasn't much to see from the freeway: lanes of traffic and more traffic, and here and there a hillside of hardwood trees somebody hadn't got around to logging off so he could build more houses.

They stopped for barbeque just out of Charlotte, North Carolina. Deek said he wasn't feeling social, that he'd hang out in the car, just bring him something good.

Beeker swung open his door, caught a lungful of late summer and stepped down on that hard-pan dirt. He couldn't help feeling dizzy from it all. Taking in that smell of the smoker out back, waiting in the hot sun until he could put in his order, taking in the buzz and bark of folks jawing at one another around the picnic tables—it was like he was an orphan come home. Only this time he had a different name and a face with enough age on it that nobody would recognize him.

A family with maybe four hundred kids invited him

to join their picnic table. He didn't even like kids. But being there, forking down that food, seeing how the boys went at each other—not being mean, just being boys—it was good barbecue and they were good people. Then it came on him why his mom had moved them north and he couldn't swallow. He made an excuse he needed to take his brother's food out to the car, climbed in behind the wheel, and they made their way back onto I-77, heading for low country.

Just out of Charlotte they started seeing signs for the interchange at Columbia—any fool with a map could see that meant they were closing in on Savannah. But Beeker didn't need a map. His hands began to burn like he'd grabbed a fistful of nettles, and he could hardly breathe. More than once, he'd had to play his fingers against the steering wheel just to get the feeling back.

"Remember the last time we came through here? You were maybe seven and Dad brought you along to our game."

So, the back seat was awake again.

Beeker remembered. He'd been nine, not seven, and he didn't want to think about Deek's football games. He most especially didn't want to think about anything from the year he was eleven.

Deek must've got the hint because he pretty much shut up until they jumped onto I-95. Then, all of a sudden, he said, "We could stay down here awhile, you know. Do some fishing. Catch a mess of striped bass maybe."

Beeker's left hand went numb at the very idea. He glanced at the steering wheel, back to the road, hunched his shoulders to shake off the feeling that he was being pushed down and down. He hadn't had it for years, but it was back. And worse than ever.

Beeker changed to steering right-handed and went to whipping his left hand up and down, just to get some feeling back. He didn't want to think about killing anything.

The miracle about their drive south (miracle, that's what his mother would've called it) was that those first ten hours had been mostly fine. It was the last two that left Beeker feeling low, low as he'd felt for a long time. Not low like a bad football game. More like the low he felt when his mother moved them to Cleveland and he had to start all over again as the kid with a corn-pone accent.

A swarm of motorcycles roared up behind them, startling Beeker back into watching the road. Seven Harleys passed the Navigator and took their racket on ahead. And that quick, Beeker realized how tired he was. After those folks at the barbecue, he couldn't help wishing things could have gone the way they'd been when he was little. Before the mall and the rest of it.

Suddenly Deek said, "Remember the first time Dad let you come fishing?"

Where'd that come from? They were nowhere near water or wetlands; they hadn't seen anybody hauling a boat.

"I sure as hell remember," Deek said. "The night before your first fishing trip, Dad sat you down in his chair and spread a map out on the kitchen table. Man, you shoulda seen your face when he talked up that river. It was like he was singing you to sleep. He talked you from the bridge crossing the Savannah, and right up onto the Black River where we used to go. You were still talking about it that night when I came to bed. How you were gonna catch fifty-hundred yellow perch and three kinds of trout; and about a million other kinds of fish. You had it that Mom and the neighbor ladies were gonna throw a big fish fry for the school. Jesus, Beeker, you were one weird kid."

Weird. The word was like needles in Beeker's hands.

They passed a sign. Columbia was coming up. He couldn't screw up the connection over to I-26. He hunched over the wheel. "Give it a rest. Okay? Just let me think how to take this interchange."

Besides, he didn't need Deek to remind him how it was, going out with the men that first time. He'd been too young to go hunting with his dad and Uncle Charlie, but he'd begged and they finally gave in and took him fishing.

He'd never forget that morning, waking in the dark with his dad leaning over him, the smell of his dad, and being lifted up and bedded down in the back of the pickup. They took the dogs and their rifles. Deek and their dad went for alligator; Uncle Harold loaded his tackle and Beeker into the old punt and they headed downriver. Uncle Harold poled along and Beeker knelt in the bow right in front. And he more felt than heard his uncle's husky whisper, *you keep a sharp lookout for water moccasin.*

They'd spent the whole day on the river. That time and the other times after, they came back with bass, or redbreast sunfish, a couple of times a shortnose sturgeon. And once, when they went a new way, he spotted the pointy head of a longnose gar just hanging there in the still water.

Those four summers were perfect.

Everything went to hell when the NFL dropped Deek, then the troubles between Mom and Dad, then the mall.

Suddenly the Navigator was going *raa-aap raa-aap* and Beeker whipped them back across the fog line, into his lane of the highway. Okay, he would not be thinking about the mall. Stupid of him to go there—like reaching into an open fire to pick out a roasted potato. You could do it but you had to be ready. You had to do it just right. Otherwise, you could lose more than your hand.

Maybe an hour before dusk, Beeker pulled off the freeway and took the road he'd seen so many times from the back of his uncle's pickup. It'd be good to touch down along the Black River before they dropped in on Pete Webber.

He assumed Deek would work himself into a lather because they didn't go straight to Pete Webber's place. But for once, Deek seemed content to kick back and take in the land at sundown. And after a while, Beeker almost forgot he had somebody with him.

The shack he remembered wasn't more than a couple of rotten boards so overgrown he'd have missed them entirely if he hadn't known where to look. But in spite of the way things had changed, Beeker managed to find the old track and drive down as far as he could toward the river. He had his seatbelt off even before the Navigator stopped. And the moment he touched down on that loamy earth, he was off down the path to the river. He found a place to sit and just breathe in that heavy air.

Except for a heron working the far bank, he was finally alone. For a long while he watched fish rings popping the surface of the water.

His first real memory of Deek, Deek was already a

big deal football player. The kids in school talked about Deek like he was a God. Deek would come home sore from practice and brag about how banged up he got. After high school, Deek got a football scholarship to UGA; by his second year there, Deek was starting at linebacker. A few times Beeker got to go watch UGA games with his dad. Nobody ever said Deek got hurt. They might've said he got planted, like the SEC championship, but getting planted was just part of the game.

The Green Bay Packers took Deek in the fourth round of the NFL draft. He lasted only part of one year. He came home, not so much changed, as mean. He drank even more than high school. And (their mother said) there were drugs. The cops picked him up all the time, but he never went to jail. They just brought him home to cool off. Only he never cooled off.

On the far bank, the heron flapped off upriver.

Beeker turned his phone on flashlight and scanned the water. He knew he should be going. He knew, back in the Navigator, Deek would be having fits.

He turned off his phone and stuck it in his pocket. *Not yet.*

Nobody ever came up with an answer why Deek headed for the mall that day. Nobody knew he'd taken a rifle. Nobody in his family knew what had happened until the TV reporters showed up saying there'd been a shooting, that the mall was locked down, and the police had identified Deek's body. The TV news kept showing Deek's picture from when Deek played at UGA and when he was taken in the Draft. For days after, the reporters wouldn't let up.

His mother sent Beeker to stay with his cousins over

in Hinesville. Turned out, that wasn't near far enough.

He was still sitting on the stump in the dark when Deek yelled so loud, they must've heard him in Atlanta.

"Jesus, Beeker! We gonna do this or what?"

Chapter 8

Beeker pulled the Navigator into Pete Webber's driveway and turned off the ignition. Across the street, an old lady was puttering along behind her dog. No point in being recognized. He waited to climb out until she was down the block.

He tried again to explain to Deek how he intended to convince Pete Webber to quit officiating college football games. "You think you can convince Pete to quit, you just go for it," Deek said. "And when he tells you no way, then use that needle of yours on him. I'll see you later."

Beeker climbed out, grabbed the beers he'd brought for Webber, and headed for the porch. He could hardly believe how much easier it was going to be without Deek breathing down his neck. Of course, it made him a little nervous, but he couldn't help feeling good.

Pete Webber was on the phone when he opened his front door. First impression, Webber looked older and with more gut than he had in that Ohio State game; and he was shorter than Beeker expected. But he still had that the good ol' boy grin Beeker remembered from his childhood.

"I called," Beeker said.

"Well, I'll be damned," Webber said. "Beeker Sloane. I'd know you anywhere. You still got your old chemistry set? Man, you look just like your dad. Lemme just—"

Except for a couple of airline employees, nobody'd called him Sloane since he was twelve, when his mom couldn't take it anymore and moved them back to her family in Ohio and changed their name.

Webber motioned Beeker on back through a house that was fancier but not all that different from Beeker's old house in Savannah—one-story, a fireplace, family room, a TV the size of Texas. Webber parked the phone he'd been talking into on a little table next to a recliner, then pointed Beeker through the sliding glass doors.

Beeker headed out to a deck overlooking a back yard and set the two six-packs on a fancy outdoor table. For a good five minutes, Webber wandered the deck, enthusing about his showplace yard, his azaleas, his rhododendrons and camellias. The longer he talked, the more sweat slicked his face. Beeker was beginning to sweat too. But he was pretty sure it wasn't from the humidity.

Now that he was facing Webber, how was he going to convince the guy to quit officiating? What was he going to say? Because he didn't want to kill anybody. Not even Webber.

He knew Deek was all for it. But killing to stop kids being hurt? There had to be a better way.

Beeker's brain swarmed with noisy, fuzzy questions—impossible to hold onto. Should he interrupt Webber and lay out his thinking? Should he argue? Should he show Webber the needle and threaten him?

What if he called Deek?

Deek breathed into Beeker's ear: *relax, it'll be okay.* And the air seemed to lighten a little. The medicine smell of the eucalyptus backed off, and he found a question that seemed to fit.

"So," he said. "What are you doing, besides your yard?"

"Real estate." Webber shot Beeker a wide smile. "I have it just about as good as a man can have it." Then, instead of asking Beeker how he was doing, or talking football like a regular guy, Webber delivered a whole comedy routine about his divorce and how he'd screwed his almost-ex-wife but good. "A done deal now," he gloated. "I just have to sign the final papers. And get this: she's gonna have to pay me."

Beeker didn't have much use for marriage, but he was developing a load of sympathy for Mrs. Webber. And damned if he could figure what to say.

He must've tuned out for a second or two. Because, next thing he knew, Webber had launched into a whole song and dance about how Savannah had changed, the developments on Coffee Pointe, how he'd built up his real estate business, and the fact he was a paid-up member in the 10 Million Dollar Club.

Beeker raised his eyebrows the way people did when they were impressed. "Ten Million. Now that's something."

Finally, Webber said, "So, how long's it been? You were just a kid. Then you and your mom moved away. Hell of a thing to happen. I never could figure what was wrong with Deek, you know? But the past is past, right? How about a cold one? And what are you doing now?"

Beeker motioned to the two six packs on the table. "Brought those for you."

"Well, I'll be damned." Webber picked up two bottles and offered one to Beeker. "I guess you're old enough now, huh? You still playing with that chemical set or what?"

Beeker joined Webber where he had bellied up to the deck railing. "Yeah, but I'm retired now," Beeker said. "A few months ago."

"Well damn. What are you, forty, forty-five? How'd you manage that?"

"Sold my company."

"Retired... You still living up north somewhere? That's where your mom went, didn't she? Lemme tell you, you don't want to be living up in the cold. If you're retired, why don't you come on down here? I got some great places I could show you. You golf?"

Beeker made a close inspection of the label on his beer bottle, then looked out at the perfectly groomed back yard. True, most people would've said Savannah was a beautiful place. He'd been thinking that too. But standing there on Webber's deck, breathing in the thick, humid air, it felt like somebody had stacked a load of hot lead on his chest.

Webber took a quick swallow of his beer. "I have a couple of places gonna come on the market over in Hilton Head if you're interested, or I know of a great place closer in to Savannah."

Was Webber ever gonna mention officiating? Or the threatening letter? Or the DVD he'd sent?

Beeker pushed himself away from the deck railing. "I saw you maybe a month ago."

"Yeah?" Webber drew back. "Where was that? How come you didn't speak up?"

"At a football game."

"You don't say. Where?"

"You were officiating. That game at Ohio State."

"You gotta love traveling to those games." Webber

slowly finished his beer, opened another, and his face folded into a sly grin.

Maybe it was nerves. Beeker began to pick at the edge of the label on his beer bottle. *Just get him talking football. Be a fan.* "All that real estate, I guess your football gig's just a hobby, huh?" Beeker forced an aw-shucks grin. "Officiating, I'll be damned. Tell me: during a game, what happens if somebody makes a mistake? You know, one of the officials?"

Webber shook his head. "There's always some fan claims we've screwed up. You learn to turn that stuff off."

A trickle of sweat ran down Beeker's back. He needed to sell Webber on quitting. He took a sip of his beer. He was out of time; he could feel it. But one more try. "You ever think about that Ohio State game?" he said. "You know, the one where I saw you? A player got hurt real bad, you know."

Webber chugged his beer, set the empty aside, and shook his head like Beeker was just another stupid fan. "Kids get hurt. That's part of the game. Their schools take care of them, you know. They can get a medical redshirt if they can't play for the year because of the injury. It's not part of officiating."

Beeker weighed the bleary look on Webber's face. Should he push Webber to face what a rotten job he'd done in that game—Deek would want that.

Just to give himself the time to get his nerves under control, Beeker slowly drank most of his beer. It tasted flat and moldy. "What I remember about that game…besides the kid and the other players and coaches… I remember you, Pete. When that kid got hurt and he was spread out there on the field, you just stood there. Your mouth was open like a fish. I don't think you even knew what happened."

Deek would hate he was saying all this crap to convince Webber. But if Webber quit, if they didn't have to kill Webber, he was willing to take the heat from Deek.

Beeker let out a breath. "You sure had me fooled. I was thinking you couldn't sleep that night. You know, knowing that kid was in the hospital and all."

Webber was staring out into the yard, looking not that different than how he'd looked the day of the game, except his face had turned dead white.

"Talk to me," Beeker said. "That kid, the one in that game, he died. You must know that."

Suddenly Webber set his jaw. "I know he died. Some nutcase sent me a bunch of crap a month ago, claiming it was my fault. He had his tail in a knot about a couple of calls he said I missed. Can you believe it? Like I should quit officiating because he says so."

Deek had been right all along. The jerk really was a waste of real estate. And now, he was a dead man.

He could feel Deek, right behind him. He slipped a hand into his pants pocket. "Shhhh," Deek said and slid the syringe out of Beeker's pocket. "I'll take care of it."

Webber squared himself off, full of outrage and ready for a fight.

"Well, I'm here to tell you, I call what I see. And the review box didn't overturn any of my play calls, not one. Yeah, I remember that game. When a game is over, they look at the whole film, and they didn't give me a bad time about it. I did my job just like the other guys."

It was like Beeker had stepped back inside the house. Like he was looking through a window.

BAM, Deek slapped that syringe into Webber's shoulder.

"OW!" Webber winced and twisted away. Then stumbled part-way down the steps to the yard. "What the hell?"

Webber's flailing brought Beeker back. Suddenly he was standing on the deck again.

The pale shape of Webber was like a noisy river sweeping Beeker away: the syringe floating, the thump of the shoulder, the arms waving, the stumbling then falling, Webber on his knees, the piney smell of the night air.

The whooshing noise in Beeker's head ran and ran until he was cold and dizzy. He glanced down. The syringe, it must've been one of his, was lying on the deck. He picked it up and stuffed it in an empty beer bottle.

Beeker bent close to Webber. "Must've been some kind of a bug, don't you think?"

Webber made an awkward grab like he wanted Beeker's help to stand. "I—shpray for bu—" His voice cracked. He struggled to step up but slipped and fell all the way down the steps into the yard. "Srry, bu thish—maaa—I naaa—"

Beeker couldn't swallow. Couldn't move. He watched as Deek caught Webber under his arms and waltzed him up onto the deck. Webber's legs jerked and pawed at the deck's surface, hooked onto the leg of one of the deck chairs. Deek kicked the leg free, carried Webber into the house and dumped him into the recliner that Webber pretty clearly used to watch TV.

Deek leaned closer and closer to Webber' face, whispering. Webber's skin looked all pale and sweaty;

his face like a balloon, his eyes wide and crazy.

So much for talking Webber into quitting. Beeker couldn't feel his throat at all, his tongue, his palate. He knew the words he wanted to say but he couldn't speak at all. He couldn't leave Webber the way he was now. But he also couldn't bring himself to give Webber the rest of the FL430 that would finish the job.

The minutes dragged on: Deek whispering, that panicked look on Webber's face. At last, Beeker felt his own heart thud against his ribs. His throat was coming back, and his tongue. He licked his lips; he took a breath. "What do we do?"

"Do what I tell you," Deek said. "Check the house for the computer." Deek plucked the second syringe from Beeker's pocket and assumed one of those poses that nurses adopt when they ask you something but don't ever believe what you tell them. "How're you doing now, Pete?"

Webber stared into space. "Haw-ahl."

Beeker headed down the hall, looking for an office. But Deek's voice played like a soundtrack coming from the living room. "*Hospital*? You're saying *hospital*? You want me to take you to the hospital?"

Even when Beeker couldn't hear them, even as he rummaged through Pete Webber's bedroom, he couldn't get the talk out of his head. Webber making that noise and Deek saying *Hospital? Something about hospital?*

How could it have gone so wrong? Webber was supposed to resign. Instead: *Find the computer?* What was the point of that? The computer was in Webber's office. Beeker could see that from the doorway. If Deek wanted the computer, he could get it himself.

Beeker started up the hallway toward the living

room. He was done. They had to leave. Somebody would find Webber. It'd take weeks, months maybe to get him back among the living, but the right hospital could do it.

Something electric split the air. Then Deek's voice shook the whole house. "Beeker, dammit. Quit messing around, find that computer, post what we talked about. Do it now."

Beeker blinked, then stepped into Webber's office. He shifted the computer's mouse across the mousepad and the screen came to life: Webber's email and three other programs were wide open.

Working the computer actually settled Beeker down. And, once he got back to the living room, it was obvious: the first dose had blocked Webber's voluntary muscle control completely and he looked exactly like Beeker's field tests of the drug had predicted. It would take another full dose, though, to stop the heart.

"Done," Beeker said, "I sent a group email to all the officiating addresses on his system. I kept it short: *Sorry but I've decided to retire.*"

Deek bent down into Webber's field of vision. "We are right about that, Pete? No more officiating?"

"Aw-ahl."

Leaning a little closer… "I'm not going to lie to you, Pete. Nobody's going to the hospital. See, what you have here, you have the same kind of problem as some of those kids had. The ones who played when you were officiating. You know what kind of a problem that is, right?" Deek narrowed his eyes. "Nobody. Cares."

"Nnnn."

"So, here's the deal," Deek said. "We'll just handle a few things here and then we'll be off. You wait right here."

Webber stopped trying to talk. His eyes stared out into the room in the general direction of the television. Beeker turned it on.

"High in the mid-90s and a low of 75 for all this week" boomed into the room.

Deek went out to the car and a minute later came back with a bag full of supplies. They cleaned, vacuumed, dumped the empty beer bottles in Webber's recycling.

By the time they loaded Webber into the Navigator, the full moon was mostly hidden by low-hanging clouds. It was nearly 2:00 a.m. and the temperature had dropped to 76 degrees. Beeker's arms and legs felt like sacks of jelly.

Deek piloted the big car across the river, headed north, and turned onto what used to be an old access road close by the river. Now and then the moonlight glinted back from the black water—it seemed like proof that the great river was still alive and spreading itself south.

Forty miles outside of Savannah, the overcast began to clear. Long grasses along the verge swayed as the Navigator eased its way along the narrow road next to the great black water swamp. They cruised in air-conditioned silence as if there were no humidity, no muddy ruts in the road. Deek slowed the vehicle to a crawl, powered down the driver's side window and turned a high-power flashlight on the undergrowth.

The green-earth smell of the land hit Beeker like a familiar blanket.

Deek was leading him, shining the lights on high, going deeper and deeper into the marsh. Somewhere near here was the narrow gap his uncles had used to put in their punt. And if he remembered correctly, they were close to the place they'd taken a gator.

Those nights on the water were the best. The sounds of the marsh, the voices of the men. That first gator hunt, he kept asking when they'd get to see one. But really, he was hoping there wouldn't be too many and that they wouldn't get too close.

Beeker glanced in the back seat. Webber lay on his back, his eyes still staring.

Nearly there.

Deek began switching the headlights on high then low, and would've missed the turnoff if Beeker hadn't spotted the right combination of trees, stumps, and that low place between. Deek braked, backed up, and squeezed the Navigator between the scrub and an old spar at the edge of a small clearing. This was the little landing they used to use that gave way to the marshland trails and bogs, just like Beeker remembered. From here on, the trick was to get as close to the water as possible without the Navigator sinking down so they couldn't get out of there.

Beeker jumped out onto the loamy earth.

It was almost sunrise and the air felt thick with night and the smell of the place. Bald cypress rose over him like painted blue-black shadows. He stood under what was left of a huge one that looked to be dead. The old tree had snapped maybe fifteen feet up, its tall stump rooted where land, real land that is, gave way to marsh. It might stand there another century, cypress being cypress.

He was hyperventilating. He headed back to the car.

The Navigator's tinted glass made Deek's shadow look like a man with his hair standing on end. Beeker stepped around to the other side of the car, stuffed his shirttail back into his pants and climbed in.

"I can't."

Deek made a sound like he'd let the pressure off his air brake. "You pussy."

Beeker twisted around in the seat. "And we can't leave him here. If we get him to a hospital, I can explain what we gave him."

In an instant, Deek was out of the car, swearing at Beeker, fanning open the back door and jerking Pete Webber around, boosting Webber out of the car and up onto his shoulder like a fireman.

All Beeker could do was watch. Deek carried Pete Webber back down the path and across the clearing, to a tree half-submerged in the backwater. Deek flopped the inert body down. As if it was nothing, Deek pulled the other syringe out of his pocket, squatted, and emptied the FL430 into Webber's shoulder.

Beeker couldn't think how, but it felt like he had been right there, close up, close enough to see it. Webber's eyes were wide open, pearls in the moonlight.

Chapter 9

Savannah divorce lawyer Reggie Ford jerked open the door to his best paralegal's office and peered in. "Chandra, you have any idea where Pete Webber is? I had him down for a half-hour ago."

Chandra closed the cover on a thick file and looked up. A quick shake of her head, no, and she speed-dialed their receptionist. "LuAnn, Pete Webber turn up yet?" The phone's speaker crackled. "Nothin' here. You want me to—"

"Let me get back to you," Chandra said and peered at Reggie. He grimaced, turned on his heel, muttering, "What was so damned important Pete couldn't pick up that check so we could close out our file?"

Reggie's office went through the usual drill for MIA clients—phone calls to Webber's house and cell phone, e-mails, text messages—by end of day Thursday, still nothing. Chandra delivered the bad news to her boss.

A no-show made no sense to Reggie. Because the minute his client finished signing off on the paperwork, Reggie was gonna hand Webber a check for $228,764.68. Not a fortune, but a damned pretty piece of change since the client was also coming away a free man with the house he lived in, his car, a boat—all paid for—plus his entire 401K.

When Webber still hadn't showed up by late Friday afternoon, Reggie took off, saying, "Who knows where he is? Maybe old Pete started celebrating his big win a little early."

Reggie may have wished them all a good weekend with a wink and a smile, but that was just to get him out the door. It was irritating as hell to be hunting the AWOL Pete Webber. Nothing to do but go after the man. The office agreement had always been *your client, your problem.* So, at his car, Reggie popped the trunk and loaded in a banker's box of stuff he needed to prepare for a deposition on Monday morning. Then he hauled off his jacket, draped it on the front seat, climbed behind the wheel, and drove out to Webber's place in Garden City.

Thanks to Friday evening traffic, it was almost forty minutes before he pulled up at Webber's address, a one-story brick ranch house with a manicured front lawn and the predictable azaleas and trees. From the street, the house looked just fine. Drapes mostly closed. But it had just turned October and with the house facing into the sun, most everybody had their drapes shut. Reggie checked his watch and pulled into the driveway.

He piled out of the car and knocked on the new-painted front door. He tried twice, got no answer, and headed back to his car. Considering what traffic over to Wilmington Island would be, if he took off now, he'd be forty minutes getting home and maybe longer. If he waited another half-hour…

He ended up sitting there maybe five minutes. Something just wasn't right. A realtor not answering his phone? That didn't make good sense at all. And Webber wasn't even responding to texts. Or email come to that.

The sun was close to setting, and it felt plain stupid sitting in the driveway. Reggie took a last look at the front of the house, started the car, and checked the street for traffic. On the other hand, …

Would it hurt if he just checked around a little bit? He turned the engine off, stepped out, and put his phone on flashlight. At the corner of the house, he aimed his phone light into the plantings all along the bedrooms, all the way to the back yard fence. No footprints that he could see. But any fool could open the side yard gate.

Through that gate, and, my, my, my. Whoever was taking care of the front lawn had busted their ass on the back yard. Newly trimmed azaleas all over the place, a big old pine tree that somebody'd limbed out, and the kind of measuring stakes made him think Webber was setting up to put in a pool.

All that greenery, anybody could've hidden in there. For that matter, Pete Webber could've passed out and nobody'd see him. Or worse, Webber could be lying under one of those big spiraeas with his head knocked in by some pissed-off former client.

Reggie's heart gave an extra thump. What about the guy who put that DVD together?

Damned good thing he'd talked Webber into letting him keep it with the case file. Pete might have dismissed it as the work of some football nut, but *he* was not discounting a threat like that.

It was ridiculous, but he couldn't help checking. He aimed the phone's flashlight into every dark corner…he was not seeing a body in the shrubbery. Not even footprints, which was definitely a relief.

Reggie backed off the bark-dusted plant bed and pivoted as he had so many times in the courtroom. He took in the look of the backside of Webber's house—in this case, a very large deck full of furniture and a barbecue/smoker setup that would've been right at home on Reggie's own terrace.

He stepped up on the deck and peered into the house through a sliding door that seemed to lead into the dining room. From where he stood, everything looked just fine. Without quite thinking about it, Reggie pulled at the handle. The door rolled quietly open, and the little hairs on the back of his neck stood straight up. Right then, without proof of anything, Reggie scrolled down his phone's contacts list and pushed the little green icon.

Twenty minutes later, Sheriff Butch Masters pulled into Webber's driveway wanting to know what was up and why Reggie had said no lights and sirens.

Reggie laid it all out. The missed appointment, the money, the way Pete had spoken of his wife. "There's been plenty of action between the two of them but that's all settled if you check the file in the sheriff's office. The thing I'm worried about: about a month ago—nothing to do with the divorce—Mr. Webber received a threatening letter."

Butch's big flat face was the picture of skepticism. "His business, I'd have thought that was part of the deal."

Reggie raised his eyebrows. "Now Pete's disappeared. Without a word. Without picking up his settlement check? And he left the house unlocked? I wanted to check it out, but I didn't want your boys to come roaring out here and haul my butt off to jail because somebody called about a break-in."

The sheriff eyed him. "What, you got something better to do than jail?"

"Matter of fact," Reggie said. "I do."

The sheriff shot him another suspicious look. Then, like he was about to perform one of the lesser labors of Hercules, he bent himself double and excavated a flashlight the size of a baseball bat from under the front seat of his car.

Reggie led the way around the house, through the gate, and into Pete Webber's dining room.

It wasn't long before Butch made it clear, he believed he'd been dragged along on a snipe hunt. He headed back out to the deck and parked himself in one of the chairs overlooking the yard.

"Looks to me like your client's gone off with one of his buddies. That'd explain his car being here, wouldn't it? Best we just leave everything like it is."

What? Unlocked sliding door and all?

Knowing Butch though, there was no point in arguing. Once the big man took off, Reggie climbed into his own car and drove home.

It still didn't make sense that Pete Webber had failed to collect his two hundred grand. In fact, it nagged at Reggie all weekend. First thing Monday morning, before he took off for his deposition, Reggie put Chandra on it.

"It's football season, isn't it? Call whoever it is with the NCAA that handles officials and see if they know anything."

Reggie's deposition ended at 4:30 p.m., and not one minute too soon because he was about ready to pick up one of the conference room chairs and belt the witness over the head with it. He fumed his way back to the office thinking of all the ways he would take real pleasure in woodshedding that s-o-b in front of a jury. Truth be known, in the heat of that deposition, he'd almost forgotten about Pete Webber. That is, until he walked into the office and got a look at Chandra's face.

"My office," he said and kept going through reception, parked his briefcase on the sofa and hung his jacket on the bentwood rack his wife had given him.

Chandra got right to it, saying first, she'd called Mr. Webber's answering service. Mr. Webber hadn't picked up messages since late Wednesday.

"And for a man in real estate, you know you just can't do that," she said. "I did get hold of the football officiating people. According to them, Pete Webber sent them an email Wednesday night saying that he was retiring. Did he mention he was retiring to you?"

Reggie was busy tipping his drink back and forth, watching the little ice cubes tumble and slide. He looked up. "No, he did not. Matter of fact, he was talking about flying off to work some game somewhere in the Midwest."

"Well, there's that. And then, I've been thinking…" Chandra steepled her hands together. "I know it doesn't make a lot of sense, given how this case has gone. But is it just possible this is like the Brauns?"

Reggie restrained a groan. "You mean have the Webbers got back together?"

Even as he said it, Reggie was dialing Pete's wife's lawyer. His desk clock showed it was after 5:00 p.m. But good news, the guy was still in the office and he was quite certain that the Webbers had not had a reconciliation. "Why? Did Mr. Webber think they were gonna reconcile? Does Beverly need to worry about that?"

"No, no," Reggie said. "Just one of those missed communication things probably. Talk to you later." He hung up the phone, poured himself another stiff one, and, once he confirmed that the two-hundred grand check was still in the office safe, he told Chandra to get herself a drink, pull up a chair, and explain that look on her face.

Reggie took a mouthful of bourbon. "Go ahead."

Chandra licked her lips. "Well wouldn't you like to know what his last appointments were on Wednesday and Thursday morning? They'd be on his computer and maybe his phone."

"Would be nice to know who he's been talking to, wouldn't it?"

She nodded. "And then there's that DVD."

"I've been thinking about that. We never pursued it, because it didn't seem important at the time. Can you get somebody to look at that thing? See if we can track who copied those games. The other thing—" Reggie poured himself another splash.

"Be nice to know why Pete wrote an email saying he was retiring. If he's the one wrote it."

Chapter 10

Mimi dumped her coat and purse on a big kitchen island and turned to face him. She took a deep breath and looked into his eyes. "I'm sorry," she said. "I just wasn't ready for Dad's *when's the big day?*"

Ben scooped her up and held her. This was what they'd both needed. Not some damned family dinner.

Eventually she pushed free of him and took him on a tour of her house.

They'd already made it through the mudroom and kitchen. As for the rest of it, the guest rooms and bathrooms and third floor gym...he hardly heard what she was saying. Because everywhere he looked there were pictures and art glass and woven baskets, piles of books—the kind of stuff you'd pack first if you were moving. He'd assumed she'd long ago paid somebody to box up for her. *How do I turn this around?*

She opened the door to her bedroom, motioned him in, and stopped at the foot of her white quilted bed. Her not even queen-size white-quilted bed.

"What?" she said.

At five-foot nothing, it fit her. It was pretty. A load of different fabrics and pillows.

But it was way too short for him. They'd been sharing the biggest, longest bed he could find when he'd moved into the Lake house. He couldn't help laughing. Not at her, but man...it was gonna be a couple of

73

interesting nights.

He saw it dawn on her. "Oh," she said.

"I'll make it work," he said. And he did.

****

Six hours later, Mimi turned off the alarm. He flailed an arm away from the sheets and glanced at the window: still dark outside.

"Sorry, fella," she said and came around to his side of the bed. "I did say early meeting." She disappeared into her bathroom saying, "What are you going to do with yourself today?"

Shave, was his first thought. "I need to follow up on the request from the officiating people."

"What's that mean?" she said.

"Well, nothing risky," he called.

The water in the bathroom turned on and off about a hundred times, then the shower went on.

He climbed out of bed. While she was showering, he did a few stretches, then headed for the bathroom door. She was standing in the big glass surround, drying herself off.

"I'm trying to do something good here, you know?" he said. "Something useful with whatever time I have."

"Don't talk like that," she said.

"It's the truth, isn't it? We don't know how much time I have left, right? I want to help these guys."

She stepped out of the shower and tossed the towel she'd been using in a wicker hamper. "I get it. But your medical reports have been super. So, I'm thinking we have decades ahead of us. As long as you don't get clonked on the head."

Decades ahead of us.

Us.

She angled past him into her bedroom, disappeared into a walk-in closet, and reappeared with an outfit to meet with the lawyers.

Panties on, bra on, she slipped a blouse over her head and turned back to him. "As for how much time we have? That's a long talk, isn't it? And I have to get out of here. So…tonight? Hopefully we're formalizing the settlement this afternoon."

"The settlement: your dad's gonna be okay?"

"No jail time," she said. "He can't be a corporate officer. That'll hurt, but otherwise it's securities restrictions, which really doesn't matter for him. And money damages one way or another. He's humiliated, that's the main thing. Rex has to divest of some companies it took over. Don't call. Text me, okay?"

Fifteen minutes later, she took off.

He ate the last of the bagels and cream cheese, then set up his computer in Mimi's dining room and downloaded the three other video files Jackson had forwarded—at first glance none of them were much different from Pete Webber's.

The way he saw it, the officials weren't working as a team, that was the problem. And because they weren't, they were missing penalties all over the place.

He spent nearly four hours scrutinizing one play after another. Just after ten o'clock, he shoved himself away from the dining table. He'd seen enough.

He did a little research on the power brokers at American Football Officiating and made a couple of calls to the right people. His last one went to Walt Taylor, the AFO's head man.

Taylor answered the phone. "I know who you are, Mr. Leit. What I don't understand is why a man doing broadcasts for a sports network is calling me."

Clearly, a long-winded explanation was not going to work.

"Somebody is threatening to kill your officials," Ben said. "And I don't think you understand what's going on. Whoever is making these threats is serious."

"It's a very busy day, Mr. Leit. My people keep me informed about what's going on. How is it you're even involved in this?"

Ben cleared his throat. "Your people got me involved. And I'm pretty clear you should be way more than just informed. Because, when one of these men is attacked or worse, and it hits the news, you're the man who's gonna be stuck answering the questions from the press and Congress, and God knows who else, about what AFO did and didn't do."

Taylor gave a little grunt. "Security is handled at the conference level."

"I don't see that as a really smart sound bite to put out there, do you? If you want to stick with that, fine by me," Ben said. "I just hoped you were ready to take a more leadership role."

Silence.

"My point is," Ben said. "I suspect you don't know about these threats. I'm asking for a few minutes of your time, in person, to show you what I'm talking about."

Taylor was still on the phone, still breathing.

"So where are you? I can come there." *Meet me half-way, you imperious jerk.*

Finally, Taylor said, "I have a layover in Denver. I get in about 2:30, my next flight leaves at 5:20. I don't see how—"

"Meet me at the Hilton inside the airport. I'll be

there by 3:00."

In the minute before his flight took off for Denver, Ben posted a text to Mimi.

Flying to Denver to try for a handoff to Officiating's head honcho. Back this evening. How about a take-out dinner? XOXO.

****

He checked into his room at the Hilton with fifteen minutes to spare. He got the hotel's IT guy to configure his laptop so he could play the threat videos on the TV and was running the Lex Mincey video when Walt Taylor showed up.

Taylor—six feet, fit, nearing fifty?—stopped in the doorway looking like a bear with a sore paw. He was carrying a briefcase in one hand, with a serious wrist support on the other.

When, finally, Taylor did step into Ben's hotel room, he kept his coat on. He laid the briefcase on the bed and adopted one of those military "at ease" stances not two feet from the TV.

Ben eyed the heavy-duty wrist thing. "That doesn't look good."

"Carpal tunnel. It's already been a long, trying day, Mr. Leit. And my next flight leaves in a couple of hours. Just so you know."

Behind Taylor, the TV blasted a replay of a U. Georgia player hanging a massive hit on a U. Texas player. Taylor glanced at the screen and his jaw did a re-set as the players were helped off the field.

"The individual conferences have their own commissioners," Taylor said. "They do their own security. You understand that, right?"

Ben pulled a chair away from the room's little

writing desk and turned it to face the TV. "Have a seat. Like I said on the phone, you need to see this. This video was sent to an official named Lex Mincey, along with a note suggesting he should retire. Or else."

Taylor's gaze shifted to the TV but he didn't sit. On the screen, Lex Mincey was wiping his hand across his nose instead of looking at the game.

Taylor needed to get it. Mincey should've called a penalty a load of times: on the crackback block, on three egregious instances of clipping, and on a horse collar tackle. In all, fourteen major screw-ups. Any one of those incidents could have resulted in a bad injury.

Taylor shifted his weight, then actually watched the game clips for a few minutes.

Ben cleared his throat. "You do know, at least one kid has died already?"

Taylor shifted his sleeve up, glanced at his watch. "This all looks cherry-picked to me." He shot Ben a look. "Mr. Leit, no one is perfect. Seen together these incidents look bad. But they're rare. Our officials are, on the whole, doing a good job."

"I don't know that I agree," Ben said.

Taylor picked up his briefcase. "We do a good job. Not perfect. But a good job. In a demanding situation. Everybody's an expert these days. And sometimes fans get a little crazy. But that's what Security is for." Taylor glanced at Ben, then opened the door to the hallway.

Ben caught the door before Taylor could close it. "And the threats?"

"As I said, the individual conferences are responsible. Their security will take care of it. Mr. Leit, someone on our staff has wasted your time and money. I hope you'll accept my apology."

Ben shut the door behind Taylor and turned off the TV

If Taylor wasn't going to take some kind of action, it was up to him. Because somebody had to identify Videoman before one of these officials got hurt.

Skip Jackson had said it: if Videoman was that obsessed with college football officiating, he had to be haunting the college football message boards. Why couldn't the website security team track Videoman down? It couldn't be all that different from what he and Mimi had done when they hunted his dad's killer using the internet.

Now he needed to convince Mimi.

Chapter 11

By the time they left Pete Webber for the gators, Beeker had a migraine going. One so bad he was barely able to climb back inside the Navigator. No way he could drive. "You slide over," Deek said, "I'll drive a while." Beeker laid his throbbing head onto the inflatable pillow and closed his eyes. He was asleep in seconds.

As if he'd had only a few minutes' dreamless sleep, he was climbing up from the bottom of a well. He woke sprawled on the Barcalounger in his media room, still wearing the clothes and shoes he'd had on at the swamp. He took in a huge gulp of air.

The TV was running ESPN full-blast.

Deek must've driven the whole way back. Must have carried him in and dumped him in his chair. He made a mental note to check himself over for bruises once he hit the shower.

He sat part-way up in the recliner and scrubbed his eyes. According to his wristwatch, they'd left Savannah thirty-six hours ago. But how could that be? If he went by how his body felt, he hadn't slept in days.

He flopped back and stared at the ceiling.

That look on Webber's face, that was a different kind of awful. They'd finished it. Deek had killed Pete Webber using the anesthetic he'd invented to help people through heart/lung surgery. And thinking about that, he felt as bad as he'd ever felt. As bad as two years ago, watching his mom waste away. As bad as when their daddy ate his gun. Almost as bad as when Deek shot up that mall.

But Deek had been right. Pete Webber was a waste of real estate. It was Webber's fault that boy had died. Putting Webber out of his misery had likely saved some other kid. An eye for an eye and all that.

Whether it was right to do it or not…you could probably argue whether killing old Pete was the right thing to do 'til you were out of breath and still not figure it. But, sure as God made little green apples, it would be a long time before he could feel right about himself. And even longer before he could forget what they'd done.

Beeker closed his eyes to the talk on the TV. He must've slept some more, because he woke up rubbing that place at the inner part of his left eye. Both eyes burned, but the left one felt like somebody'd aimed a dry hot wind at him. He pulled himself upright, stretched, and in the process discovered he was clear-headed and his migraine was gone.

Where was Deek? A frisson arced along his arms and, instinctively, his fingers worked their way into his pants pocket. Good, the car key was there. He trudged out to the kitchen: dishwasher running, sink clean. What had Deek done?

Or, more likely, what kind of a con was Deek working? The ham sandwich on the counter was just like the ones his mother used to make, with sliced tomato that always slid out when you took a bite, and mayonnaise that oozed where she cut the finished sandwich into two triangles. There was even a lacy edge of lettuce showing all around the crusts of the bread. The salt/smoke smell made Beeker's mouth water.

He took a bite, then another. Heaven. The salt, the sweet ham and tomato, the crunch of the lettuce, he couldn't believe how satisfying it was. Four bites, he finished the first half and went after the second.

"Like it?"

Deek. Beeker swallowed. What was going on?

Pain flooded the back of his skull and that muscle at the top of his neck ratcheted tight, tighter, tightest. Beeker braced his hands on the counter and dropped his head down...*let go, letting go, I'm letting go.* He slipped into that soft gray zone where he couldn't tell time from light from cold. The pain belonged to someone else.

If he stretched out, closed his eyes, the feeling would move on. He headed down the long hall. If only he could get away.

"C'mon Beeker, what's first? Websites or TV?"

Beeker stopped in the media room doorway. Sofa or Barcalounger? At least if they were watching TV, he wouldn't have to talk about Savannah. But he would not be watching sports. Not ESPN, not ESPN2, or ROOT, NBCCSN, GOLF, Fox Sports, NFL, FXX, ESPNN, the five big sports college networks. None of them. He couldn't take it.

"I'll be back." He spun around in the doorway and took off. He didn't want to hear Deek's offer to come along. "Stay home!" he shouted.

He powered through the front door, slammed and locked it behind him. They'd been through this before. Every time he went for a walk, it felt like Deek was shadowing him. Or else it seemed like he'd landed on another planet, that the people on the street weren't really people, and the only person he knew, the only person who understood him, was back in the house, abandoned and miserable.

An hour later, Beeker unlocked his front door, stepped back inside, and headed down the hall to his office. He footed aside a pile of AAA books, sat in front of his computer, and leaned into the screen. The monitor swarmed with websites for hotels and cafes, cruises, Ticketron, a video promoting the St. Louis waterfront, another of a dude ranch somewhere.

Deek's voice buzzed in his ear. "Doin' better?"

Beeker straightened up in the chair.

He had to flex his jaw and ease a load of air into his lungs just to keep from going crazy. He stared around the room. The floor in front of a file cabinet was littered with roadmaps—Illinois, Missouri, and Oklahoma lay on top, and at least six others, plus the AAA travel books he'd pushed aside. He hadn't cracked them open since he couldn't say when.

Almost a whisper, Deek said, "You ready for it?"

Beeker leaned back in his office chair and closed his eyes. Nothing could be worse than talking about Savannah. "Fire away," he said.

"Road trip, Beeker. You're gonna love it."

Beeker's neck came alive with pinpricks. Deek had said road trip like *I know something you don't know.* Like that guy in The Graduate who said *Plastics.*

Deek's voice almost quivered it was so hot to do this thing. The sound of it took Beeker back to the days when he believed in Deek. When he would sneak into Deek's bedroom instead of going to sleep. Deek would make room on the bed and talk Beeker through the football play charts he was studying. Those Xs and Os were the neatest thing on the planet.

More than thirty years ago and it felt like last week.

You're gonna love it was what Deek always said about the next game. In his big brother soft voice. That promise that he'd love it meant everything. Most of all, because Deek made it sound like Beeker was in on a secret.

But after Savannah, a road trip with Deek was the last thing he wanted.

Beeker took a deep breath and held it. Why couldn't he just say he didn't want to go? Why couldn't he fix Deek with the blank stare he'd always given his junior research people, and say *Didn't we just take a road trip?*

He knew why. There was absolutely no point in saying no to Deek's plan. Because *no* would never be the end of it. But he was resolved. It didn't matter that a road trip might be fun. There was not gonna be another one.

Beeker shifted in the desk chair and finally managed, "I don't know, Deek."

"Right, right," Deek said.

But then, there he was again, typical Deek. "I was just trying to give you a break. I wasn't thinking freeways. More like backroads and fruit stands, you know? You always liked driving, so why not a road trip? What else you got to do? You're moping around here like an old man, acting like it's your fault college football's so screwed up. I was just thinking I'd get your mind on something else, you know?"

Beeker's chair bumped closer to the computer. He was looking at some kind of a tourist site for Chicago.

"Think of it, Beeker. We could be in Chicago in a day. Route 66 starts there, did you know? Right by Wrigley Stadium. We could take in a ball game if you want. No more football, we're done with football, right?"

The screen started morphing from one map to

another. So fast, Beeker had to close his eyes to get away from it. But even then, there was the snick, snick, snick of the mouse, and Deek was saying, "Wrigley Stadium. Or if you'd rather, you know it's not my thing, but if you're wanting art, they've got a jillion museums in Chicago. There's even one with dinosaurs. And a surgical museum. We could see if you're famous. They must have the stuff you invented, at least your name. Or look, a planetarium; maybe we could go there and look at the stars, whadya say?"

Beeker thought he said *Cut it out, Deek*. But did he?

A knock at the front door and some woman yelling. "Mr. Beacham? Are you there? Are you all right?"

More knocking. He was rescued.

He launched himself out of the chair, out of his office, and out to the front door. He fanned it open. He didn't recognize either woman though the fatter one looked familiar. He couldn't think from where. The blonde one seemed to float in the air, her hair blooming out and fading. It made him dizzy.

"We saw you a few minutes ago," the fat one said. "You seemed so troubled. There is help you know." She had a soft smile. Pink lips and big teeth. Her eyes looked straight into his eyes. She held out a couple of colored pamphlets. "The Lord can lift even the heaviest heart," she said. "You have only to ask."

The air had this humming feel. And the women kept floating, smelling like he couldn't think what, but it was nice. Like cookies.

Part of him wanted to thank them for coming. For their soft voices, like his mother's. For the way they talked to him, their concern for him. He would have invited them in. Found something for them to eat. Or a soda. But outside, on the porch, he was away from Deek and the road trip scheme. He was safer there.

He forced himself to smile and nod at the women. He took their pamphlets and thanked them. The paper felt dusty, and he wanted to wipe his hands against his pants. He thanked the women a second time, stepped back inside, and closed the front door. He pressed his forehead against it. He could feel Deek listening, waiting to seize on anything. The little pamphlets fluttered to the floor. He stared at them. Finally, he said, "Sorry, Deek, I can't do another thousand miles in a car."

"You're probably right," Deek said. "I thought it'd be fun, the two of us, the back roads…but I get it. It was a dumb idea."

Five hours later Beeker hit the sack. Deek hadn't breathed another word about a road trip, and as a result, Beeker slept through the night—all the way through—and woke the next morning feeling alive, refreshed, and more than ready for the coffee he could smell even in his upstairs bedroom.

He was halfway into his second frozen waffle when Deek said, "It's all on me, Beeker. Pete Webber was my deal, not yours."

Beeker stared down at his hands. His fork toyed in and out of the maple syrup, making little loops on his plate.

"I just thought a road trip west…" Deek's voice was low and soft. "We could put it all behind us, you know? Take Route 66? Have some fun, drink a few beers, hit some barbecue."

Beeker took another bite. A road trip didn't sound so oppressive once he'd slept on it.

He dipped a finger into the syrup. Maybe. But Route

66?

For the second time in less than a week, he wasn't sure what to do. He'd never in his life heard Deek apologize. He stuffed the last of his waffle into his mouth and chewed.

When Deek spoke again, it was almost a whisper.

"I just want to make it up to you," Deek said. "It'd be good for us to get away, you know, like it used to be. You're all I have, Beek. I kept hoping we could… I kept hoping it'd be like old times. I just… I love you, Beeker. I want you to know that."

They spent the next morning packing. Took off for Chicago early afternoon and pulled into the Hotel Zachary just after eight that night. Less than five minutes after they checked in, Beeker took his headache to bed.

Chapter 12

Next morning, Beeker glanced out the hotel window. Wrigley Field. He couldn't get over it. They were right across the street from the ball park. Their tickets were waiting down in the lobby at the concierge desk. He was as excited as a kid.

Taking in a baseball game had been Deek's idea. For once, a really good one. But what were they going to do until four o'clock?

The desk under his hotel room window had a whole pile of suggestions—hotel services, a big book called Chicago at a Glance, a newsletter full of the month's events. Beeker squared the hotel's big book around on the desktop and flipped to the What-to-Do section. He'd take a pass on the walking tours. It was still too hot to be walking on pavement, though the architectural one sounded interesting. Better go for something indoors and air-conditioned. His finger trailed down the page: movies, more movies…games, stuff for kids… Not theater, definitely not musicals. The Chicago Museum of Science and Industry, now that was a possibility.

"Why not see if they got your name right?" Deek said.

Beeker couldn't help smiling. Was Deek actually proud of his little brother's accomplishments? Probably not. But it felt great. For once his big brother wasn't hassling him.

"I'll leave checking on my name up to you," he said. "Come with me. There's lots to do in Chicago. No point in hanging around the hotel 'til the game."

Deek snorted. "Maybe I'll go out later."

"Okay then." Beeker unhooked his phone from the charger and stuffed it in his pocket. "I think I'll take your advice and check out what the museum has to say about me. Game's at 4:00. I'll leave your ticket with the hotel concierge, okay? See you there."

Six and a half hours later, Beeker found their seats at Wrigley Field. The sun was pounding down, but their seats were in the shade and there was a little breeze. So he actually felt cool. And they had a perfect angle for seeing the game: midway on the third-base line. How good was that? He stowed his bag under his seat and took a deep breath. He probably should've taken a look for Deek in the concourse under the stadium. But his feet hurt and it felt good to sit.

Deep breath...and there was that wonderful smell: the hot dogs, barbecue, and pizza from the food court inside the building, popcorn and more dogs walking the stands.

He stared up and down the aisle nearest their seats. Old men, young men skipping work but still on their phones, now and then a woman—fat people, skinny ones, bald and weird-haired. And their section was more than half full already. He glanced at his watch.

Where was Deek? Looking for *him* at the food stalls? That would be like Deek.

Beeker pushed his way up the aisle, through a battalion of old men in team shirts, and weaved his way through throngs of fans, out to the long avenue of concessions. More than once, he thought he saw Deek, but no. Nobody walked like Deek, not really. He ended up buying a cap and a memorial program.

He made the long trip back to his seat and asked the men sitting next to him if Deek had come looking for him. But no luck.

Part of him began to worry.

But then, it occurred to him, maybe Deek hadn't left the hotel. He called their room. Deek didn't pick up.

It felt miserable to admit Deek wasn't coming. But he wasn't. That's just the way it was going to be.

Beeker settled back in his seat. He would enjoy the game anyway. It was Deek's loss.

He stayed for all nine innings. The high point was Javier Baez hitting a three-bagger into the left field bleachers in the bottom of the ninth that drove in the winning run for the Cubs. But even before he got out of the stadium, the excitement of a win fell flat.

It wasn't the first time he'd left a stadium victorious but feeling robbed. This time, though, it wasn't about win/lose. It was that old thing, from as far back as he could remember, about being left behind.

He headed back to the hotel. The maids had tidied their room. No sign of Deek, but it didn't matter. He dragged out his suitcase, splayed it open on his bed and dumped his stuff from the game and the museum inside.

As long as he could remember, he been Deek's fan. He couldn't recall when it happened exactly, but it was before Deek went to UGA that things changed. From sometime in high school on, he'd been the butt of Deek's jokes.

"How was that museum?" Deek said.

Beeker's teeth clamped tight. He pinched the bridge of his nose. He was *not* taking the bait.

"They get your name right?"

Beeker squatted and pulled a water bottle out of the little refrigerator.

"You can't ignore me, Beeker. And don't tell me they didn't have something about the stuff you invented."

Beeker forced a swallow. "You lied to me."

"No picture? Write-up not big enough? No mention of your company?"

"Shut up, Deek." Beeker jerked open a dresser drawer and tossed his pajamas into his suitcase. "The whole way over from Cleveland, all you talked about was going to the game. I got us the tickets. I got good seats. I told you I'd meet you there. I got there early and hunted all over looking for you. Don't tell me you were there, because you weren't."

Deek's voice went soft. "Jesus, Beeker. I musta fallen asleep or something."

"I don't think you ever sleep."

Beeker headed for the bathroom, pulled together his stuff on the bathroom counter, and went to work coiling the charger cord for his shaver.

"Okay, maybe I didn't show up," Deek said. "I went for a walk, next thing I knew I was lost."

Beeker re-folded his pajamas and layered them into his suitcase. He was hyperventilating. He knew it, but he couldn't help it.

"This was just like when you came home from the NFL," he said. "Remember *Toy Story?* You and Pete were supposed to take me to see *Toy Story.* Mom gave you the money. I remember if you don't. You took me to one of those Freddie Kreuger movies. You think a horror movie is okay for a kid of ten? And you left me to walk home after dark?"

"Jesus, Beeker, how long ago was that?"

"I couldn't sleep for a week."

Beeker stuffed his ditty bag in his case and glanced around the hotel room—was he forgetting anything?

"What do you think you're doing?"

"This road trip thing…" Beeker closed his suitcase and slipped into his shoes. He snorted. "It was a stupid idea in the first place."

He hadn't intended to shout. They were in a hotel after all. But the hell with it. He hoisted his bag, left his key card on the little desk in the room, shut the door behind him, and took the elevator to the garage.

Five minutes later, his bag stowed in the Navigator, his seatbelt fastened and car doors locked, Beeker pulled out onto the street and followed his GPS back to the freeway.

In another six hours, he would be home in his own bed.

****

A thump on the wall woke him. He must've slept. But his back and hips and shoulders felt as if he hadn't. Not at all. He took one look around the room, lay back, and closed his eyes.

He must've stopped in South Bend, or maybe Toledo. That made sense. It was a long drive. Stopping and sleeping was safer than driving all the way home. At least he'd left Deek back in Chicago. He could have a little peace and quiet.

Time? He picked up his phone…not possible. How could he lose fifteen hours?

He arched his stiff back against the mattress, then curled himself off the bed. He shoved the blackout drapes wide and stared out into the blinding day.

What the hell? The St. Louis Arch? Every ounce of blood drained out of him. How had he ended up in St. Louis?

A fresh wave of panic sheeted over him. Had the ball game even happened?

The hat...he'd bought Deek a hat. He'd bought a program.

He ransacked his suitcase: shaving stuff, jeans, a jacket. No program. He fingered a red cap with a bill. This wasn't the hat. This is nothing like what he picked out.

Beeker laid the hat aside and forced his trembling thumbs to work his phone.

According to the call history, somebody had been using the phone for most of the night, making phone calls and running a load of internet searches. Every search linked to a football site—five or six searches went to his usual football website, a handful more went to American Football Officiating.

Deek.

Like he'd been shot, right over his left eye, Beeker's head suddenly hurt so bad he thought he was going to pass out.

Chapter 13

Ben left his St. Louis hotel just at sundown and headed across the wide green lawn for the riverboat ticket booth. Wouldn't you know it, Jack Halprin was already waiting for him, stumping from one foot to the other, checking his watch. The idea of a touristy boat ride on the Mississippi didn't do it for Ben. But Jack had already set one up.

Why? Because, there was an official going to be there, Lee Greer. And Greer had worked with Pete Webber. That was Jack: always a step ahead.

Jack had been a key player on the website board right from when Ben's dad first organized it. Maybe more important, Jack turned out to be Ben's avuncular friend (and website mentor) after his dad was murdered.

Jack reached out a thick hand and clapped Ben on the shoulder. "Good you decided to come. What's the story again with Mimi?"

Ben explained about the business thing she had going in Minneapolis, and dodged the question, when are you gonna make it official, by stepping back, like he'd never seen a sternwheeler before.

"So, Jack," he said. "Whadya call a thing like this? A floating pinata? A Victorian train station? A waterside wedding cake?"

Jack raised his nose like he was sniffing the air. "Smells like more train station to me." The old man lumbered onto the sternwheeler's bottom deck where a herd of tourists jockeyed for position in the buffet line. "Head up on top?" he said, "Unless you're hungry."

"Top, it is," Ben said. Jack dodged through the throng and led the way up the stairwell like a pro.

As the boat shifted out onto the river, they snagged a spot at the top deck railing where the stink of the diesel engine and the barbecue smell of the steam tables was mostly just a memory.

Ben squeezed back against the railing to let a wolfpack of giggling old ladies pass.

Jack was right. The sternwheeler was a good idea. How often did he get to step away from TV travel and conferences, and do stuff like this? If he could shut out the whump, whump of the paddle wheel and the player piano from the bottom deck, the boat ride might be the break he needed.

Below them, the river was running a wide blue-gray, and glinting here and there with reflections of the city's lights. The spread of trees and lawn along the river promenade had already shifted to a shadowy green.

Jack was staring at him. "You serious, Walt Taylor at AFO blew you off?"

Ben kept his gaze out over the river. "That's one way to put it. According to Taylor, American Football Officiating does a great job training their people and we should be impressed by their effort. They handle complaints and so on at the conference level. I believe him about that, so maybe that's why he hadn't heard about the threats... I shouldn't put words in his mouth. He didn't say he didn't know."

"But that was your take," Jack said, took a half-step back from Ben, and looked out across the folks in the middle of the deck. "Jesus, Mary, and Joseph."

Ben let go a sigh. "Anyway, like I said, if the board will go for it, I figure we can help. If this video guy *is* just blowing off steam, then it's nothing we have to worry about. But if we can ID the guy from our website, then if he goes after somebody, we can really help the cops out. Don't you think?"

Jack leaned back, planted his elbows on the painted wood railing, and dangled his hands out into the breeze. "Still playing detective."

"I'm not playing detective. I'm being honest. At this point, our website may be the best place to look for this guy. And we can search without his knowing we're onto him."

A hand clamped down on Ben's shoulder and he turned. Not a foot away, a guy big enough to play nose tackle, his face shining with sweat. "You're Ben Leit! Man, you look good. I just gotta say we miss you. Don't mean to interrupt, sorry. But, man, the Giants screwed up letting you retire. We need you, you know?"

The guy nodded and turned back to a woman nearly as big has he was and the two of them waved touchdown signs at their friends across the boat. After a couple of bear hugs, the pair squeezed their way back toward the stairway behind the wheelhouse.

Jack shot Ben an appraising look. "How much you pay that guy?"

"A hundred." Ben grinned. "And fifty more if he remembered to say it how I wrote it."

Jack's shoulders pumped with that old man wheezing laugh.

For a while they stared out at the lights on the river. Eventually Jack turned and surveyed the top deck. "Turn around," he said and gestured with that lantern chin.

Ben turned. Three men were standing on the far side of the deck, talking. He'd noticed them before. Not all three, but two of them looked familiar. The third guy, the one in the baseball cap, looked more like a teacher. Shorter and too stocky. Baseball cap guy was standing a little to the side of the other two.

Jack cleared his throat. "The guy in the blazer is Lee Greer. The other man is…John something. It's a plain last name. If it were Zaradnik, I'd remember it. Getting old. Lee said he lives here in town."

Ben licked his lip. "John Brown? That's a simple name." If it was John Brown talking with Lee Greer, he'd much rather talk with John Brown. Brown was the one on Videoman's list, not Greer.

Greer looked straight at them and started threading his way through the crowd to Ben's side of the boat.

"Could be Brown." Jack said. "But I keep thinking the name's Downs, you know, like the game… He's god-awful." Jack shook his head. "Sorry, can't remember. Not for certain. Lee will know."

Half-way over to them, Greer got hung up between the throng of people coming out of the stairway up to the top deck and people headed down.

Then somebody yelled for help.

Ben couldn't quite make out what was wrong, but it seemed like Greer's buddy John was having a fit, his red shirt jerking and bucking. And the third guy, the one in the baseball cap, had hold of the red shirt, struggling to get a better grip on John. Trying to hold him up.

Ben zigzagged through a half-dozen tourists blocking the aisle. Then jumped up on the bench seats and edge-walked toward the action, yelling for somebody to get the crew. He dodged plastic shopping bags, coats, and God knows what else as he worked to get across the top deck; he caught a shoe on something, and somebody grabbed at him and tried to steady him. He went down like a fool but managed to roll out of his header into a squat, and stood.

He'd lost track of the action. It took him a minute because five or six people were grabbing at him, asking if he was okay, straightening his jacket, getting in the way of his seeing.

He centered himself and took one of those snapshot looks he used to do when he was still quarterbacking. And he got it. There was a full-blown melee going on at the railing. A woman screamed. The guy in the baseball hat was making a dash for the stairwell. A tall woman in a tan jacket, older, was leaning over the railing, pointing. Next to her, another woman with a scarf on her hair, was shouting to someone below. Greer's friend John had vanished.

The big boat shuddered, the paddle wheel stopped, then reversed, and suddenly it felt like they were more or less hovering on the river.

Greer rushed past Ben, side-stepped, and pushed his way through the crowd to the stairs down. Ben yelled after him, "What's his name?" But Greer was gone.

Where was the crew?

Inflating a small rubber boat, it turned out. Two men climbed in and pushed away. Minutes dragged by with everybody on board talking and milling around. A police launch appeared, then another. They circled the area, getting farther and farther away, the current taking them downriver.

The talk on the top deck shifted from death and

drowning to who had seen what or said what or done what. And the voices kept on keeping on, lifting then fading then lifting again until the sternwheeler eased its way into place against the dock.

The passengers seemed to divide into two groups: the ones who hung along the railing and watched the police setting up to interview the passengers, and the ones already lining up to disembark early and get their interviews over with. Still no sign of Lee Greer or the man in the cap.

Eyeing the line forming at the top of the stairs, Jack said, "You gonna tell them?"

Ben took one more look around for Greer—where had the guy gone?

Jack was waiting for an answer. *Should he tell the police?* He'd been thinking about that. He craned his neck to get a better look at the line of passengers snaking down to the deck below them. He turned so he could catch Jack's reaction.

"Answer me this, Jack: before he went overboard, what did it look like to you?"

"You mean was he shoved or did he jump?"

Ben gave a slow nod.

"I dunno," Jack said. "You want the truth, I'm not sure I could say either way."

Ben nodded. That was pretty much his take. Though maybe he was ready to say "jumped."

Jack squinted at him. "You didn't answer my question. You gonna tell them about the threats?"

"It depends," Ben said. If "John" was John Brown, then he needed to be straight with the police about what he knew. But without the man's name…

Jack pulled out his phone and started calling. "Lee

could tell us who it was." No answer. He tried another number, no answer.

By the time they got back on solid ground, Jack wasn't looking good—sweating, his skin seemed gray. And he still hadn't got hold of Lee Greer.

"You okay?" Ben said.

Jack shook off Ben's concern. "Just want to get done with the police. You decide what we're gonna say?"

"I'm thinking," Ben said, "tell them what we saw, and say, if the man who went overboard is John Brown, then they should be in touch with me. That make sense?"

Chapter 14

Heading to Joplin, MO

Beeker spotted the Route 66 medallion signpost…a few seconds later, another sign painted in the middle of the highway…then another old-time tin sign: all for the next roadside attraction on their list. He'd been hoping they could skip this one. But Deek barked, "This is it."

Beeker obediently tapped the Navigator's brake and pulled into the gravel parking lot of Gary's Gay Parita. This would be stop five of the day if you counted the sandwich break at the state park right on the Meramec River.

Deek was thumping around in the back seat. "The Route 66 stuff I looked at says it's one of the best."

Oh good. Beeker glanced at the clock and let his hands drop to his lap. He was not getting out of the car until the dust cloud settled. Then, he would give Deek ten minutes. Ten minutes. Then they'd be back on the road.

"Come on, Beeker," Deek said. "What if we try to find you a cute little apron to use in your home lab?"

Beeker pushed the Navigator door open and stepped out onto the gravel. The heat and humidity nearly knocked him over. He shifted his neck to unstick his skin from his shirt collar, then craned it to see what Deek was talking about. One more Route 66 museum: part old-time gas station, part cemetery for rusted-out oil delivery trucks, part open field that somebody had populated with outhouses and sheds. Just terrific.

He was thinking about the dinosaur logo on a pair of Sinclair Oil signs when a camper pulled in next to his Navigator. A carload of grandma shoppers piled out with enough straw bags they must've been starting a store. As the old ladies passed him and headed for what used to be a gas station, their heads swiveled back for a good gawk.

Just look at them all, blundering around, poking their heads in. Deek knows how he hates crowds. All counted, there must've been fifty people wandering around. Fifty-six counting the old ladies.

Beeker mopped the back of his neck. The gravel made his feet feel awful. Rubbly and sharp. He hated it. He'd seen enough and he hadn't even left the parking lot. And it was too hot. He needed to get out of the sun. There had to be shade somewhere. Somewhere that didn't involve being crammed together with a rusty tool collection, home-made jam, flour sack dishtowels, and a herd of sweating humanity.

He scanned the wide property. Nothing that didn't involve going inside a dilapidated building. But then, two big pecan trees across the highway. One of them leaning out over the grassy verge.

He made his way across the gravel, across the narrow road they'd driven in on, and climbed up the angled bank. He braced a hand in the deep grass and lowered himself down. He felt exhausted. The pungent smell of the trees washed over him like the summer air. Birds flittered away in the tree's canopy above him. The occasional leaf gave up and rattled its way through to the ground. Farther down the bank, a pair of bright blue damselflies hovered, touched down, and hovered again.

Eventually, he sat up and stretched himself to get a better look at what was going on at Gary's Gay Parita. What was that name about, anyway? Whatever it was, he'd seen enough. If they didn't get moving, they'd be getting into Oklahoma City in the middle of the night.

It seemed like there were way more folks wandering around than when they'd got there. But no red baseball cap. Had Deek taken off without him? Beeker patted his pocket—no, he still had the car key.

Beeker angled his forty-three-year-old body up off the bank and headed back across the road, weaving around a couple of old men commiserating and mopping their bald spots. He stopped at the doorway of a long clapboard shed and peered into the shade. Was that a red cap?

He stepped inside. The air had that stink of what used to be. Like a storage shed somebody'd shut down years ago and never bothered to clean out. A couple of lights fizzed overhead, and he had to ditch his dark glasses just to see across the room. Two more steps...

The dizziness hit him like a shovel, and he thought he was going to pass out. Deek was ranting about a yellow truck crammed against a wall. It was just like the one in Uncle Toby's back pasture. But this one was painted bright yellow and shiny like it was brand new. Beeker's head went from dizzy to humming right between his eyes and it felt like he was just dropping away.

He pivoted, slid past an old man blocking the doorway, and landed outside feeling like he'd just escaped falling down a rabbit hole. He needed a drink, that was it. Dehydration. But no water pipe, no soda machine in sight. Maybe in the old gas station. If it was like Georgia back country, there'd be a soda counter, a couple of old bent wire chairs, a little round table, and a whole wall filled with souvenirs.

He stumbled back down to the little building that obviously had been a gas station back when. But then he had to wait for three ladies to leave just to make room so he could step inside. One whiff of the air in there though, and he couldn't. He backed out and stood leaning on the doorway under the high canopy that sheltered the old-time gas pumps.

The next thing he knew, he was sitting on a rusty bench. His head hurt. Deek was saying whadya think?

"What do I think about what?" Beeker said.

"Sir? Excuse me."

A woman's voice. He looked up, forcing himself to focus on the face. A woman in a white floppy hat was standing next to him. He caught a breath but couldn't seem to talk.

"Excuse me," she said. "Sir?"

She had on green pants and a white blouse with little flowers. She leaned closer. She was wearing perfume. The space between her eyebrows pinched together.

"You doing okay? Maybe if you had some water. How about some water?" She turned, looking back over her shoulder. "Jerry, can you get me a water?"

She was taking his wrist in her hand; she was checking his pulse. "Sir? Are you diabetic? Do you need some sugar, a candy bar?"

Beeker pulled his hand away, smiled—smiling would reassure her—and forced himself to look into her blue eyes. "I'm fine. Just thinking. But, thank you."

She pressed a water bottle into his hand. "Please

take this. But drink slowly, okay?"

He nodded. And drank. The water felt good flooding his tongue, the back of his throat. He used some of the water to wet his handkerchief and press it against his neck. Then drank some more. The sun had shifted around so it made it under the canopy, blasting away on his feet and knees.

Feet and knees…feet and knees… It was like he was coming back from he didn't know where. Maybe that was what caused it, that or the dust. He hated dust. He must've looked down at the bottle he was holding in his hand. His shoes were all dusty with wet splotches. Must've spilled.

His head finally came clear and he looked around. A spoked car tire leaned against the clapboards right next to him. One after the other, four car doors slammed; a family crunched their way across the parking lot.

The people that brought him water had stepped inside the old-time gas station. But he could feel the woman standing in the doorway. He turned to look. She was still watching him. He thanked her, and she disappeared inside.

He checked his watch and the time landed on him like a brick. He'd lost an hour and a half. He remembered being in the long shed where Deek was going on about all the junk. And then what? Maybe he wasn't over whatever he'd come down with in St. Louis. He'd been down for a whole day with a migraine.

He started for the car. Deek would show up when he was ready to. He climbed in, stretched his seat back and got the AC going. He closed his eyes. Losing time. How could that be? Because for years he remembered everything that happened to him.

He could remember the little white edge on his first shoes. He remembered every day from when he was three years old and he knew about calendars, that the days had names and numbers. His mother had some pants she wore for working at home. She wore them for three hundred eight days; she tore a place in the left knee on a nail, patched the tear, and kept wearing them. Two hundred eighty-three days after that nail she threw them in the rag bin. He remembered his first day in school. Mrs. Curry's hair stuck out behind her left ear, she had an ugly brown dress, his classroom was on the east side of the building and the sun shined in the window but never got high enough up the wall to shine on the clock. He read his textbooks once and could recite them back. His dad had four sick days off from work in his whole life until the day of the mall and after that, he wasn't sure he remembered, but he thought his dad missed work for a week. The mall was seventeen days before his birthday. After the mall, his mother stopped answering the door and the telephone and his father moved out. He remembered every step he took in developing his first anesthetic, every test they ran and every result they got before they were approved by the FDA.

He wanted to believe he remembered Deek driving them from Chicago to St. Louis instead of going back to Cleveland. But he didn't. He remembered being furious at Deek, and that Deek said he'd passed out, that he'd been sick. But that was a lie. His mom had done the same thing, lying, saying he'd been too tired to remember when she moved them from Savannah to Cleveland. "Nobody remembers everything," she'd said. But back then, he did remember everything. That was the point.

Chapter 15

Ben waited in the doorway of the hotel meeting room for one more detective and another interview. You had to wonder how long the St. Louis P.D. was going to ask him to hang around. Not that he objected to helping them out, but he'd have been way happier spending the day back in Minneapolis, doing what he could to take care of Mimi.

Detective Ally Lattimer folded herself into a conference room chair and pulled a couple of pages out of a little notebook she was carrying. Except for the lack of nail polish, she looked more like a sports model than a cop.

"Mr. Leit. I appreciate that you've told us your story already. But there've been some developments and we have a few more questions. I'll try to make this quick."

"Developments?" Ben took a chair opposite her.

She smiled and pushed a pen and a drawing across the table to him.

"If you could describe your movements on the boat, and as you do that, if you could mark where you stood or walked and note the direction you walked with arrows. An A-B-C system will work fine. Start from when you and Mr. Halprin arrived on the top deck.

He gave the page a quarter turn so it was wider than it was tall and he could look at it from the same angle as he had that night. He laid out the high points: A wheelhouse, B railing, C the bench where he fell, D where the man went overboard.

"We boarded and went straight to the top deck. The stairs end by the wheelhouse—"

"You didn't stroll around?"

Ben shook his head no. "Just grabbed a good spot at the railing."

"And you were there to meet with Mr. Greer?"

He leaned back in his chair. "Sort of. Jack Halprin, the man I was with, knows Lee Greer. Greer's a football official for the Big10. During a website Board meeting, I mentioned to Jack I wanted to talk to a few college football officials, and Jack tried to set up a meeting with Lee Greer. As it turned out, I never got a chance to talk with the guy."

She was looking from one page of her notebook to the other…back…forward…back.

He said, "The papers didn't say. Who was the man who died?" He watched her for any kind of a reaction because, after all, they were in Big10 country. Two of the men who got videos, Pete Webber and John Brown, officiated Big10 games. But then it hit him, she'd said *developments*. No way did *developments* mean this was an accident.

She laid her pen aside and said, "Let's not lose focus. You heard someone yell for help."

"Yes. I didn't see who," he said. "We looked over— Jack and I—and there was a fight going on. Or, not a fight. Actually, it looked like somebody was having a fit. The guy in the baseball cap was trying to keep the other guy from going overboard."

Lattimer cleared her throat. "And you never met Mr. Brown."

Ben's gut dropped to his knees. *That changed everything.* His brain went off in a dozen directions about the follow-up he needed to do.

"John Brown? An official for the Big10?" he said. "That's who it was went overboard?"

She kept her gaze down on her notes. "And you never met him."

She wasn't denying it, so it was Brown. "Correct."

"What about the man in the baseball hat? Meet him?"

Ben shook his head no. "Never met him. Don't think I'd ever seen him before. Except, you know, we saw him across the deck. We looked for him after. But no. Never met him. Never talked to him."

"Okay." She laid her pen aside. "We have your description of him. But sometimes people remember something more after they talk with us. So, if you don't mind, could you describe him for me—the man with the baseball hat."

"Other than the hat," Ben said. "Maybe five foot ten. But your men must've talked with him."

"Five foot ten. Hair color? Caucasian, Latino, Black?"

They're looking for him. He must've got away without talking to the police. Ben closed his eyes. "I'm guessing sandy hair, maybe even gray; short enough the baseball cap mostly covered it. The cap looked new. You know, clean, no fading. What else? Thick body. If I said, like a linebacker, would you know what I meant?"

"Think so," she said. "Not fat but strong shoulders? Sturdy, would you say?"

"Close enough. Can't do eye color. He was too far away. His hands looked small, you know, against John

Brown's arm when he was grabbing? Just an impression, but yeah, small hands."

She made a note and regarded him. "Anything else? For example, he wore a baseball cap. How about a team jacket? A tee shirt. Sports shoes? Did you see a watch? Wedding ring? Tattoo? Can you characterize the type of clothing he wore?"

"Regular jacket." Ben shook his head no. 'I only saw him for a couple of seconds. Sorry."

"Okay," she said. "Somebody yells for help. You see who?"

Ben shook his head no.

"How about the voice. Was it a man's or woman's voice?"

He stared at the diagram he'd marked. Maybe something about it would jog his memory. Man's voice or woman's? He'd been thinking it was a man's. But putting himself back on that deck: he's standing there, watching Lee Greer get swallowed up trying to get past the pack of fat ladies.

"It was a woman's voice," he said. "But I didn't see who."

"Okay," Lattimer said. "I believe you said he was trying to restrain Mr. Brown, to keep him on board. Is that right?"

"Yes."

"You said restrain. Why'd you say that?"

Why had he? "Because the guy in the cap had Mr. Brown wrapped up, like in a tackle. He kept grabbing like he was trying to get a better grip. He kept trying to hold Brown down."

"Okay," she said. "You never had the impression that Mr. Brown was trying to get away?" Her eyes widened. "You have a problem, Mr. Leit?"

"Not a problem," he said. "But it wasn't a fight. Nobody threw a punch or anything. It was more like jerking…flailing his arms. The baseball cap guy had one arm holding Mr. Brown. That's when I took off to get over there. So I didn't see most of it."

She nodded and made a note.

A sour taste flooded his mouth—his whole system. He should be telling her that John Brown was one of the guys who'd been threatened. Why the hell had he given his word he wouldn't talk about the threats except to the website directors? On the other hand, how likely was it that she'd take threats from some football nut seriously?

He pushed the diagram across the table like he was done. He said, "Thinking about it, having a fit doesn't make sense. Like, not epilepsy. I don't think he could qualify to work as an official with that kind of a medical problem. But the truth is, I don't know. Has anybody checked?"

Lattimer stopped messing with her notebook and regarded him. Still that blank face. She glanced over to where a gardener had started working in the atrium and, finally, she closed her notebook and pushed it aside.

She took a deep slow breath, like she was annoyed. Like she knew he was holding back.

Screw Football Officiating.

"Off the record?" he said.

She sat back in her chair and folded her arms.

"A little over a month ago," he said. "I got a call from a guy at American Football Officiating. That's the organization that handles officiating at college football games, okay? And I gave them my word I would not talk about this, so, you know."

Her eyes shifted to her notebook, then back to him. And he laid out the whole story: the phone calls, the conferences, what the website was doing to try to help, his meeting with Walt Taylor. Most of all, the threatening letters and the DVDs.

"And John Brown is one of the men?" she said. "If you could provide us with copies of the letter and DVD?"

"Sure," he said. "You know, I must've watched that John Brown DVD a dozen times. I sure didn't recognize him."

"Sometimes it's like that," she said. "It's why so many perps are never identified." She opened her notebook, turned to a fresh page and began taking down the contact details for the people she should talk to at American Football Officiating. That done, she worked a business card out and handed it to him.

"Mr. Leit, I said there had been developments. A minute ago, you said *off the record.* And I'm okay with that. So… Remember when I said developments? They're not for publication. You okay with that?"

"Absolutely," he said.

"It's just, you may be in a position to help us. And we appreciate that. So, what has not been made public… We don't know *what* killed Mr. Brown," she said. "But it was not a natural death. The coroner is certain. Mr. Brown did not have a heart attack, or anything like that. But he was dead when he hit the water."

Chapter 16

Joplin

Beeker figured the girl behind the reception desk of their hotel had to be a trainee. For the better part of a full minute, she had stared at the equipment in front of her as if she only vaguely remembered seeing it before. She looked up, clearly surprised he was still standing there. "You're all checked out, Mr. Beacham. Is there something else?"

She had brown eyes. He hadn't noticed that before.

Suddenly he couldn't think. Or rather, he couldn't make the right words come out of his mouth. And yet he heard himself say, "My brother seems to have disappeared. I'll be right back. If you see him—"

Her dark brows narrowed, and she leaned across the desk. "I'm sorry?"

Beeker forced a smile, repeated what he'd just told her and added, "He looks like me. Only older." She still didn't get it. Well damned if he was going to draw her a picture. He headed for the men's room.

He was standing in front of a sink, his hands soapy, dripping. The lights bouncing off all that white tile left him feeling like he'd taken hallucinogens. Someone had left a sheaf of papers on the marbled counter. Not his business. The men's room door opened then clicked closed.

"Sorry," Deek said. "You've been looking for me."

"Where've you been?"

"Catching up," Deek said.

Beeker grabbed a handful of paper towels. Then took a long time drying his hands.

"C'mon, Beeker," Deek said. "No reason to get huffy, I just saved you doing your homework. Check out what I pulled together."

Beeker glanced at the end of the counter, stuffed his used towels in the waste bin, and scooped up the loose pages. Thumbing through, it was all Route 66, fourteen pages' worth. Deek had been on a computer somewhere, and that did not feel good. For a moment, Beeker held his breath. Without comment, he folded the pages in half, crammed them in his pocket, and headed for the car. "Let's get moving," he said.

On their way out of Joplin, they must've passed a zillion two- and three-story brick buildings all tricked out with murals from the Route 66 way-back machine. There were plenty of national maps and "Welcome to Joplin." Most of the pictures featured pin-up girls or old-time US highway shields, or both. The girls all had long hair and swingy skirts that were blowing a little in the wind, and they all had big smiles and leaned against the fenders of shiny new cars. "New" being maybe 1952 or thereabouts. Suddenly, Joplin disappeared in the rear-view mirror.

"You're taking the Historic highway, right?"

"I am," Beeker said.

Back when he'd traveled on business, he'd barely noticed the outskirts of cities. A few times on cab rides in from the airport—warehouses, business parks, light rail. He was making up for that oversight now, for sure.

He opened his window a crack and sucked in the farm country air. The thick row of trees lining the road smelled like a summer morning even if they had already hit October. In a way, it felt good once they were out among the little farms and patchwork fields. Much better than all those roadside attractions Deek had come up with.

Just into Kansas, they cruised into the little town of Baxter Springs. There was a nice old bridge just out of town. But, stopping again? How far had they gone since Joplin, thirty miles?

Beeker's gut was killing him from all the greasy food they'd been eating. He'd vowed over breakfast to be more careful today. But they still had to stop at every "museum" along the way so Deek could stuff down another corndog and soda.

Baxter Springs Independent Oil & Gas turned out to be another step along the road to hell. Besides the usual junk food, the Baxter Springs folks were hawking a full-on refresher course on Bonnie and Clyde. When your claim to fame is "a seventy-year-old crime spree stopped here," what does that say about you?

Beeker dutifully inspected pictures of the shoot-up from that movie, which did nothing to help his gut or his mood. He carefully returned one of the Bonnie postcards to the little wire rack and wiped his hand on his pants.

Was the whole damned trip going to be stopping and dust and rust and junk food? Was that what driving Route 66 was about? Too late to turn back. And besides, when he'd tried that, he'd failed anyway.

Beeker crunched his way across the parking lot back to the Navigator. He resettled himself behind the wheel, and, figuring he had a few minutes before Deek showed up, he took a look at Deek's printouts. At least seven more "attractions" that, according to Deek, they should visit.

Beeker's heart sank. They weren't a fifth of their way to Oklahoma City. If they skipped the rest of the "attractions," they'd be lucky to be there in three or four hours. And they still had to come up with a hotel.

Right on cue, Deek said, "Ready?"

Beeker started the car. "Was that the thirteenth or fourteenth old-time gas station we've stopped at?"

No answer.

"Okay," Beeker said and pulled out onto the old highway.

It should've been a pleasure driving the backroads— a flat landscape covered with cornfields. But with the bushes so close to the road, it felt like he was driving down a tunnel.

It occurred to him Deek was not talking. He snaked a finger under the car's seatbelt just to loosen it across his lap. The silent treatment was fine by him. He could drive in peace. Drive long enough and he could actually think about things, how they might have worked out.

What if Deek had never played football? Or if Green Bay hadn't drafted him?

They passed a sign. They were leaving Kansas.

Or, what if Deek hadn't played right away at the pro level?

Because right away, the NFL thing took over their lives. Sure, it was fun at first...

It was like living at the circus. Getting ready for the Draft, then going to it. When the time finally came, their whole family flew to New York. Dad had booked a hotel suite right in the center of everything—the Marriott:

gleaming and loud, full of players, their families and girlfriends. Every hallway was rocking. So much, Beeker's mother said she couldn't sleep. At eleven, Beeker couldn't see why she would want to sleep, it was all too exciting. When the teams finally started picking their players, the whole family watched the action alongside the other UGA guys.

Deek was hoping he'd get taken in Round Two, but his call came in the middle of Round Four. Deek would be going to the Green Bay Packers. And everybody in the room went crazy. Beeker spent an entire month's allowance on tee shirts and bobbleheads and a foam block that looked like a big chunk of cheese that Green Bay fans wore like a hat.

Once they got home from the Draft, things stayed nuts for a while with Deek getting ready to take off for Wisconsin. Then, like a magic trick, he was gone. Dad was still so proud, he had a tee shirt made, "My Son NFL Round Four." He wore that shirt until everything turned sour. As long as Deek played, Dad flew to every Green Bay game. He was in the stands when they carried Deek off the field on a stretcher.

A shiny black motorcycle whipped by the Navigator and refocused Beeker on the road. Not that long after, they crossed into Oklahoma, and a battered gray pickup nosed out onto the road and stalled. Its stack of hay bales swayed ominously. Beeker dogged the brakes so hard, the Navigator's tires slipped onto the gravel shoulder and rapid-fire spray exploded on the car's undercarriage.

Beeker managed to angle the big car back onto the asphalt, but good God! Any minute that pickup's load was going to turn loose all over the road.

He re-set the cruise control to thirty-two miles an

hour and waited for the thud in his chest to settle down. He was tired. And he didn't give a damn about traveling a historic highway. He'd only gone along with the road trip idea in order to shift Deek's focus off of football and Savannah.

Beeker's gut did a flip-flop. Savannah where they'd killed Pete Webber. Where Deek had killed Pete Webber.

He should've known he couldn't convince Webber to quit officiating. They never should have gone to Savannah.

Deek was doing okay now though. And he wasn't insisting they kill the other men they'd sent DVDs. At least that was something. Keeping Deek happy and focused on anything but football was gonna be the key to surviving until they got to the end of Route 66.

Suddenly Beeker felt Deek's hand cup the back of his neck. The skin of Deek's palm, tough and cool. Beeker managed to keep his eyes on the road, but all the tension he'd built up drained away in that singular moment.

"You know," Deek said, "if we by-passed Tulsa and drove straight through, we'd be in Oklahoma City before supper. How about we do that? Bag our list of places to stop. Just get into town and find a hotel?"

When they were kids, everybody acted like Deek was some kind of a God. So did their dad. Beeker thought so too, but not because of football. Not because Deek had so many friends. It was like Deek could do anything he wanted. As long as he was happy, nobody was a better brother than Deek.

Until his junior year in high school, Deek was the one that listened. Back then, he never acted like he was ashamed of Beeker. Deek had this way of slinging an arm around him like they were buddies. And if he didn't feel like talking, Deek was good with just hanging out.

Their dad's take on Beeker had been different.

If something went wrong for Beeker, at school or on the way home, their dad would throw down whatever was in his hand and say, "For Christ's sake, Weirdo!"

Even then, Beeker knew. That was what it was really about.

He was a weirdo. His dad hated it. In grade school, they had him doing high school math, reading stuff the other kids couldn't figure out. At home, he didn't do sports like his dad wanted; he made stuff up with his chemistry set. His dad didn't get it, and not getting it, and not being able to do anything about it, made his dad mad. Anybody could see that. Anybody with a brain.

Every time, after one of those blow-ups, once the house calmed down, Deek would slip into Beeker's room and talk about football, or Night Rider or Battle Star Galactica or the A-Team.

Deek set up ways to make Beeker the hero. Like sometimes he'd ask for help with his algebra. As far as Beeker could see, high school algebra was easy. But Deek would make out like he didn't get it and then copy down the answers Beeker worked out.

Deek always said, "You're the man, Beeker. I'm just lucky to have football. If I didn't, I'd be selling burgers for a living." They both knew that wasn't true. It didn't matter anyway. Deek was going to UGA because of football. And then he was going to be a big star in the NFL.

Well, everybody knew how that turned out.

Chapter 17

Ben stretched his body full-out on his super-king bed and stared at his bedroom ceiling. He couldn't sleep. Worse, he couldn't decide if coming back to Seattle had been the right move. Maybe he should have hung out in Minneapolis.

After St. Louis, he had flown back to Minneapolis. They'd finally had that sweet dinner at her place like he'd promised. And he'd told Mimi the whole story. He'd said he knew in his bones, Videoman had murdered John Brown. He'd said he couldn't prove it, but it had to be true. He'd offered to hang out with her in Minneapolis and work remote with Thui. "I'll be okay here," she said. "You need to go home. Tell Thui I said good luck."

Every time he closed his eyes, his brain did a rerun of John Brown flailing at the people that were trying to keep him from going over the railing.

He glanced over at the luminous numbers on his clock. 6:18. It would be light in an hour. If he couldn't sleep, he might as well get going. He could shift website security into high drive.

An hour later, he drove the three and a half miles from his place on Lake Washington over to the website's office in South Lake Union. As soon as he let himself in, he could hear classical music, Vivaldi. He headed for Thui's office.

Wire thin, intense, Thui always reminded him of a

starving bird with a long neck. Partly because of the man's habit of holding his head way forward to stare at the computer screen. Thui was the Website group's first big-time hire. And man, had they lucked out.

It was Thui who had set up the website's vast network. Where a fan for a particular college could access the parts of the website that were dedicated to his school. A fan could search just about anything that school's alums would want: players, potential recruits, news, gossip. Or he could post comments on a news story, ask questions, toss out a pithy idea for discussion, or just generally grouse.

A hundred-fifty schools with four fan sites for every school… Thui had designed a masterful system. And now, it looked like he was engaged in a mind-meld with his creation.

"Hold on," Thui said but kept his gaze on the pair of computer screens he had going. As his fingers clacked over the keyboard, what looked like computer code spilled out over the screen at a neighboring desk. He stopped typing and piloted his desk chair over to the screen with the code, rolled back to his keyboard, did a few more clicks and turned to Ben. "They're sure John Brown was murdered?"

Ben nodded, brought Thui up to date, and added, "To the extent we uncover anything solid, we need to keep Ally Lattimer in the loop."

Thui's jaw looked way too tight.

"Have a problem?" Ben said.

Thui shook his head no and drained what had to be the last of a take-out coffee. "It'd be a help if we knew more what we were looking for."

"Isn't that what you're doing now? Looking for

Videoman?"

Thui explained what he was doing, which wasn't looking. At least not yet.

While Ben cleaned out yesterday's coffee and made a fresh pot, they brainstormed until Ben felt like he'd run out of ideas. "What we need is an expert," he said. "U.W. must have a criminology department."

Thui's dark eyes glimmered and he cleared a computer screen.

"Wait, wait," Ben said. "I know they do. I know a guy, Karl Hessman…"

It took him a minute to unzip his jacket pocket and dig out his phone. Why hadn't he thought about Karl before? Karl was an expert in criminal psychology. Karl climbed inside the heads of these nuts for a living, didn't he? Karl could give them the insight they needed.

He hadn't seen Karl for a while. Still, you get to know somebody in AA. It's a different bond.

Karl answered his phone on the second ring, but said he wasn't taking on projects just now.

Just from Karl's tone, Ben got it: explaining the threats he was investigating wasn't gonna change things. He tried a Hail Mary pass: "Look, one of these guys was just murdered. There's three other men, their lives are at stake. If I could just run what we have by you, maybe you have some insight into this nut."

He could hear Karl breathing into the phone.

Finally, Karl said, "I can't get away until after noon. You know Luigi's, on Capitol Hill? I'll walk over. See you about 1:00."

Ben was talking his plan through with Thui when a text from Mimi rolled in.

Sorry. I deci…thou…

He closed out the message and tried accessing the text again but got the same garbled nothing. He thumbed a text back to her, *Ur text broke up, send again.*

Mimi's answer came back as, *Sorry, I…*

When rebooting his phone didn't work, Thui said, "Problem's in the message. Or her phone."

He tried calling her, and landed in voicemail.

The rest of the morning, he hung with Thui and worked on the chat room, screening the stuff members had posted. He tried calling Mimi a couple of times but never made a connection. Just after noon, when he still couldn't get through to her, he headed over to Capitol Hill.

A little rain squall hit soon after he left the website offices, and he had an image of Karl showing up at Luigi's cold and soaked—not good for a successful pitch. But the farther south he drove, the more the storm backed off, and by the time he passed Volunteer Park, the downpour was mostly over.

A half-block down from Luigi's, he climbed out of the car and planted a foot into a slide of leaves disguising a pothole. Clearly, they were heading into a full-on Seattle winter. And it was only October. He zipped his jacket and started for the restaurant.

Luigi's was mostly full when Ben looked in the front windows. No sign of Karl. And not on the street either. He checked his phone. Nothing from Mimi, nothing from Karl. Couples edged by him, disappeared inside the pizzeria, and reappeared carrying boxes that smelled like—God he was starving.

Twenty minutes past one, and no sign of Karl.

It occurred to him that maybe Karl was drinking again. He'd sounded depressed. And it happened sometimes, falling off the wagon. He'd come way too close himself. After his dad was murdered, he just wanted to numb it all out.

Rain started bucketing down, and he stepped back against the old brick building to get some cover; then had to move out of the way to let in two women and their kids. When he turned back to the street, there was Karl, walking toward him on the other side of Harrison: head down, shoulders drooping, shoes slopping the leaves and water.

Karl headed across the street, worked up to a smile though it wasn't much of one, and tapped Ben on his shoulder. "Saw you a couple of weeks ago on ESPN. You going to do TV now?"

They headed inside. The smell from the pizza ovens could almost wipe away the rotten weather. But even better than that smell, the enveloping warmth of the red brick walls. Once they ordered and shed their coats on a spare chair, Karl did a little rant about the rain. And followed that up with a memory he had of dinner with his wife at Café Olivera, a restaurant Ben remembered well that was just around the corner. Karl's story was beautiful, about earrings he'd surprised Ann with.

There was something tender and lost about Karl, different from how Ben remembered him at AA meetings. Then, as their pizzas arrived, Karl said, "Sorry to eat and go but I can't stay long."

Ben said, "You just got here, now you need to leave?"

"Ann's terminal." Karl's chest rose and fell, and finally he got himself under control. "I, uh…not your fault. I shouldn't have left her. Opal's there, but…"

"Opal is your helper?"

"Practical nurse." Karl slumped back against his chair. "We bought the house because we loved the neighborhood. We moved. A month later she went to the doctor…" Between bites, Karl shifted their talk around to the life they'd planned to share, the trips they dreamed of taking.

Ben kept flashing on the days after his dad's murder and how he couldn't talk about it because, if he did talk, he went on and on, until whoever had asked him about his dad was wishing to God they'd never asked him anything. It seemed like he couldn't stop talking because stopping meant the end of his dad, again.

"Man, I'm sorry," Ben said.

"You didn't know." Karl flashed a weak smile and glanced at his wrist. "What was it you wanted help with?"

"You got enough going on," Ben said.

Karl's face went from curious to concerned. "You have another stalker."

"In a way," Ben said. "But not me personally. You don't need to take on my stuff."

"I can give it a few minutes. I just get jangly when I'm away from her, that's all." Karl straightened his chair around so he was sitting directly across from Ben. "I don't know how much I can help. I'm not working. Because of Ann. I took a leave from the U. and shut down my consulting so I could be with her."

"If you could maybe point me to somebody."

Karl leaned into the table. "Tell me."

"We're looking for a killer," Ben said and explained about America Football Officiating, the threats, the letters and DVDs, and the death of John Brown.

"The police are on it," Karl said.

Ben nodded. "As far as John Brown goes, yes. But there are three *other* letters to other officials. And those are just the ones we know about. The officiating people asked for our help, looking for crazy posts on the fan feedback. The idea is we could maybe pull together enough specific information to give the other cities a heads up. Thing is, we don't know what to look for. And…that's when I thought of you."

"You said letters. Talk to me about the letters."

"I can do better than talk," Ben said and pushed the folder he'd brought with him across the table.

Karl fished his glasses out of a shirt pocket and opened the folder. He read the first letter, glanced at the others, and the color came back into his face. For the first time since they'd walked in, the guy looked totally dialed in.

"He cares about something," Karl said. "At first read, I'd say it's the *game*. Does he see it in some idealized form would you say? Or is he focused on protecting the players? A father perhaps. Could he have lost a son? Or had a kid badly injured?" He fingered one of the letters; read it again. "Ordinary paper. Computer printing. You probably noticed he writes in complete sentences."

For Ben, it was like having so many of his fleeting suspicions confirmed. But he'd never considered the thing about idealizing the game.

Karl was nodding to himself.

"Losing a kid," Ben said. "You're thinking older, then."

"Possibly. The language is wrong for a kid. And the style of the writing. Too self-assured. Direct address. No misspellings. Proper punctuation. Curious there's no vulgarity." He placed the letters back in the envelope and leaned back in his chair. "Funny how your guy makes his threat. How well do you know your Shakespeare?"

Ben arched an eyebrow. "Not so you'd notice. What's the connection?"

"There's a line in King Lear. He's ranting about the wrongs done to him. He says, *I will have such revenges on you both that all the world shall—I will do such things.* Recognize that emotion? *I will do such things.* Rage but a lack of specificity about what he intends to do?"

"Well, it's specific now. I was there," Ben said, and explained about John Brown's death in St. Louis. "Anyway, you have enough on your plate. But maybe you could give me a name of somebody. You know, once we get some stuff pulled together."

"Uh-h-h, one death already," Karl said and glanced out at the rainy street. "You said DVDs. You have a copy?"

"Seriously," Ben said. "If you could just give me a name."

Karl shook his head no. "Ann sleeps a lot these days. There's nothing I can do, so I sit there beside her. Just in case, you know. But you can only do that so long. I remember you talking about your mother. So, I know you know how it is."

'I don't want to impose," Ben said.

"I can't teach, not now. And I can't do the regular consulting because I can't travel. But I could dig into this. You know, after Ann is asleep. Maybe it's what I need, a project like this. That work for you?"

Once they got out on the street, Karl said, "I'm not sure how much help I can be. But send me some examples of the fan site posts. That's enough to get me going, give me an idea what you're looking at."

Ben started to apologize again, and Karl waved him off. "Whoever is working for you, tell them to send it as a PDF attachment. And text me. Same number you reached me at."

Fifteen minutes later Ben barged through the website's front door. No one. He headed back to the research center, his voice loud enough to be heard wherever his team was, even if they did have their ear buds in.

"Thui, can you pull together a PDF of the posts you and Devonne are flagging? We need to get it to—"

As he pushed open the door to their main work room, Thui and Devonne shifted their eyes away from the computer monitor they'd been staring at.

But it was Mimi who spoke up.

"Hi yourself," she said. "I texted you I was coming back early. After what you said at the airport, the more I thought about it... I figured you could use some help." She lifted her hands off the computer keyboard and did a little mock shrug.

She had that smile going that always flattened him.

First Karl agreeing to help, and now Mimi back? Could it get any better?

Chapter 18

Oklahoma City

Beeker was lying on his back in the middle of a king-size bed. His stomach wasn't doing backflips anymore and his eyes actually were focusing. The armoire loomed at him from the far wall where the television screen gleamed like a great granite tombstone.

It seemed like he remembered the sun knifing its way through a gap in the hotel room's blackout drapes. But that must've been hours ago. Because the light had moved across the room and now it was rebounding off the full-length mirror in the bathroom door. He'd been sick. That had to explain it.

It would be good to know the time. But he couldn't seem to summon the energy to roll over and check the clock on the nightstand.

In spite of an exhaustion he couldn't explain, he pulled himself upright, swung his legs over the side of the bed and touched his feet to the floor. His whole body ached. Like he'd been doing calisthenics or running on a treadmill. For weeks it seemed like. There were painkillers in with his razor. He braced his hands on his thighs, stood in spite of his aching body, and checked out the bathroom.

He'd...he'd...slept in his clothes. He never did that. But he didn't remember going to bed either.

What was wrong with him?

His phone lay on the bathroom counter next to a wadded up white towel. He grabbed for the towel, not his phone. Google flashed open on a football website he'd been haunting for years and, though it seemed like he hadn't touched it, the internet connection shifted him into the Big10 Hardcore Football Fan chat room.

Most of the chat room posts were gossip, but there was usually some good news in there too. His eyes scanned down the chat subjects, mostly arguments about one game, a particular play, some recruiting idea. But then...*Fan Blamed for Murdered Football Official.*

It was like a siren going off in his head. Beeker's thumb quivered. His phone flipped sideways and tumbled away from him. He scrambled to catch it midair, but missed. It went skittering across the bathroom floor and out onto the carpeted bedroom where it ended up under the armoire. He managed to retrieve it using a coat hanger. At least it wasn't broken.

By the time he got to his feet, his heart was hammering. He knew it. They'd found Pete Webber. Somebody had seen them. Some cracker remembered seeing his car. Sweat poured off of him. He stumbled over to his little hotel room desk and sank into the chair.

PeteWebberPetewebberPetewebber.

His breath finally under control, he carefully tapped the headline and scanned the first entry, then down the next few responses from fans.

"A fan gave some Big10 football official what he deserved."

"I saw the TV coverage. The guy fell off a boat."

"Wrong, I talked with somebody who was there. He committed suicide."

There was a half-dozen more entries, all arguing about something they pretty clearly didn't know anything about.

Beeker laid his phone aside and stared at his hands. If the dead man fell off a boat, this was not about Pete Webber. But the police were saying it was a murder. So, who died? And where was he killed? And how? And when?

He Googled Pete Webber—nothing new. But according to The St. Louis Post Dispatch, John Brown had been pulled out of the Mississippi River, dead. Beeker's mouth turned to sand. A drop of sweat splashed down on his cellphone screen. *His* John Brown lived in Springfield, Illinois. That's where he'd sent the DVD.

Cold and sweating, he dug a handkerchief out of his pants pocket and mopped his face. He forced himself to finish reading about a riverboat accident that turned out to be *not* an accident, but it was about John Brown, Big10 official, and there couldn't be two of them. The worst of it: the police were saying it was a suspicious death. They weren't releasing details.

Beeker made another swipe with his handkerchief.

They'd been in St. Louis. Three days ago. He'd spent the day in bed with a migraine. Deek had gone out. But where? He couldn't see it, not Deek on his own. If Deek had been planning to do something…

"He would've needed help," Beeker said, and pocketed his phone.

Talking to himself. Now *that* was ridiculous. He finished packing. They were finally on their way truly West. Deek was probably already down in the lobby, pacing up a storm.

By the time they finished loading the car, Beeker

was feeling better. And he didn't think about Brown again until they were almost out of Oklahoma City. But then, *JohnBrown ... JohnBrown ... JohnBrown.* The name thumped in his brain every time they crossed a seam in the old cement highway.

As they passed their zillionth Historic Route 66 sign, Beeker said, "You remember John Brown?"

There was a definite pause before Deek said, "Who?"

Beeker gripped the wheel. "John. Brown. The other Big10 official we wrote to."

Deek snorted. "You been looking at football websites. I thought we weren't doing that."

"That's not the point. Do you remember him?"

"Remember John Brown? Jesus, Beeker, of course I do. So what?"

Beeker gritted his teeth and passed a too-wide, long-load truck.

"He was murdered," Beeker said.

"No shit? Somebody killed him? He dropped out? He's been traded? He's playing for another team?"

"Not funny."

"If you say so," Deek said. "How'd you hear about it?"

Beeker's hands were leaving sweat marks on the steering wheel. "The St. Louis papers say it looked like he drowned. But the police say it's a suspicious death. I think that means murder."

"I guess he won't be wrecking any more kids then, will he?"

Beeker couldn't come up with the right words. Eventually he said true enough and kept on driving west.

Coming up on Chickasha, the gas pump icon on the

car's dashboard suddenly blinked red. Beeker pulled off the highway and found a Conoco station. As he leaned against the back fender and listened to the whoosh of the gas, a little dust devil made its way across the far parking lot.

Wait a minute...how could the tank be empty? They'd filled it just before Oklahoma City, hadn't they? Easy enough to check his charge card but he'd have bet money he remembered. He climbed back in the car, moved it to the side of the station and parked. "Back in a few," he said. He needed antacids. He needed out of the car.

Inside the station, he grabbed a pack of Tums, headed up front and glanced down at the empty news rack. "Out of papers?" he said. The cashier climbed off her stool and leaned over the counter. "Guess so," she said. "That be it?"

Beeker nodded, paid, popped a mint lozenge, and strolled back to the men's room. The stink of chlorine combined with the antacid vapors nearly knocked him over. But better that, he decided, than not clean. He stood in front of the door, blocking it with his back in case Deek came after him, and pulled out his phone.

In seconds he was looking at the Buckeye football fan site...nothing about St. Louis. His thumb seemed to work on its own: *Somebody's killing officials.*

He read what he'd just tapped into the message line. He should delete it.

The restroom door banged against his butt. "Sorry," they said.

A boy. Not Deek.

Beeker's heart was hammering. A whole tank of gas, gone in, what, fifty miles? He pressed send. He turned his phone off, washed his hands, and slow-walked the whole way back to the Navigator searching the asphalt for signs of a gas leak. At the car, he squatted and scrutinized the area under the rear axle. No gassy smell, no droplets. Not from the gas tank and not—once he walked around to the front and checked—not under the engine either.

He climbed back behind the wheel and for the first time since they'd started the trip, he made a mental note of the numbers on the mileage gauge. He started the car and made his way back onto the highway.

As they hit cruising speed, Deek said, "So what's going on?"

Beeker kept his eyes on the road. "Just checking for a leak."

"You got your tail in a knot about John Brown."

"You were there."

"Where? St. Louis? Me and a couple hundred thousand other people. Jesus, Beeker."

"You were there."

"You think I killed him? Like I knew he was in St. Louis? Damn, Beeker, talk about paranoid. You want a run-down of what I did? I spent most of the day at the Cowboy Museum, I saw a lot of old photographs, a bunch of sculptures, I walked around, ate some street food, came back and hit the hotel bar. I didn't know I'd need the names of witnesses."

Beeker stared hard out at the road in front of him. He shouldn't have mentioned it.

Chapter 19

Mimi climbed out of her spot behind the breakfast table and headed for the foyer. She stopped there just long enough to change from her trainers into her wetland shoes. "Heading out. I know you need to call that guy, but want to join me?"

He still hadn't reached the California official, Redweather. And he'd promised Thui that by end of day he'd finish his review of posts on the University of Nebraska website. On the other hand, if she wanted to talk, he shouldn't put her off.

"You bet," he said.

They walked west through the Laurelhurst neighborhood toward the Union Bay Natural Area. It was the perfect day for a walk. The high clouds that blocked the sun left the sky a pale silver. The lake itself was smooth as glass. They stopped at that place where the marsh path came closest to the water. He wrapped an arm around her and she leaned into him, stretching her arm around his waist. A long V of snow geese split the sky and turned south.

She waited until the whole flight disappeared, crossing the hills over South Center. Then she said, "I did a lot of thinking after you left Minneapolis."

A tingle shot down his arms. He said, "Buddy, I—"

She pulled away from him and put her hand up. "Let me just say this, okay?"

He nodded, but to be honest, he could barely breathe.

"I know all summer I kept saying I wanted my own life. Well, I got a good taste of my life while I was back in Minneapolis. I made all the decisions, pushed people to do what needed to be done. I felt like I was on thin ice from daybreak until I fell asleep, if I slept at all."

She fished a tissue out of a pocket, then balled it up in her hand. "What I need to say is, I shouldn't have walked away from you in Minneapolis. I was just so mad at my father. And when you said maybe we should get married... I knew you were asking because Dad had been such an ass about it."

The way she was standing there, he knew not to touch her. But God, he wanted so much just to hold her.

"I shouldn't have shut you down the way I did. Not when I love you..."

Finally!

"It scares me," she said. "Not because of CTE. It scares me because marriage scares me. I mean, you've met my family. What kind of an example are they?" She stepped back and checked his face. "Is that okay?"

God, he loved this woman.

"More than okay."

She put her lips together and did that popping thing she did. "One more thing before we talk about the officials. And don't take this the wrong way. But the next time you ask me to marry you? If that ever happens again, I want a real proposal, you know?"

She ducked her head. "We're already a team, aren't we? We just, when this is over, I want us to— Let's think how we can work together without somebody dying, okay? I think we could do something really good. Deal?"

She stuck out her hand like they were signing a business contract. But her eyes were shining at him.

He used her proffered hand to pull her close and kiss her.

She pressed herself away from his chest. "Didn't your criminal psychologist say maybe this was connected to a football injury? If you're okay with it, I have an idea."

She talked strategy most of the way back to the house—beginning with a couple of tweaks to a program she had. She seemed pretty confident she could come up with a nation-wide injuries list.

A program that could filter twenty years of sports reporting down to information they could actually look at sounded great to him. But most of the way back to the house, all he could really think about was that it'd been a year, or nearly, and she'd finally said she loved him.

The house phone was ringing as they unlocked the front door. Ben managed to grab it and listen. A hot nerve ran up his neck. "Hold on." He put the phone on speaker and motioned to Mimi. "It's Skip Jackson," he said. "From American Football Officiating? The Texas official is dead."

Mimi pulled a notepad around, sat, and grabbed a pen.

"Lex Mincey's hired man found him in their horse barn this morning," Skip said. "They don't know how he died but, uh…"

Ben lowered himself into his desk chair. How long had it been? Three days since the St. Louis murder? "A horse ranch where?" he said. "Texas is a big place."

"The ranch is outside Ardmore. Oklahoma."

"I thought you said Texas."

"The ranch is up in the Texas panhandle."

Ben cleared his throat. "You tell that sheriff about St. Louis?"

"I told him you were following up on some letters to a couple of officials."

A couple of officials. Now that would be four as far as they knew, wouldn't it?

"You didn't tell him about St. Louis?" Ben said.

"Well," Skip said, "mostly I tried to get a handle on how Lex died. Because, you know, if he had a heart attack or something, it doesn't matter, does it? But they don't know how he died."

For a second, Ben's gaze dropped to his desktop and the little stack of files on the men who'd been threatened. Four men threatened, two dead...

"Is that sheriff calling me or what? You did put out an inquiry to all your officials, didn't you? Has anybody else received threats?"

"He'll call you," Skip said. "And, yes, we did a blanket reminder to the conference officiating groups."

"And?"

"So far, just those four men."

Ben chewed his lip. Did nobody reporting a threat mean nobody else was threatened? "You have talked with Webber and Redweather, right?"

"Not exactly," Skip said. "It turns out, Pete Webber quit officiating. I didn't know that when you and I first talked. I did try calling him, you know, just to check with him. But he's not answering his phone. He's resigned though, so I figured it didn't so much matter."

Ben glanced over at Mimi—wasn't Pete Webber the very man they needed to talk with? "But you have talked with Redweather, right?"

"Not exactly," Skip said. "Security for Pac 12 has been trying to get hold of him. I haven't heard back."

Mimi was scribbling EXACTLY on her notepad. He gave her an eyeroll.

"So, what are you doing, exactly?" he said. "You're not waiting to hear from the Pac12, are you?"

"Sorry?" Skip said.

"Tell me you, yourself, are getting hold of Mr. Redweather."

He kept pushing Skip for who would take responsibility for protecting Matt Redweather. Eventually it seemed like nobody at Football Officiating was gonna follow through. For sure, nobody had a clue about what steps to take to keep Matt Redweather safe.

"Let's talk tomorrow," he said. "Ten o'clock my time." He hung up and checked Mimi's face: eyebrows up, eyes wide.

This was exactly what he did not want. When he took this job on for Officiating, he'd agreed to check the website's fan posts. That had been the whole deal, no running around, playing detective, nothing risky.

Mimi was still looking at him. "Slippery slope," she said. But she had that crooked smile going. "Good thing there's two of us working on it."

Chapter 20

New Mexico

Beeker eased the Navigator into the left lane, hit the accelerator, and swept past the big rig they'd been trailing for miles. He was loving desert driving. For one thing, the stupid roadside attractions were fewer and farther between. But the open range, the distances, the power in his car—it was all exhilarating. He pushed their speed to eighty-four and settled back in the right lane in plenty of time to negotiate a long sloping curve.

Once they got to Tucumcari, he should be able to find a full-service car wash. The Navigator needed it, especially the interior. It smelled like a garbage pit. Why hadn't he noticed that before? Maybe because every time they loaded the car, they had all the doors wide open. Whatever the cause of the stink, having the car detailed would feel better. Feel like a fresh start.

Besides, in Tucumcari, he could take a few minutes alone. He could make sense of that missing tank of gas. Alone time would give him the privacy he needed to research what had happened in St. Louis and think through whether Deek could have been involved in John Brown's death. He upped the speed to ninety and reminded himself to keep his mind on the road.

Tucumcari turned out to be a little town, spread out along Route 66. Plenty of motels, a few places to eat, and one car wash. Yes, the woman in charge said, they did detailing.

Beeker handed off the keys and paid the cashier. As he reached for his phone, the cashier rolled her eyes. "Reception ain't so good here," she said. "It's our roof. But there's restaurants with Wi-Fi back on the highway."

Deek said he'd hang out with their bags if Beeker brought him extra fries. Though Beeker's stomach lurched at the idea of smelling French fries, especially after having the car detailed, he agreed. The fumes of fried potatoes seemed worth it if he were getting some time alone in the trade.

He walked the six blocks to a restaurant with a life-size steer mounted on a neon sign. Yes, they had Wi-Fi. He asked for a table on the patio, where his phone worked fine. It took him less than a minute to check his credit card: he *had* bought gas. Right before Oklahoma City, he'd filled the tank.

It couldn't be fifty miles from Oklahoma City to where he'd had to buy gas at Chickasha.

Did it make sense that while they were tucked up in their Oklahoma City hotel, a complete stranger had stolen the Navigator, used up six hundred miles worth of gas, and then returned the car to the hotel garage?

Had to be Deek. He must've driven all night. Where'd he go?

Beeker leaned back in the patio chair. The lunch crowd had thinned to nearly nonexistent. What was three hundred miles from Oklahoma City? He considered calling up a map on his phone, but then...if Deek used the GPS, the trip would be there in the history. He'd check when he got back to the car.

Next item on his agenda: what was the story on John

Brown?

He checked the Big10 news. The AP had more detail about John Brown—murder for certain, and the police were looking for a witness who had disappeared, a man wearing a baseball cap. Again, not a whisper about old Pete.

Beeker stared out across the street for a moment. Deek hadn't denied killing John Brown. In fact, Deek had danced around every question Beeker put to him.

And that baseball cap… He'd bought Deek a cap at Wrigley Field. Was Deek wearing it? He couldn't remember. And that itself was worrying. Whole pieces of his life seemed to be slipping away.

And now he wasn't alone on the patio. A couple and their two boys, tourists obviously, claimed a table maybe twenty feet away. Beeker forced himself to sit up and at least look like an ordinary person.

The boys quickly busied themselves on a laptop, setting up some kind of a game—the older one playing teacher, the little one fiddling with a cowboy hat and kibbitzing. They looked like good kids. The older one maybe twelve. The little one, six or seven, kept giggling. The man and woman smiled at Beeker and nodded.

Beeker forced himself to smile back, then made a point of feigning more phone research.

There'd been times like that with Deek. Going places, Deek schooling him all about hunting and football. Not with a laptop of course, not giggling like these boys. Giggling wasn't their style.

Deek was the star, so people didn't stare at Beeker's old coke-bottle glasses or how skinny he was. And he didn't have to talk. With Deek, he was a regular kid, only sort of invisible. His whole childhood, right up until

Deek was a high school junior, Deek had been his friend. Deek had protected him from the other kids. Deek had been more like a father than a brother.

No. That wasn't entirely true. Deek had been mostly good to him before the NFL, but always. And for certain, not after. It still made his heart crack.

Nobody could understand why Deek got dropped from Green Bay's roster.

So what, if Deek had been planted a couple of times? Deek gave as good as he got. Okay…he'd been planted lots of times.

Of course, when their mom was over the moon about Deek coming home from Green Bay. Those first few days were great. Except for Pete Webber. Pete made an ass of himself trying to impress Deek with all the big deal people he'd met while Deek was away.

Everybody said as soon as Deek got healed up, he'd sign on with another team. And then Deek's sports agent quit. And their dad shifted his pep talks to *We'll get you a new sports agent. Who do you hear is good?* And *Who's the best bet for a new team?* But Deek wasn't signing with anybody. And he kept dodging their dad's questions. And getting madder and madder.

One night their mother said something about Deek's concussion and their dad said, *Well, he can damned-well get over it.* After that, Deek started doing drugs right in front of them. He'd been doing drugs before, but it wasn't a secret anymore, it was like he didn't care. And the drinking got way worse. Where it used to be beer, he'd do anything he could find.

Deek never hit any of them, not exactly. He punched out a lot of walls; threw stuff, stomped stuff, set the garden shed on fire and laughed when the firemen tried to save it. There were fights with neighbors and the police got called a lot.

But everybody, *everybody,* cut Deek slack. People kept saying it was all those injuries. Deek hated that. But Beeker understood, even then. You hate it when people look at you that way.

It was a Saturday in November, and cold. He was working on extra credit at the back of his math book. Deek opened the bedroom door and stuck his head in. It was an hour until lunchtime, but early for Deek to be up. His voice sounded almost like the old days.

"It's you and me, Beeker. Come on, let's hit the road."

It didn't matter to him where they were going.

Deek was feeling good, and Deek had asked him to come along. That was the thing. In less than a minute, Beeker was waiting on the driveway. Deek piled a gym bag in the backseat of his Cherokee and off they went.

It seemed kind of weird to Beeker when they drove past the gym, but he didn't say anything. At the mall though, when Deek pulled the big bag out of the back seat and was going to take it in with him, Beeker asked how come. Deek locked the car and said, "Don't want somebody breaking in to get it, do we?" Okay, that made sense. They headed on in.

People were already Christmas shopping. Everywhere you looked, there were glittering trees and ornaments and fake snow. "Christmas in Dixie" was echoing around and around. Somebody cut in on the PA, saying something Beeker couldn't make out. Maybe because of the echo or maybe because Mr. Wilkins, his school principal, stepped out of the Brookes Camera shop right then and Beeker couldn't think what he was supposed to do, so he kept looking from Mr. Wilkins to Deek to Mr. Wilkins and the lady with him.

Deek caught Beeker's arm and jerked it hard, so hard something snapped and it hurt so much he couldn't get his breath.

"Move it," Deek said like he was mad that Beeker wasn't keeping up. Then Deek plowed past some ladies with a stroller, shoved his gym bag out in front of him, and hopped on the escalator. Deek was talking to himself, F-this and F-that, louder and louder, the way he did sometimes at home, like he was going to start punching the walls. And people were looking and looking.

There was no way Beeker could keep up. But it was going to be bad if he didn't. And really, really bad if Deek went off right there in front of everybody. So, Beeker climbed the escalator fast as he could and ended up bumping into Deek at the top because of all the people at the top that were heading for the food court.

"Sorry, Deek," he said.

Maybe he was crying because Deek was so mad. Probably he was crying.

Deek started messing with his gym bag. And when he turned around, he was holding their dad's AR-15 rifle and his face was really scary. "Shut up," he hissed. Then he started turning in a circle, pointing the rifle everywhere and nowhere.

The minute Deek turned away from Beeker, a bunch of high school girls in the food court ran into the Bebe's store. And some lady Beeker didn't know grabbed his arm and tried to pull him away from what was happening.

But Deek turned back, the lady let go, and Deek

shouted, "Beeker, get over here." Then he shot Bra-a-a-a-t, Ra-a-a-t at the ceiling and there was gun smoke and glass and people were screaming and running and then more shots and Deek snaked Beeker up close in the crook of his arm, holding him like a football, and Deek pointed the AR-15 down the escalator at the people below. A couple of guys, high school kids, had been looking up where Deek was. Bra-a-a-a-t, Ra-a-a-t. The shots knocked one of them to the floor. The kid was lying there, the blood was running, and the other kid was trying to drag the bleeding one off and Deek shot again, pop-pop and there were sirens going off and the mall cops running. That's when Deek started firing off at the cops, yelling F- you, F- you, and he pulled a pistol out of his jacket and aimed it.

Beeker kept squirming to get away. He was begging Deek to let him go. Begging Deek not to shoot. And then…and then…there was more shooting. And somebody else had hold of him and there was a coat or something over him and he couldn't see and they were carrying him away.

The next clear thing he remembered was being home. The police were talking to his mother and dad in the kitchen. There was a blue Kleenex box on the table. His dad was staring out into the yard where the garden shed used to be, and not talking. His mother was crying.

The ping on Beeker's phone brought him back to the restaurant. He was in Tucumcari, New Mexico. He was having the car detailed. For a moment, all he could do was lean against the edge of the table and try not to shake. John Brown was dead. Deek had killed him. That meant Lex Mincey would be next. That couldn't be right. Deek had already got to him.

Checking the Big12 news: nothing about Mincey and Big12 football. That should have felt good. But what if Mincey had died and his family or whoever didn't mention the fact he was a football official?

Googling… Beeker suppressed a groan as the AP story unfolded. Lex Mincey had been found dead in his horse barn. No cause of death listed.

Sweat saturated his shirt. Somebody had to stop Deek. But who? *He* couldn't do it. He couldn't turn Deek in to the police. But there had to be some way to stop the killing.

Beeker grabbed the carafe on the table, poured himself a full glass of water, and slowly drank. Once he finished, there was this pain. Right at the center of his chest. And he couldn't get his breath.

Not the police.

He stared a long while at his hands. They were shaking. He swiped his thumb across his cell phone and his search history unfolded, down and down: the website's football fan chat rooms opened up like flowers.

If he posted something in one of the chat rooms, they would monitor those wouldn't they? He wouldn't name Deek; he wouldn't leave his own name. But if he posted a hint that one man was killing these football officials, the website guys would follow up on it.

Beeker pulled up the website's form for posting a new message. The question was, what to put in the subject line so he'd get their attention? What else?

FOOTBALL OFFICIALS ARE DYING.

He was cold all over. His hands were shaking. He could barely punch in the message.

HE'S KILLING THEM ALL.

Beeker let out the breath he'd been holding and

stared at the screen. He half-expected Deek to come bursting out onto the patio.

One more step and he'd be done. Was he sure he wanted to do this? A swarm of nettles prickled its way up his back.

All he had to do was click on that word: *submit.* Do that, and in a nanosecond, the website would publish what he had written and a million fans would read it.

But if Deek figured out what he was doing…what he'd done…Deek would kill him too.

He should delete it. He must be crazy to even think about posting it.

He clicked *submit*, removed the phone's SIM card and buried it in trash can. He would get new SIM cards when they got to Albuquerque.

Chapter 21

Ben couldn't help smiling. It felt so good seeing Mimi in her place at the kitchen table, he hadn't really been listening. Whatever it was she'd said, she looked happy enough. She popped a little pork dumpling in her mouth, leaned back against the banquette, and sighed.

He shifted the paper take-out bag aside. "You want the last hum bao?"

Mimi shook her head no and pushed her plate away. "Too full already," she said, and flopped a chart she'd made up onto the table. "We have *Somebody's killing officials* posted four days ago in the Buckeye Nation fan site. Does that mean he's connected to Iowa?"

"Maybe," Ben said. "But *He's killing them all* was posted on the Texas site. Which is a different football conference."

She thought for a second. "But this should be simple. Hasn't Thui checked the name on the account against your subscribers?"

The question launched Ben into one of those explanations he hated. It was a problem with the billing software conversion that messed up their records. Should he give her his version or Thui's explanation, which he couldn't understand?

He said, "Thui's working on it," and hoped she'd be satisfied with his non-answer.

Just to be safe (and to cut off the "subscriber"

questions), he jammed the rest of the big white steamed dumpling into his mouth and chewed.

Mimi scooted out from her side of the table. "I'm going to re-check all the Big10 sites for anything else from this guy, okay?"

After an hour or so working in his office, he said (not exactly yelling, but loud enough she could hear him, even in the dining room). "What if we answered this guy?"

She showed up in his office doorway and leaned her back against the door jam, her eyebrows arched and brown eyes extra-wide. "You mean in the fan site?"

He got her point, but, "Yeah. What if we wrote, something like...*Finally somebody's doing something about the officiating*? Maybe we could get him to say more."

"It's an idea," she said and came round to his side of the desk. She leaned her butt on its edge. Her focus flicked away from him to something out the window, then back to his face. He could see that analytical brain of hers going over it.

"You think it's...irresponsible," he said.

She brushed something off his shoulder. "Maybe too much attention would scare him off. Or, if it encouraged him, wouldn't that make us responsible if he, or some copycat, went after somebody else?" She chewed her lip. "In fact, don't you think we need to make sure that no one over at the website does respond to him?"

She was right. "Maybe we run it by Karl."

"Karl?"

"Taught criminal psychology at U.W. I told you about him, didn't I?

"Right," she said. "You did. Hessman."

Hessman answered on the second ring. "I don't have a helper today, so how about you come by tomorrow. Say one o'clock?"

"Tomorrow then," Ben said, sat back in his chair, and simply breathed.

They were actually getting somewhere. But then he got a load of Mimi's face. "What?" he said.

"Well, maybe this guy has a reason to be angry. He's focused on Targeting…"

She was assessing his reaction. He got that. She didn't have to say CTE was getting to her. Obviously, it was.

What was worse, the research she'd been doing on injuries wouldn't include the stats about the average number of hits a player takes to his head. Nobody was collecting that. But do the math: figure eight or ten hits to the head every season for at least five players on each team, times how many seasons? No wonder players were ending up dying.

He took a breath. "Are you saying you think the killer has CTE?"

"I think we haven't considered that head injuries are part of it," she said.

"CTE? A former player taking it out on officials?"

"Just a thought." she said, and her face shifted like, *Back to business*.

"You know, we still have Mike Redweather and Pete Webber to talk with. If you can get hold of them, maybe you can learn something more. Meanwhile, I'll try tracking them on the internet. And maybe I come up with something useful."

She tapped the doorframe and took off.

He watched her cross the foyer and couldn't help but

smile. If they could get hold of Mike Redweather and Pete Webber, they could hand this whole thing off to the local police where these guys lived, and he could get back to his life.

Pete Webber's voicemail was full. What was it with these guys? At least Redweather's voicemail wasn't full; he just wasn't answering.

Ben left Redweather a message (for the seventh time) and decided he should pull in a few favors. Who did he know in Georgia, or L.A., that might know Webber or Redweather? Or, if he was lucky, who lived close enough to talk to them in person?

He made a little list and asked everybody he could think of, including the website board, to step up. For the good of the game.

Messages out. Seeing Karl tomorrow. He should be hitting the fan site for U. Texas. But truth was, he was on the verge of hitting the downstairs gym when Mimi walked in and parked herself in one of his guest chairs.

"Maybe this will make you feel better," she said. "Matt Redweather went through a divorce that was final about six months ago. That gives us an address and a lawyer's name. I have a call in to his lawyer, I hope that's okay. And I have more on Pete Webber." She shuffled the papers she was holding. "You said Pete Webber is an official for the Big10, right? Well, he lives in Savannah, Georgia."

"We knew that," Ben said. "Skip said—"

"Okay, I didn't know. Did you know he works in real estate? He has his own company? You said his voicemail is full. I figure you meant his personal voicemail. I tried his business voicemail. It's full too, did you know that?"

She fixed him with those brown eyes and said, "You ever hear of a real estate guy with a full voicemail box? Anyway, when nobody answered at his office, I called some other Savannah realtors."

"Okay, and?"

"Pete Webber is missing. That's their theory. Another thing: he had a divorce in process that looks like it's done except, when I looked for it in the court records, there's no decree on file."

"How'd you get into the court records for a divorce?"

"You don't want to know," she said. "Anyway, I left a message for his lawyer, a guy named Ford in case he calls you. His assistant says he'll get back to us tomorrow."

"I don't think we wait to talk with a lawyer. Not if Webber is missing."

Ben Googled the City of Savannah, Georgia, and in less than a minute he was talking with some deputy in the office of Sheriff Walter "Butch" Masters.

Chapter 22

Arizona

A road sign for the Petrified Forest jogged Beeker back to reality. A minute later, he pulled the Navigator through the park's official gate, circled around, and stopped. The desert was taking on the beginnings of evening, all pink and rosy. Even without heading down the scenic track, there were fallen and broken logs to be seen—petrified trees from 225 million years ago. He couldn't conceive of time like that. Or that these hills and gullies had ever been studded with trees, green, trembling and big enough to leave the thick petrified trunks that lay everywhere he looked.

A big white camper rolled in past the national park sign and slowed as if it might join them in the gravel lot. But then it swung left and cruised on down the road, heading into the park.

As the dust settled, he took two or three breaths and tapped a thumb against the steering wheel. He did not turn around to look at Deek. He did not even glance in the rear-view mirror. It was now or never. "I know what you're doing, Deek. John Brown? Lex Mincey? It has to stop." Had he imagined it, or was his voice shaky?

After an interminable silence, Deek said, "You've been visiting football sites again."

Beeker reminded himself, *stay strong*. "That's not

the point," he said. "It's bad enough you killed Pete Webber. At least we'd talked about that. We never discussed doing the others."

"Doing the others? Beeker, you really disappoint me. You're saying *I* killed the others? You know this how, exactly?"

Beeker fixed his gaze straight through the windshield, at the orange-purple sky. "You know what you did. At Pete Webber's, you knew I hated it. Don't insult me by denying it. And the minute we got back to Cleveland you're all about going on a road trip. You talked like doing Route 66 would be like old times. Like it'd be an adventure. All lies. It was about killing the rest of them."

Even before Beeker finished his sentence, Deek snorted. "Your life in Cleveland was such a kick in the butt? I can't think how we were ever able to tear ourselves away from the place."

Beeker wacked the steering wheel with his hand. "How could I not see what you were doing? Route 66 put you on top of John Brown. And Lex Mincey? You were howling about buying gas right when we got to Oklahoma City."

He could hear his voice cracking. "Remember? You said *If we get gas now, we can get a good start tomorrow morning.* I just wanted to get to the hotel. But we stopped and bought gas. I put it on my credit card, so I have proof. And, the next morning, the tank was almost empty."

"You're pissed because you had to buy gas?"

"I'm pissed because you conned me," Beeker shouted. "I'm pissed because you used me to get next to John Brown. To kill him and kill Lex Mincey. And tonight, after we got to Flagstaff, after you made sure I was asleep, you were going to drive down to Mesa and kill Chris Matsen, weren't you?"

Beeker shut his mouth just as a herd of hikers climbed out of the gully and congregated right in front of the Navigator. They conferred over a map; then, as suddenly as they'd appeared, they headed across the road and disappeared into another gulley.

"Don't deny it," Beeker said. "And don't try to change the subject."

"Jesus," Deek said. "Why not Chris Matsen? A couple of months ago you were screaming for his blood. The same way you went nuts about Pete Webber, and John Brown and Lex Mincey."

Beeker slammed the steering wheel so hard it hurt his wrists. "You cannot—"

"Have you forgotten about that kid who died after the Ohio State game? Man, you were so freaked out at that game, people must've taken you for that kid's dad. And don't start up with *I don't remember*. For damned sure *I* do. You nearly took out a phone pole on the way home."

Beeker hunched down in his leather seat, clamped a hand over his mouth, and shut his eyes.

"You started the killing, I didn't," Deek said. "You and your research, you made up the DVDs, wrote the letters. What was it you said? 'Quit or retire. You'll regret it if you don't.' Wasn't that it? Now what? Living up to your promise is too much for your delicate sensibilities?"

Beeker pulled his fist away from his mouth; his thumb was bleeding. He struggled a handkerchief out of his pants and wiped it.

He hadn't forgotten why the killing started. Yes,

he'd been furious at those screw-ups. He'd wanted to make those incompetent fools hurt. Putting those DVD's together, he'd wanted every one of those cretins dead and buried.

But Pete had stared at him the whole time they were out there on the Black River. The air stirring the water. The egrets. The night sounds. All that beauty. And those terrible eyes. He never wanted to see that again.

You can want to make a man pay for the kind of screw-up Pete Webber had done. You can imagine fifty ways to make him suffer and die. But wanting and imagining is a whole world away from how it feels to kill a man.

The car was too quiet. Beeker caught his breath. Wiped his face. "Deek?" he said.

No answer.

Disappeared. Where Deek had gone, and for how long, Beeker couldn't guess. But for the moment, he was alone.

Phone out, he checked the posts he'd made on the football websites. There were plenty of responses. But mostly they were just gripes and juvenile opinions. Nothing to indicate the website manager had taken his message seriously. Well, if Ben Leit's people weren't reading the stuff fans posted there, they must read their texts.

It took him less than a minute to find the right phone number and tap out a text message. *My brother killed John Brown and Lex Mincey. Help me.* He stared at the phone's screen…that ought to blast them into action. But not *help me.* Definitely not. He deleted the last two words of the text and pressed send.

He could stall for time in Flagstaff. That would give

the police a chance. Maybe he could keep Deek busy for a day or two at the Grand Canyon, sabotage the car or something. Maybe the website people would set up protection for Matsen. Maybe Matsen would go underground.

The sun had shifted low enough in the sky that it began to cut through the driver's side window and warm his face. The air in the Navigator seemed, alternately, to shudder, then go still. The silence was exquisite. He could feel the thud of his heartbeat, the expansion of his ribs.

He was so tired. It was like his body didn't want to move. He closed his eyes just for a minute.

****

It was almost dark outside when he finally came to.

Deek was saying, "You finished?"

Out of instinct, Beeker's hands grabbed at the steering wheel, his eyes wide.

Deek didn't wait for him to answer. "Doesn't matter what you did. If it made you feel better to give Ben Leit and his cronies a little tingle, that's okay."

Deek's voice wasn't angry at all. But Beeker couldn't help the feeling his world was going to end.

"Listen to me, Beeker. Remember how Dad used to come in and sit on the foot of the bed. He'd say, 'Here's the truth of it.' Remember?"

Beeker let go of the breath he'd been holding. "I remember."

"Good. Well, here's the truth of it. You can call me whatever you want. But I am not Deek."

"But—"

"Beeker. You know I'm not Deek. Deek's been gone for thirty years. Deek shot nine people dead at the

Savannah Mall and then offed himself. You remember."

Beeker made a desperate grab for the rearview mirror and cranked it every direction he could to see into the backseat of the Navigator. But the mirror kept slipping in his sweaty hand and his eyes were tearing so bad he couldn't see a damned thing.

"Get out," he said. He didn't know what he would do without Deek, but he had to say it, "Get out."

"I can't, Beeker." The voice sounded exhausted and sad.

It felt like somebody had touched his shoulder. But when he reached up and felt for a hand, it was only a muscle spasm.

"Have a drink of water."

In spite of himself, Beeker took a long pull on his water bottle. "You just want me to stop fighting you about Chris Matsen."

"Don't get hung up about Chris Matsen. Or that text you sent Ben Leit. It made sense doing that text. You're the smart one. You obey the law. Pay bills and, mostly, you drive the speed limit. You needed to send that text. That's who you are. You also needed to kill these men. That's who you are too."

The voice he would always think of as Deek, the voice that was Deek, went on and on about it: every detail of how he, Beeker, had killed Pete Webber, how he'd attacked John Brown on the riverboat and made it look like Brown had jumped into the water, and how he'd driven to Texas and met up with Lex Mincey and—

Beeker couldn't breathe. The smell of that horse barn rose up thick and suffocating. Little motes danced in the air. He could still hear the rustle of the hay, the shuffle of the horses' hooves in their stalls, their restless snorts.

He didn't want to remember. And he couldn't listen anymore. He hit the car horn with both hands and held it down until his wrists began to ache. Until, finally, his hands dropped away down into his lap.

"So. Now you remember the horse barn. Can you remember the look on Lex Mincey's face? How you got the needle ready, how you—"

Tagged him. The words flew into Beeker's mind. It was true. He had tagged Mincey just like he'd swatted the needle into John Brown, right under the shoulder blade.

Beeker flinched at the millions of ants crawling inside his skin. "No," he croaked.

"Not you alone." The Deek voice was calm, almost comforting. "*We* killed 'em. Pete, John Brown, Mincey. You and me. You were there for all three of them. Think about it, Beeker. Why else would you be so tired?"

"No-o-o-o."

"Yes. Just like Dad used to say. That's the truth of it. You need to think about it, that's okay. If you want to call me Deek, that's okay too, just as long as you know I'm not Deek. Just as long as you know you're talking to yourself."

Beeker fought back his tears.

Maybe part of him was doing the killing. But that part, that killing part, wasn't him. He was the good son. He was Winslow Beacham, Beeker to people that knew him. His mother had moved him away from Savannah and all the terrible things that went on down there. She'd loved him. She'd seen to it he got better.

Chapter 23

The sky opened up in a cloudburst just as Ben and Mimi made the block-long dash from their car to Karl Hessman's place on Capitol Hill.

They raced up the steps of the big craftsman house and began stamping the soaking leaves off their shoes. Mimi swiped a hand over the top of her wet hair and glanced over. "You did send him a copy of the blog posts."

Just like her, to make double sure they were prepared. She'd probably stored copies of the things on her phone in case he'd forgotten to forward them. "What blog posts?" he said, and rang the bell.

Seconds later, Karl opened the shiny black door. He looked like he'd been up all night and hit the wall. They shouldn't have come.

Karl flashed a smile at Mimi. "What a day, huh? Stash your wet stuff and go on in. I'll be right back." He tapped a hook on an ornate hall coat rack and disappeared down a hallway.

Ben and Mimi headed into what people used to call the front parlor.

The house was like so many Seattle houses he'd been in when he was growing up. Except someone had hung sheets over the French doors that separated the parlor from the dining room. Karl must've moved his wife down there.

They'd done that for his mother in her last year, moving her hospital bed into the big room at the front of the Scottsdale house so she could enjoy the art she'd collected. All that year, neighbors brought flowers for his mother, and dinners for the family. It sure looked like the same thing was going on for Karl. There must've been a year's supply of coffee beans and treats piled under the front window.

Ben settled himself on the sofa across from what looked like Karl's regular chair and checked out Mimi. She was warming herself at the fireplace, but she was also watching him. She moved over and sat next to him.

If they'd had more time, they would've figured an exit strategy. But Karl parted the sheets over the French doors and stepped through into the living room.

"Sorry," he said. "Ann was just saying was how good it was I was finally being a criminal psychologist again."

"You sure this an okay time?" Ben said.

"We're good," Karl said. "So where are we with this?"

"Two men dead now," Ben said.

Had Karl blanched? He didn't say anything for a second. Finally, he pulled out a pen, grabbed his notepad, and flipped to a clean page. "I assume the local police are handling the investigation? Not the FBI or…"

"Right," Ben said. "As far as I know."

"Tell me what you can about the murder scenes."

Ben laid out the whole sternwheeler story with more detail than he had when they met before. Then he said, "As for Lex Mincey—you have the stuff on him, right? —he was found in a barn, in a horse stall. There's no cause of death but according to the sheriff, there's a puncture wound on his back, which is also the story in St. Louis."

"He lives at the ranch?"

"No," Ben said. "His hired man said he was up there to sell a horse."

Karl nodded. "Send me your contacts, okay? And… where are we with the blog posts and letters?"

"Nothing new," Ben said. "As far as we know."

"Well then. What can I tell you?"

"Who are we looking for?" Ben said.

Karl set his pad aside on a table next to his chair. "There is a pathology called shared psychosis or Shared Delusional Disorder. There are various forms but what's more commonly seen is a 'Primary' who forms a delusional belief and imposes it on another person. I suspect that's what you're dealing with here."

Two? "You're serious. Two men?" Ben said. "You know, the guy in St. Louis definitely was alone."

Karl's wiry eyebrows arched up his forehead. "Entirely possible you saw only one man. But the blog post says *he* not *I*. Which is why I take this writer at his word. He's writing about another man. So: two men involved. I know it's not a lot to go on, five letters, the DVDs, two or three blog posts, and one text."

Mimi glanced at Ben, then said. "Maybe it would help me to understand. If you could take us through your thinking?"

"Of course." Karl leaned forward, his elbows on his knees as if he were confiding in them. "Most often, there is a triggering event. Something powerful enough to get the Primary moving into his fantasy. In this case, I have to think that's connected to football officials. It may have cemented the two men on their path at that time. Or it may have inspired the Primary. And the Secondary man may have come into the fantasy later."

Mimi's face had that puzzled, tight expression. "A single event could cause him to…"

"The pathology doesn't arise from the triggering event. There is usually an earlier psychic injury. Think of the triggering event as opening a door into that."

Ben let out a whispery breath. "We need to come up with the triggering event?"

"Well," Karl said, "There may have been a series of events. But I'm suggesting that around the time your letter writer began contacting the officials, something happened to trigger the Primary. Something dramatic enough to push him from a festering wound to a full-blown disease. I assume your people are looking for that dramatic event. And I think you're right, Ben. The letters clearly demonstrate the Primary's idea of how football *should* be played."

"But you're sure it's two men," Ben said.

"I am," Karl said. "Typically, there is an aggressive or dynamic leader and a nervous but obedient follower. His communications, the follower's, make it pretty clear. It's not uncommon for the weaker personality to be uneasy about the crime or about being caught. But he's been convinced of the killer's belief. Convinced that the Primary's solution to their problem is the best solution available."

Karl fixed his gaze on Ben. "You're shaking your head no."

"I guess I'm just stuck in St. Louis," Ben said. "That guy was by himself. I noticed it because everybody else was in groups—couples, tourists, families. And everybody waited to talk with the police, everybody except that one guy in the baseball cap. If it is two men, where's the other man? What's he doing?"

"We don't know what he is doing. And he may not have been on the boat with you," Karl said. "But think about this: St. Louis was six days ago; the first post is a day later—not before the murder, not even the same day. And the death in Texas was what, two days ago?

"Three, isn't it?" Mimi said.

"Mincey was found first thing in the morning," Ben said. "According to the sheriff, he'd died the night before."

Karl shifted his focus to Mimi. "I see your blog man as the secondary man. He's troubled by the murders. Perhaps he's afraid of the Primary. But based on the timing of the blog posts, I'd say the writer is learning about the murders after the fact. Which supports your observation, Ben. He probably wasn't on the boat but learned about that death after the fact."

"So he's not the killer."

Karl seemed to consider the idea. "From your own description, the St. Louis killer spent a fair amount of time talking with the victim. Mr. Mincey thought the killer was interested in buying a horse and traveled all the way out to that location to meet him. That has to mean phone calls, emails, texts, … communication. Doesn't it? I have to think your Primary is intelligent, but especially, he's approachable. People aren't afraid of him."

"And the Secondary?"

Karl's eyebrows shifted up. "Let's stick for the moment with the Primary. He's patient, calculating, authoritative, and determined. He's a good planner and he's comfortable with his actions. He maintains a distance, even in his letters to the officials. They're all full of—"

"Direct address," Ben said, "always with the *you should, you failed.*"

"Exactly. As if he is completing a picture of how things should be. And your Secondary seems to be afraid. He wants help, wants to stop the killing, but isn't willing to contact the authorities directly. And why do you suppose that is?"

They talked through the idea that the blog posts were a way to get some publicity and discarded it when Karl said, "What about the other men that were threatened?"

Mimi scooted forward on the sofa. "We know Pete Webber and Matt Redweather are at risk and we're working on that. But doesn't the text mean the Secondary is at risk, too?"

"Likely, yes." Karl dragged off his glasses and polished them on the bottom of his shirt "Other things we know: the Primary knows his way around college football. I would think he's a season ticket holder."

Mimi perked up. "And one of them has to have enough money to own the equipment he used to put together those DVDs."

"Okay," Ben said. "Maybe it's the second guy who set up the DVDs."

"Makes sense," Karl said. "That might be his role, technical wizard."

For a moment, it seemed like they were through. But then Karl started up again. "Based on what the St. Louis coroner has discovered, it seems clear that at least one of these men has access to pharmaceutical chemicals. Doesn't have to be a doctor. Could be a pharmacist, a nurse, a former medic, an EMT, a pre-med student, a veterinarian, even a chemistry teacher. And we still don't know what the toxin is, am I right?"

"Right," Mimi said.

They all heard the voices in the dining room. "You need to stop?" Ben said. "We can take off."

Karl's face looked like his answer to that was no. "I need to check in, but don't go. We haven't discussed their relationship." He unfurled himself from his chair and disappeared through the glass doors.

Mimi waited for the click of the latch, then turned to face Ben. "Why were you doubting his two-man idea?"

"I wasn't doubting him," Ben said. "I just, I saw one guy. Nobody else was around, nobody followed him, everybody else hung around to talk with the police. Was I rude, do you think?"

"Karl didn't seem to take it that way," she said. She hauled her phone out, her thumbs tapped something. "He called it *shared psychosis,* right?"

Ben's phone pinged. When he looked, a text from Thui. He'd follow up in a minute.

"Found it," she said.

"Causes?" he said. *Don't say head injury.*

"Causes unknown," she said. Her finger hovered above the little screen. "But the main contributors are stress and social isolation."

Another ping. Ben grimaced and grabbed his phone: Urgent. He opened the app and his gut did a backflip. "Jesus," he muttered. "Mimi? You need to see this."

Helpmehelpmehelpme.

Her lovely skin was still ashen when Karl reappeared, saying, "We were talking relationship. The Secondary is likely a family member. Or has a social connection to the Primary that resembles family. That's the most common situation."

Ben offered his phone with the *help me* message.

Karl read and handed the phone back. The corners of his mouth shifted; his left hand kept fiddling with a shirt button. "A week ago, this man was reporting. Now, we don't have to guess, he's afraid."

"Should we answer him?" Ben said.

Mimi had that iron determination look going. "Just don't—"

"Why not let your detective in St. Louis make that decision?" Karl said."

"Right. Just one more thing then," Ben said, "and we'll take off. The official in Georgia that resigned? Webber? Turns out, he's disappeared. The sheriff thinks the guy went off by himself because, apparently, he does that sometimes. But Webber's lawyer is convinced his client's been abducted."

"Missing since when?" Karl said.

"Eleven days."

Karl scrubbed a hand across his mouth. "Maybe it's a sore point with me. Maybe... Lemme put it this way: I worked a case a few years ago, the first victim wasn't found for more than a week."

For a full minute, nobody said anything.

"In a series of killings—if this is a series—we tend to think the first victim is special. For one thing, a killer is most likely to make his mistakes in the first killing. Also...maybe more important from your point of view, there's a reason the first victim is first. Odds are, there's a connection between your killer and, what was his name, Webber?"

Ben's heart was already going like a jackhammer.

"If I were you," Karl said, "Wherever this man

Webber lived, I'd grab the first flight and follow up with that lawyer."

Chapter 24

Flagstaff, Arizona

Beeker's eyes burned, his ears had a jet roar going, and his hands trembled so hard it was all he could do to work the touchpad on the laptop. Finally, he just couldn't. He slumped back against the miserable hotel desk chair.

"I understand what you said. I do. I understand I was there. I understand I was part of it. But I still feel…separate from you. I can't help it. I hear you in my head and you're Deek. You're not my brother. I see that. He's dead. I know. But… I need to call you Deek, that's what it is."

"Have some water."

Right. Water. Beeker pushed himself away from the little desk and headed for the mini fridge. It felt like Deek had been talking for hours about Chris Matsen. How Matsen was every bit as bad as the rest of them. He grabbed a Perrier and downed half of it.

"You've forgotten what you saw in those games. That's all," Deek said. "The Matsen stuff is on the jump drives in my suitcase pocket."

Well, he was not gonna check the suitcase.

Finally, Deek said, "You need to do this, Beeker. You know you do. You can't go on forever blaming me for what you do."

Beeker clamped a hand on the top of his head, just to keep it from blowing off. He knew he needed to look at those games. But seeing them again would make him remember those men the way they were when they died. And he didn't want that. Not that fear in their eyes.

But Deek was right. He needed the truth.

He grabbed a handful of USB plug-ins from the suitcase he still thought of as Deek's. He found the one for Matsen and jammed it into the laptop's port. Almost on its own, the game's action restarted.

"See that?" Deek said. "That look on Matsen's face? Back it up. Take a snapshot of that, and enlarge it."

Beeker paused the game, took a copy of the screen image, and enlarged the still picture so he could see Matsen's face clearly.

One of the players had just landed a crippling, illegal hit, and Matsen was completely clueless. Beeker stared at the face for a long time. He could see it in the man's eyes: blank as a brick. He coughed, then couldn't get his breath. He ended up nearly choking. He knew he should stop watching. It was the man's eyes upsetting him. But he couldn't stop. Not if he was going to understand what happened.

He tried screening a different game, but it wasn't different. Deek was still there in his ear, saying *now wait for it, wait for it*. And there was always a loud whack reverberating the football stadium, two more kids on the field. And the nearest official—it was Matsen again—walking away.

Walking away! How had college football reached a point where the people responsible for keeping the players safe didn't give a damn?

Beeker dug a handkerchief out of a pocket and

mopped his face. He'd forgotten what it felt like to see a kid hurt like that. No. That wasn't true. He'd tried to push away that feeling. But he remembered. He closed his eyes.

"You're remembering, aren't you?" Deek said. "It was the same for your brother. His head rocking back like that, right when their helmets collided."

He couldn't remember. Why couldn't he? He thought he'd remembered everything. Had his mother kept it a secret, how Deek got hurt?

"You want the truth, don't you? I downloaded copies of his Green Bay games off the internet. Take a look. Deek delivered those kinds of hits. Man, he was a brute on the field. You gotta wonder he didn't break his own neck."

Beeker's eyes filled with tears. How long had it been since he'd seen his big brother on film? After the mall, their dad had destroyed their old tapes of the games.

Beeker mopped his face and scooted closer to the little screen, better to track Number 25—it was Deek all right. After five plays, Green Bay's defense, including Number 25, was off the field. He rubbed his eyes and tried to refocus. It seemed like, on nearly every play, even with the laptop's rotten sound system, there was the THWACK of another helmet-to-helmet hit.

He watched the whole jump drive of the Green Bay games. It left him sick to his stomach. No wonder his big brother went crazy. How many concussions had he had?

When Green Bay dropped his brother, what if the family had known what was going on? What if they'd known Deek was bad hurt? What if they'd known about CTE back then?

Beeker slumped back in his chair. "I need to stop."

He closed the lid on the laptop and headed for bed.

It felt like the night went on for years. Like he slept but didn't sleep. Like he dreamed but it wasn't a dream exactly because he was sweating. And Deek was alive with a broken neck, then he died, then two other guys had broken arms, then Deek died on the field, then the night turned into a collage of separated shoulders and needles and a paddle wheeler and hands grabbing at him and Deek being alive again with a concussion and the ambulance was coming out onto the field and then there were fifteen ambulances and the doctors and the sirens and Deek was waving goodbye and everywhere men in striped shirts black and white and the yellow in their hands.

Over and over, he woke sweating. It was their fault, those officials. He'd proved it creating the DVDs. He'd told them. He'd warned them. Even threatening them hadn't worked.

His body gave up an involuntary shudder. *He'd* threatened. Not Deek.

What else could he do but finish the job? And he was right to stop them. Those men on the field, their screw-ups weren't only damaging kids. They were setting up families for catastrophes like what happened at the Savannah mall. He was not blaming it on that other part of him, not anymore.

At nearly five a.m., he took a pill and finally, truly slept.

When the alarm clock went off at nine, Beeker took a deep, cleansing breath and stretched his neck. He felt clear-headed, like he'd awakened from a fog. For the first time in two years there was no buzzing in his head, no kibitzing from Deek. Even his body felt good.

Deek had written *You need to call Matsen* on the bathroom mirror.

Well, that gave a pretty good bump to Beeker's mood. "Call Matsen and say what?"

"Find out what time we see him," Deek said. "Matsen does counseling. We need to check in by phone."

"And say what?" Beeker repeated. Why was *he* the one who had to do the calling? If Deek called before, why couldn't he do it now?

Deek hummed for a second or two. Then said, "It's all about responsibility, Beeker. Time you did your part. You know that."

Beeker turned on his heel, headed back to the bedroom, and unhooked his cellphone from its charger. Matsen's number was right there in his contacts. Of course, it was. But he could feel his mouth filling with cotton, his palms sweating.

"You got the ball," Deek said. "Run with it. I got your back."

But it was a woman, not Matsen, on the other end of the line. "The Lord is good," she said. "How may I help you?"

Beeker's ears were buzzing. The room was going light and lighter. He was gulping. Suddenly the words were right there, his mouth worked, and he said, "Sorry to bother you. I have an appointment with Mr. Matsen today and I've lost my calendar. Could you check with him? What time do we meet?"

Beeker heard the clunk of the phone. She must've laid it down.

Matsen was in Mesa, Arizona. Mesa was right next to Phoenix; he knew that much. But wasn't Mesa hours away? He probably couldn't get there in time. Probably he should just cancel. Or reschedule. An appointment was a terrible idea.

And a new panic struck: who was he? He hadn't given the woman his name, how was she going to check on an appointment?

She came back on the line. "The only appointment I don't recognize is…are you Mr. Sloane?"

He was drenched with sweat. And his childhood name landed like an electric shock.

"Yes," he said. "Yes. I'm sorry. Didn't I say? Sloane."

"No problem, Mr. Sloane. He has you scheduled for this evening. Eight p.m."

"Oh, of course it is," Beeker burbled. Plenty of time to drive to Mesa. He'd sounded like an idiot. Certainly not like himself. He thanked her, confirmed the address, and said he would be there at eight.

Was it relief? Part of him was still laughing when he stepped into the shower.

Free for the day. It was like he'd been released from jail. His breakfast tasted wonderful. He took a walk. The air at that altitude felt fresh, alive. As he made the drive up to Grand Canyon, it seemed like he was driving through the wild west. He passed cattle in pastures and horses. The belly-high grass; the broken and rising land, the sky, the whole day, left him buzzing with life.

****

Just after 4:00 that afternoon, Beeker took off for his meeting. Four hours later, he pulled into the parking lot of the He Is Risen Bible Church. A hedge of oleander softened the impact of the eight-foot cement wall that separated the church from an apartment complex.

He angled the car as close as possible to the church's side door and surveyed the area for trouble. Two parking lot lights, but the one by the door was out. Equally good, only one car in the lot, presumably Matsen's. A sign on the side door instructed Beeker to come on in and lock the door behind him.

He stepped into the hallway and heard buzzing. There was a thread of panic; but then he realized, for once, the sound wasn't in his head. A fluorescent light was getting ready to fail.

Right on cue, Deek was there. "Matsen thinks you're married to a drunk. Trust me, he'll do all the talking. All you have to do is go along with him."

Beeker sucked in a breath. Married to a drunk? But he had a wing man if he needed. He set his jaw, worked the syringe free, and headed for the open door.

It was a small office, lined with bookcases partly full of hymnals, but mostly holding stacks of pamphlets, a coffee pot and filters, and a half-dozen unopened boxes of Oreo cookies. A faded print of The Last Supper dominated the wall behind a painted steel desk.

Matsen had his back to the door and seemed to be fiddling with something on one of the bookcases. He was wearing a tropical shirt. And when he stood…he was way taller than how he'd looked on the TV.

Taller. Beeker reran his calculations on the dosage he'd loaded in the syringe in his coat pocket. The man must weigh twenty pounds more than what he'd guessed. One injection might not do the trick. But it would still incapacitate him.

Matsen stepped around the desk, smiling. "Mr. Sloane," he said and reached out a hand. "I like to begin with a prayer."

Without warning, Matsen clasped both Beeker's hands in his own and dropped to his knees, pulling Beeker down with him. "Merciful Lord, we come to you this night…"

Matsen swayed one knee to the other, his eyes closed tight. His head shook as if he were in pain. The only thing missing was the church music Beeker had heard every Sunday when he was a little kid back in Savannah.

Beeker's head roared.

"Open our hearts…a new vision…"

Beeker's knees started to go numb. He needed to finish it. The minute the man let go of his hand, the minute the guy shut up…

"…as you would have us do." Matsen stood and let go of Beeker's hand. "Now, that puts us right in the spirit, doesn't it?" He shot Beeker a reassuring look. "Your brother explained about your wife's problems. We need to help her find the way to sobriety, to be easy in herself. How about a coffee while we talk?" He pulled a pair of mugs off the shelf, filled them, and offered one to Beeker.

Beeker reached, left-handed, to take hold of his coffee, and managed to flip the mug out of Matsen's fingers. As the scalding contents flew in all directions, Beeker struck with his right hand and emptied the syringe into Matsen's shoulder.

Matsen looked up. "Wha?" he said and struggled to raise one arm. Then said, "Unnnh." His arm dropped to his side, and he collapsed into a chair.

"Hang in there," Beeker said.

It took a while to clear away the coffee mess. Once everything was tidied, Beeker capped and pocketed the syringe, cleaned away any fingerprints, and after a considerable struggle, managed to drag the groaning Matsen down the hall and out to the parking lot.

Fifteen minutes later, Beeker slid into the driver's seat of the Navigator and checked off his list: surfaces wiped, lights off, furniture in place, doors closed. He was sweating but more exhilarated than he'd been in years.

But wait. Where was he going? Back up to Flagstaff? MapQuest could get him out of town. But then what?

As he twisted around to get at his phone, Deek said, "Leave the phone off for now. From here, we're gonna turn left out of this parking lot. Six blocks on we hook up with Highway 60, then head north at Highway 17. Don't worry, I got this figured."

Ten minutes later, Beeker took the on-ramp to Highway 60.

With traffic bulleting past him, he went to work at talking himself back from laughing. It had gone that well. Matsen was tucked away in the back of the Navigator and sooner or later…

That was the question. Sooner or later, he needed to be rid of Matsen. He heard himself say "But where?"

The perfect wingman, Deek said, "Highway 17 coming up. Take that on-ramp and we're on the road to Flagstaff only we won't go that far."

What a team. Beeker took the freeway on-ramp and headed north. Past the suburbs and golf courses that ringed greater Phoenix, he glanced in the rearview mirror at his inert passenger. Time for a little truth telling.

"Mr. Matsen?" No response. But he could hear the guy breathing.

"Mr. Matsen, perhaps it's occurred to you. I don't

have a wife with a drinking problem. I don't have a wife at all. I'm the man who sent you that letter about your inexcusably bad football officiating. Remember that DVD? Remember in that letter I said that for the safety of the players, you should resign? You have to admit, I gave you the option. I bet about now you're thinking it would have been better if you had resigned. Bu-u-u-t you made your choice, didn't you? So, Mr. Matsen, you should consider this your Judgment Day."

They drove in silence for almost two hours.

"You're gonna turn off at the Fort Verde Garden Reservation, okay?"

Beeker nodded. At the big sign, he took the turnoff, followed the road a while, then took another turnoff onto a one-lane trail. He drove on and on into land that, from what the headlights showed, looked like a rocky moon. Eventually all Beeker could make out were washes, a dry creek bed, and the dirt track they'd been following.

When the track began to drop away, he decided the rest of it was for dirt bikes.

He managed to back the Navigator up to a spot that looked wide enough he could turn around. He set the brake and fished a flashlight from under his seat. He glanced back at Matsen. "Be right back."

A few minutes searching and he spotted a quiet place that felt right—maybe ten yards ahead and just off the path. He walked back to the car, his heart pounding so hard he couldn't hear his footsteps. Pounding so hard, he couldn't even hear Deek. He pulled a fresh syringe from the lock box in the back of the Navigator, climbed in behind the steering wheel, and maneuvered the car around so the headlights would give him a little light.

After what seemed like hours of sweating and

hauling, Beeker leaned Matsen up against a big boulder. He wiped his face with his sleeve, then leaned down and trained his flashlight on that frozen face. The man's eyes had that same unblinking stare he'd seen on the others.

Beeker spoke quietly. "Mr. Matsen, you must know, this hurts me as much as it does you." He stepped to the side and waited, almost as if Matsen could have responded.

Eventually, he said, "Do you have any idea how many young men have been wrecked because of you? How many families you ruined? You should've quit. Now it's too late."

He tapped the syringe into Matsen's neck and waited.

The clear sky arched above them. Wide and dappled with stars.

Chapter 25

Reggie Ford came around his office desk and headed for Ben and Mimi. Big smile, hand extended, wearing a pair of custom-made but casual shoes, an untucked linen shirt, and an impeccably cut pair of pants that had nothing to do with a business suit. To Ben's mind, the man looked more like he was headed for a lunch on Martha's Vineyard than running a big-time law practice in Georgia.

"Miss Mimi," Ford said. "And Mr. Leit. Welcome to Savannah."

Miss Mimi...

Ben checked the look on Mimi's face. He'd expected a "Southern Gentleman," and Ford did have the patrician features you see in paintings of Thomas Jefferson. But he'd expected a sixty-year-old one, not a man his own age.

Ford helped Mimi into one of a trio of guest chairs in front of a big mahogany desk and nodded Ben into the another. He thanked them for coming and launched into the usual warm-up questions: how was their trip, was their B&B comfortable, could he get them a beverage? The impressive part of Ford's routine was that he managed the whole operation without any of it seeming forced.

Eventually Ford sat, opened a file folder, and squared it in front of him. "Pete Webber had a plan for that settlement money. He'd tried to get it earlier, but the court wouldn't agree. That's the first thing didn't make sense to us—him not showing up once the money was available. Like I told you on the phone, I went over to check the house. And when the house didn't feel right either, I called our local sheriff. He'll be here any minute by the way. Well, getting Butch involved went nowhere."

Ford slowly leafed through the file.

"The more I thought about it, well, I decided finding Pete Webber was gonna be up to us. Nobody I know ever hired an investigator to hunt for a client. But I figured this was the time for it. Because, like I said, Pete Webber isn't the kind of client who takes off without saying something."

Mimi blinked. "Lawyers check on their clients with investigators?"

Ford ducked his head. "Miss Mimi, you'd be surprised. But Mr. Webber is a very successful realtor. He has a good business and a reputation for dotting all the I's. So, when he disappears in the middle of a deal? When he leaves his back door unlocked and his car is still in the garage? I couldn't swallow the idea that he just took off somewhere. I went over there a couple of times. And the more I looked around…that back door wasn't the only thing didn't make sense. Not by a long way. So, I hired an investigator."

Ben couldn't resist. "You paying for that?" He did his best to make it sound easy, but there it was, kind of an insult and Mimi caught it.

Ford laughed and shook his head no. "I can take you over there if that works. You all sure you won't have a little something? Sweet tea? Something stronger?"

Ben shook his head, thanks but no to the drinks idea. Visiting Webber's house, though, that was exactly what they wanted: a thorough walk-through and a chance to clone Webber's computer in case there was something in there to make sense of what happened.

"Done," Ford said. "Sheriff Butch is due to show up here any time, but we can drive over to Pete's right after if that works for you. Meantime, maybe *you* can convince Butch that Pete's in trouble."

Ford made a couple of notes, closed the file, and pushed it aside. "Anything else?"

Ben shifted his weight. Ford's guest chairs were handsome enough, but damn they were hard on your butt. "You said on the phone, Webber gave you the DVD."

"He did. But I'm probably the only man in Georgia doesn't follow football."

"No problem," Ben said. "I asked because our expert has based his ideas about the killer on the DVDs and the letters."

"I read the letter when Pete gave it to me," Ford said. "I confess I was impressed with how riled-up the writer was. But Pete didn't seem that concerned. He said it was likely some football nut. Well, I couldn't exactly argue with that. Football's pretty far out of my universe. But it didn't feel right."

And that quick, all the affability seemed to have disappeared from Ford's face. They were suddenly sitting across from a sharp-eyed lawyer. "What's your expert say?"

"That the man we're looking for has an idealized sense of football, like it should be perfect. And officials that screw up, you know, that don't make the right calls, they should be punished."

Ford seemed to consider that idea, then nodded. "Your expert give you any idea how this guy is connected to the officials he wrote to?"

Mimi cleared her throat. "Karl Hessman is his name. He worked regularly with the F.B.I. He says it's likely somebody close to the killer was injured playing football."

"He thinks," Ben said, "*if* Pete Webber is dead, and *if* he was murdered about the time he sent that email to officiating—which is the same time you have him disappearing—then Pete Webber would be the first victim. That's why we came. If we can come up with somebody who was seriously injured, then…"

Ford nodded. "Makes sense."

Ben scooted a little closer to the big desk. "Good. We're hoping, even if you don't follow football, maybe you've heard about somebody local who got hurt in a game? Hurt with long-term consequences?"

Ford was already shaking his head no. "I can't remember hearing anything like that. Let me…" He turned to his computer and began typing. "I can have Chandra check with the Savannah Morning News right now and somebody likely will get back to us tomorrow or the next day. Meantime she can check with the partners here. Maybe one of them would remember. How far back you want to go?"

"Good question," Ben said. "I got a quick look at the guy in St. Louis—my guess, our man is about forty."

Ford went into that lawyer habit: the string of questions that feed off your answers. But the questions stopped when they all heard a thud on the side door to his office. A barrel-chested guy in a khaki uniform stepped in.

Sheriff Butch Masters tossed his hat at a chair. "Sorry," he said. And with a quick nod over at Ben and Mimi, he planted himself in the remaining chair in front of Ford's desk.

The guy looked half out of breath. Ben gave a side-eye to Mimi—hopefully the sheriff wasn't such an in-charge guy that he'd make their trip to Savannah a complete waste of time. Clearly, she'd already zeroed in on that jowly sunburnt face. That little place between her eyebrows shifted just a millimeter up and closer together.

It was her searcher look. She always had that face going when she dived into what she was studying. Leaning a few inches forward, usually it was staring at a computer screen like she was frozen. He'd never understood how she could lock in like that. But he'd seen it plenty of times, that amazing brain clicking away. Truth was, he was counting on her to spot the phony or pick up on anything he missed.

The minute the sheriff settled himself in his chair, Ford said, "So, Ben, you can bring Butch up to date better than I can. How 'bout it?"

The sheriff swiveled around and motioned Ben should go for it.

So he did. Starting with the first phone call from American Football Officiating. In spite of the close-fisted look on the sheriff's face, he made it all the way to the murder in St. Louis before Sheriff Butch's eyebrows shot upward.

"I suppose you're gonna tell me the police in St. Louis are keeping you plugged in."

Ben reminded himself not to bite on the sheriff's snide tone. Play it straight, be clear about St. Louis and what he knew of the other murders.

"Well, yeah, Detective Lattimer checks in," Ben said. "As things have worked out, Mimi's talked with her as much as I have, so maybe you have a question or two for Mimi."

The sheriff's eyes were near half mast, not looking at either one of them. "Must be nice for St. Louis to have all this unpaid help. But what we got here is a man who quit his officiating job. Anybody tell you that, Mr. Leit? That he quit? My guess, he took off because he's got a fat dee-vorce settlement and he's looking to hold himself a little celebration."

Ford was talking even before the sheriff finished.

"Butch, you don't know what you're talking about. Pete hadn't signed the settlement, the decree isn't filed, and that check's still in our safe."

For a second, Ben studied a rough place on a fingernail. It sure looked like Ford and the sheriff were stuck in *he's just gone off somewhere* versus *you should be doing something about it.* If that was the way things were going to go down, he was watching his best hope for finding a good connection crash and burn.

Eventually Ford's voice grew more icy and polite, his arguments more "legal" sounding; and the sheriff was looking downright pissed. Shaking his head, *nope, nope, nope.* Suddenly Ford smacked the pencil down on his desk. "Butch! Dammit—"

"JO-LEENE!" The ring tone of the sheriff's cell phone cut Ford off like a guillotine. The big man twisted around, dragged the phone out, and stabbed it with a fat finger. "Masters."

Ben couldn't make out what the caller was saying. But whoever it was, was yelling.

"Tell those idiots out there to shut up," the sheriff roared. "Say that again. You seen it? ... Where you at? ... Purrysburg? Wait just a darned minute. Where's the state line? ... You sure yur in Georgia?"

Purple-faced and sweating, the sheriff looked ready for a heart attack.

"Judas Priest." Sheriff Masters lurched out of his chair, jammed his phone back in a pocket, and made a grab for his hat.

"Okay." He glared at Reggie Ford. "We got a body. Maybe it's Webber, maybe not. They say it's gonna be hard to tell."

Chapter 26

Ford angled his car off the dirt road and onto some beaten-down grass, pulled up short next to the sheriff's car, and took off through the weeds for the river. Ben had his door open and was about to take off too, when his gut did a backflip. They were in open country, but the air was beyond foul. Thick, choking. Like death. He couldn't think. Couldn't do anything but... He was gonna hurl.

A car door slamming brought him back to where they were and what they were doing there. Mimi'd climbed out of the car. The last thing he wanted was for her to see something like this. She was running her hands through her short hair. Shifting her shirt. She was fine. All business, would you believe, digging into one of her cargo pants pockets.

"Here." She handed him a little tin. "Take three."

He couldn't see that anything would beat back the smell. But he popped the breath mints anyway. Almost immediately his sinuses began to buzz. And finally, he could think.

What were the chances it was Pete Webber? Ford thought it might be; was he grabbing at straws? On the other hand, Webber had been missing what, ten days? Eleven?

Mimi leaned her butt against the car, pried the breath mint tin out of his hand and stuffed it into her pants pocket. "Ready?" she said.

Damned right he was ready. But whatever was going on, Mimi shouldn't be part of some body recovery. Just for starters, if it smelled this bad fifty yards from the river, what was it gonna smell like up close?

"I'm thinking…" he said.

"That I shouldn't go down there?" she said. "It's written on your face."

"Why don't you hang with the car?" he said. "Check in with Thui. Let him know what we're doing. Maybe he's heard something. Besides, you don't wanna see what's making that stink."

She rolled her eyes and marched away, heading toward a little knoll and the shouts coming from the river. Christ. He was living with Lisabeth Salander.

He caught up with her at the top of the rise.

The recovery scene was playing out right on the river: four men thrashing around in the water; three more, plus what he assumed was a cadaver dog, on the bank. It was like the start of some horror movie: murky river, tension in the voices, shadows so deep you'd have to guess what was hidden in the water.

You'd think they'd know better than to foul up a crime scene by dumping tarps, ropes, grappling hooks, and who knew what else over what might hold evidence.

If they'd found a body, it had to be where they were digging. Thing was, the guys in the river had turned the bank into a muddy bog so who knew what was there?

All he could see was an alligator halfway up the bank. But it was so bloated it must've been dead a while. Then he spotted a deputy with a heavy-duty rifle, stationed on a little point of land, with what looked like a good view of the water and both banks.

Mimi wanted to stick with the men in the river. No

problem so long as she was safe. He gave her shoulder a pat and took off for the gravelly point. Maybe he could pick up something from the deputy while the guy was on his own.

Deputy Jim didn't take his eyes off the water, not even once Ben stepped up beside him.

"Butch figured you guys would show up. You really Ben Leit?"

"Yeah," Ben said and shifted his gaze to the dead alligator. "That your work?"

"Naw. What y'all doin' here?"

Ben kept his gaze upriver. That was the question, wasn't it? What were they doing?

"I'm following up on something for a colleague," he said. He could've asked what the deputy knew about Pete Webber. But better to go after local football stories. Ford had said it: every man in Georgia was a football nut. So maybe here was his guy. "The specifics are still under wraps so I can't, you know. But if you follow football, maybe you remember if any players got hurt. Bad hurt, we're thinking. Or, do you remember hearing about officials that screwed up—again, big time? Like got into it with a coach or maybe somebody's dad? We're talking college, not the NFL."

"Last year?"

"If you remember something, yeah. But any year, might help."

"You could get how many injuries from the papers."

"Yeah, but we're looking for more than statistics. We think somebody got hurt really bad. Maybe a few years ago, maybe recently. Whenever it happened, it made somebody so damned mad he can't let go of it. You ever hear about anything like that?" Ben watched the deputy's face.

"So, where somebody's out of the game?" Deputy Jim said.

"Right," Ben said. "Or maybe the injury didn't happen in Georgia, but somebody from here was hurt, you know? If you think of anything, maybe you could gimme a call. Or text me." He handed off his business card. The deputy pocketed it, and a shout from the recovery team made them both look.

One of the recovery crew disappeared into the muddy river like something pulled him under. One second...two... He came up thrashing the water, laughing at the others. As for the sheriff, the stunt definitely was not funny.

Deputy Jim looked more disgusted than concerned. "Sweet Jesus," he muttered. "They spent the last hour trying to drag that body out. Before y'all showed up, they pulled off one of the guy's legs. You gotta wonder what's next."

That was the trouble, wasn't it? What was next?

They watched the guy who'd gone under slosh his way to the bank, the whole time working his grappling hook so it sprayed enough water to keep everybody away. Ashore, he dumped his pole. Then unfurled a fresh yellow tarp and floated it out toward the team in the water.

By the time Ben got over to where Ford was watching, the guys in the water had freed the body from where it was stuck and steered it over to the bank.

Now maybe they could find out if it was Webber.

Ben glanced around for Mimi, and she was nowhere.

How in hell had he lost track of her? There must be snakes around. And how many alligators were in that river? He scanned the bank. His breath was coming fast. No Mimi. He checked the slope all the way to the top of the rise, no. And she wouldn't have headed to the car without telling him. He was ready to holler for help but then, finally—his heartbeat thudding in his ears—there she was, sliding down from the tree that hung out over the river.

Christ, she'd been hanging right where the men had been working and he hadn't seen her.

She started for him, avoiding the worst of the mud, scrubbing her filthy hands on her pants. To his surprise, she marched right past him and stopped just outside where the deputies were talking.

"Excuse me," she said. She had that extra-pleasant look going—that, alone, should've been a warning.

The tan-hat brigade shuffled out of the way enough she ended up facing the sheriff.

"I don't mean to interrupt, but I think your coroner—"

The sheriff's whole face started pulsing red and redder. "Tell you what, Miz Fitzroy. When we start taking advice from amateurs, you'll be right up there on my list." The man's chest heaved with an effort to stop with one insult.

She gave her head a quick shake. "Your coroner won't have the vaguest idea what killed that man. I'm not dissing your doctor. It's just, he's up against the same poison as the St. Louis coroner, who can't identify it either. But they are working on something in St. Louis. I'm just thinking that alligator might give both coroners some more information. Give them a call. Detective Lattimer in St. Louis. Or the St. Louis coroner. Why not at least see if they want to test that gator for chemicals?

What can it hurt?"

Dead silence.

Ben stepped up next to her. "How 'bout we take a walk upriver?" She made that little popping noise with her lips, then headed up the trail toward the car.

Once they got far enough away from the action, she said, "Dumbass sheriff. You know as well as I do that's Pete Webber. Water in St. Louis, water here. Whatever that stuff is that killed him—" She shook her head. "That alligator was dead the minute it stuffed Pete Webber in the bank."

"Stuffed him in the bank?"

Eye roll. "Well, he had to swallow some of Webber when he bit him, you know, and then... Ben, if you watched the Discovery channel, you've might've learned alligators stash their victims away to age."

"More than I wanted to know," he said and set off with her, down the road.

They walked far enough it felt like they'd put some distance on the nightmare scene at the river, and the subject of alligators. Even the stink seemed to dissipate. Eventually the road took a sharp bend, the brush thinned out, and they were standing at the edge of a clearing big enough you could park a car, or even a pickup.

A couple of ghost trees stood at the edge of the river. The water looked dead still. A pair of birds slowly descended and settled on its surface maybe fifteen yards on from them.

Ben pressed the toe of his shoe in the spongy earth. If anybody walked around, there'd be footprints. And, yup, somebody had been in that clearing. Been there long enough the weight of their vehicle had left a track and four deep impressions in the loamy turf.

"Don't walk on it." They both said it, right together.

As if she'd read his mind, she went one way and he went the other, stepping one tuft of grass to another, working the circumference of the spot where somebody had parked. He stopped mid-way around. Some kind of claws had chewed up the bank. Claws twice the size of his hand?

"Mimi," he called, "I just saw tracks, either a bear or alligator. And there's probably snakes. So, keep a lookout, okay?"

"I'm okay," she said. "And I've got something."

He started over to her.

"See that tire imprint?" she said. "Next to it? Does it look like footprints to you? Over to that tree."

From her angle, yes, he could see it. Somebody heavy enough to sink more than a good half-inch into the soft ground had walked from the car over to a dead snag.

Assuming the body was Pete Webber, had he died there? Leaned up against that tree? Or was he killed somewhere else and they dumped him?

Either way, the murder was local. You'd have to be local to know about this place. Score one for Sheriff Butch.

What still didn't fit: Pete Webber didn't work for the South East Conference. He worked for the Big10. So why was Pete Webber the first man to die? Personal? Location? Something else?

Ben glanced over to Mimi, like maybe she had the answer. A shiver hit him. "Let's get out of here," he said.

Chapter 27

They'd just made it back to Ford's car when the back door of the coroner's van opened. Reggie Ford stumbled out and made a dash for the nearest high grass.

Mimi headed for Ford's SUV. "I'm going to, you know." Yes, he knew: this was all about getting on the phone. She opened the big door and climbed in.

When Ford stumbled back out of the underbrush, he was pale and shaken. He walked right past the sheriff. He braced himself against the driver's side of his SUV, mopped the sweat off his face, and then, without a word, climbed in behind the wheel.

As Ford settled himself, Ben flagged down the sheriff. "We found a place, upriver. Your guys would get there, I know. But it looks like somebody parked there, maybe dumped something in the river."

"Hang on." The sheriff offered a business card to Ben. "I'd appreciate it if you'd send me those St. Louis phone numbers."

Ben climbed in next to Ford and glanced into the back seat. Mimi's brown eyes shifted from her phone screen to his face, to the back of Reggie's head.

"How you doing, Reggie?" Ben said. "You okay to drive?"

Ford answered by starting the car and backing onto the gravel track they'd come in on.

Silence until they hit the outskirts of Savannah.

Then, suddenly, Ford said, "It was Pete Webber. Or what's left of him."

Ben sucked in a breath. He'd figured as much from the way the deputies were acting. But hearing Ford say it somehow knocked him back. Three out of the four officials murdered. Officiating would have to go public now.

"If," Ben said, "if we're still going over to Webber's house, we're gonna need latex gloves and something to cover our feet."

Ford whipped the SUV into a superstore parking lot. They got what they needed, and ten minutes later they were standing in Pete Webber's foyer. All three of them, gloved and booted.

The house smelled stale; maybe a hint of beer, but nothing ominous. The living and dining rooms looked mostly organized for TV watching, like Webber spent his time in a big leather chair and ate his dinner from an ottoman. Beyond the dining room, glass sliding doors opened onto a deck with the usual overstuffed loungers. No sign of a fight.

Mimi hoisted her computer bag. "I'm guessing Webber's office is down the hall?"

"First bedroom on the left," Ford said and straightened around to Ben. "I should be taking you through the house, showing you what I put together."

"On the other hand," Ben said, "you look fried. And you probably need to check in with your people, right?" In four strides Ben had the sliding doors to the deck open and stepped outside. "Why not take a load off?" Ford shot him a tired smile, dug his phone out of a pocket, and parked himself on one of Webber's loungers.

In spite of the mosquitos, Ben hung out on the deck,

leaning against the door frame. Evening was coming on and the sun had gone low into the big trees. The yard seemed a little too perfect for his taste, and eerily quiet. The whole neighborhood was quiet enough. If there'd been a struggle outside, plenty of people would have heard.

Now that was just nuts. Why wouldn't the killer take care of Webber the same way he'd killed John Brown? Didn't that make the most sense? Knock on the front door, Webber opens it, the killer hits Webber with the same thing he used in St. Louis, and, bam, Webber is a dead man. Why not do that?

Before he headed inside, he took another slow look around the deck. He must've looked at the steps down into the yard five or six times, thinking whether he should check out all those plantings. Funny how you look right at something and don't see it. It wasn't until he'd turned to go inside that he spotted something stuck between a couple of boards in the decking.

Without thinking, he picked up a plastic doodad a couple of inches long. A cover for a needle? That's what it looked like. His hands, his arms tingled at the possibility. If it was a needle cap, that'd clinch how Pete Webber had died. And for sure it would tie Webber's death to John Brown's murder in St. Louis.

Lassiter hadn't said anything about finding a needle in St. Louis. But the coroner was certain the killer had delivered the poison by injection. And the Texas guy had died the same way.

He made a quick check of the deck. No needle.

He headed inside calling, "Mimi, you won't believe—"

Down the hall, she was already giving him her

report. "Still cloning his system. He left his phone unlocked so I got pictures of his call history. The other thing, I grabbed copies of his emails and file history—everything that wasn't scrubbed."

That brought Ben up short. "Something's scrubbed you think?"

A quick shake of her head and she looked up at him. "No, just my usual cautious self. Sorry." Her system pinged and she was back in computer land.

No point in talking now. His news would keep anyway. Still… Had she considered everything in Webber's office or just the tech stuff? It wouldn't hurt to give the place a hard look.

But as he looked… Was anything *not* connected to real estate? No. No. No. Yes.

Webber had left a binder splayed open by a leather chair: The man was studying this year's college football regs. Now how did that make sense? He quits officiating but he's still keeping up on the rules?

As unobtrusively as he could, Ben shifted around Webber's home office, taking one new angle after another—was there anything more? He ended up right behind Mimi, hovering over her shoulder. And hold it…he had seen something, hadn't he? When she'd moved her head. What was it?

He took a step back and clicked through the images in his memory: her hair, her fingers, her computer screen, Webber's computer screen, the cords behind it, a bulletin board on the wall behind the computer screen with a mess of real estate cards, printouts, a picture, an investment flyer, hold it…

A picture. He edged a little closer. It was the bottom of a football team photo with the date in the corner: thirty years ago.

"Mimi," he said and reached over her. "Look at the bulletin board. See that shiny photo? Just a piece of it. It's mostly the kids' feet showing. I think it's a football squad. I'm gonna lift up the crap that's in the way and if you could…"

She scrambled out of his way. He grabbed one of her zip drives to use as a lifter and shoved the real estate flyers out of the way so they could see the whole photograph.

"Now," he said. "Can you get a shot of the whole thing? Make sure you get all the kids' faces, okay?"

She took a whole series of pictures, then stepped back so he could lean closer.

He'd posed for a bunch of those 8x11 team pictures when he was in school. They always took them early in the fall when the uniforms were new, then handed copies out in December along with the sports awards. The one he was looking at was of the Ben Davis Volunteers squad.

He said, "Is that Pete Webber there on the end?"

"The manager shirt?" she said.

"Right. Karl said personal, right? So how many guys hang onto their high school football picture for thirty years? Especially if they were just the manager. You think maybe among the players we're looking at the killer?"

"You think?"

"We need the names of these guys," he said. "There must be somebody who can come up with 'em." He stepped out of the way so she could get back in the desk chair, then kissed her sweet, brilliant forehead and headed into the living room.

All he could come up with there was a dried stain from a glass and four dents in the carpet like Webber's TV-watching chair had been moved. Why was that? Was it important? He couldn't tell. Maybe the police could get fingerprints off the leather.

He studied the room once more and couldn't see anything else.

Which left the kitchen. Clean except for a few empty beer bottles in the glass recycling. Checking the fridge... The beer bottles in the bin and the ones in the fridge made it pretty clear.

Ben couldn't help his grin. Wasn't that pretty solid evidence the killer knew Webber a little bit? The killer brought beer. Just not Webber's brand.

On to the garage. He'd nearly died in his dad's garage. He'd never shake the feel of that explosion and fire. But this wasn't his dad's garage. He yanked open the door.

The air was dead still and nothing about the place looked disturbed. Maybe a couple of scuff marks right by the garage door. But it didn't look like a struggle, more like somebody had scraped a shoe heel... Had they dragged Webber out through the garage?

He was still kneeling on the cement when Mimi showed up behind him.

"Okey dokey," she said. "You ready?"

Yes, except for bringing Ford up to date.

Ford met them in the living room. They shed their rubber gloves and booties—they were headed for dinner.

Only not.

Before Ben even realized the significance of it, Ford was off the front porch and trotting down Webber's front walk, smiling, calling *ma'am* at a well-dressed older lady who had planted herself at the end of the driveway and was tugging on the leash of a little dog.

Smart. Who knows what she'd seen walking that dog? And Ford was just the man to find out what she knew.

She must've said *Rusty, you stop that* a good five times before Ford caught up with her.

Ford introduced himself (almost bowed). And, as Ben and Mimi slow-walked down the driveway, they were treated to a one-hundred percent Southern Gentleman in action: the kindly head-tilt, the soft smile, nodding, an easy conversation about Rusty the dog, the lady's grandchildren, and finally an amazing dip into neighborhood gossip. Periodically, the lady clucked at her dog. She also flirted with Ford in that way old ladies do. And eventually she turned her enormous blue eyes on Ben.

"My heavens. Am I looking at Mr. Ben Leit the football star?" she said.

Ford managed the introductions: Miss Martha, Miss Mimi and, yes, Ben Leit.

"Miss Martha was saying she makes this walk with Rusty here two or three times a day. Did you all meet Rusty? He's been with Miss Martha fourteen years this November. Can you imagine?" Ford shot Ben a look, then turned to the older woman. "Now, Miss Martha. You were telling me about that car you saw."

Miss Martha shifted Rusty's leash from one hand to the other. "Well, yes," she said. Her voice as soft and warm as a breeze. "Mr. Ford, here, was asking if I knew Mr. Webber. And could I recall when I'd last seen him. As I said, it was eleven days ago. I remember because my bridge partner and I had a grand slam that night.

Well…we're talking about Mr. Webber, aren't we? That afternoon, I was walking Rusty and I saw Mr. Webber talking with the Wilson boys who do his yard. They do such lovely work, you know. And then that night when Rusty and I were out for our bedtime ritual, I noticed Mr. Webber had visitors parked up the driveway right where you all are parked now."

"And what time would that have been?" Ford said.

"Well now." She giggled. "We don't retire around here 'til nearly midnight, Rusty and I. So, eleven-thirty? Something like that." The dog shifted his focus from a bush at the end of the driveway to Mimi's shoes. "Rusty, stop that." Miss Martha tugged the dog's leash.

"Ma'am?" Ben said. "I don't suppose you remember what kind of a car you saw."

Her face softened. "I'm so sorry. This is important, isn't it? Mr. Webber being not here and… I wish I could help you but I'm just not up on automobiles."

"I know what you mean, ma'am," Mimi said.

"I'm so sorry I can't say more. But, anyway…" With a little hand wave, she started on down the sidewalk. "You all have a nice evening."

They were still standing at the end of the driveway when Miss Martha came hustling back.

"Now that car was big and white, did I say that? Well, anyway. It had an Ohio license number."

"You're sure about that?" Ben said.

"Oh yes, Mr. Leit. I'm quite certain. My grandbabies live outside Columbus. I'd know that red and white license plate from a mile away. Now I hope that's some help for you."

"Oh yes, ma'am," Mimi said.

Ben watched Miss Martha sashay down the

sidewalk, still talking to her dog. Ohio wasn't much of a lead, but if they could find an Ohio phone number on Webber's phone history…

By the time Ford dropped them at their B&B, the three of them had put together a plan that felt solid. Ford would get his paralegal to follow up on names for the guys in the football team photo; and Ford would line up interviews for Ben and Mimi with his investigator and also with Webber's widow. Ben would follow up with Thui, Detective Lattimer, and Football Officiating. Mimi would set up Ben's computer with the stuff she'd cloned from Pete Webber's system, so Ben could work on his own. And while the download ran, she'd check Webber's phone history for calls to or from Ohio.

As soon as they got to their room, Mimi went to work at the little desk. Ben turned on his cellphone, and it lit up like Las Vegas. He opened Thui's most recent text and held his breath.

"Jesus. Another one."

"What?"

"A Mountain West official. Looks like he was killed the same way."

Mimi twisted around in her chair to look at him straight-on. "What's the Mountain West? You never mentioned that one."

"This guy's name wasn't on the list Skip sent me."

He thumbed open one text after another. Looking, looking. "Chris Matsen. Maybe he didn't get a DVD. Maybe he thought it was a nut case and didn't report it. Who knows?"

"Where this time?"

Finally, Ben opened the text that explained everything. "They found him in Arizona. Dead like the others."

"Where in Arizona?"

"Fort Verde Garden Reservation," he said and before she asked where that was, he pulled up an Arizona map on his phone. "Sort of Northern Arizona. Hold on. Thui says they've put the police there in touch with Lattimer."

Ben accessed a travel app and thumbed in *St. Louis to Ardmore, Oklahoma to Fort Verde Garden Reservation*.

Oh man. "He's driving Route 66. Has to be." Ben laid his phone aside. "You do remember, there's one guy left on my list, right?"

"The one in California," Mimi said.

"Know where Route 66 ends up?"

"Doesn't everybody?" she said. "Santa Monica Pier."

"Ten points for you. Any idea how fast can we get there?"

Chapter 28

Santa Monica, California

Beeker sucked in a deep, satisfying breath and stepped back to get a better look at the famous sign— *Santa Monica Pier*. His back hurt, his hips burned, and for the last three hundred miles, his left shoulder had played up regularly. In spite of the pain, here he was, standing under the huge sign with its arc of deep blue and the flash of green. It left him breathless, amazed at his accomplishment. And proud. He'd driven Route 66, Chicago to Santa Monica. And he knew now, he had driven every mile of it himself.

He ignored the crowds pushing by him, crooked his neck, and stared up at the elegant curve of the arch spreading across the bright blue California sky. Finally, when he'd had enough, he gazed out the length of the boardwalk. He couldn't help feeling a touch disappointed because the Ferris wheel and what looked like a little amusement park blocked his view. But it felt amazing to be there.

The air smelled more of carnie food than ocean, but still, the Pacific was right out there. If he walked to the end of the pier, he could lean right over it. But that would mean making it past the amusement rides, and the squealing teenagers, the toddlers and their po-faced mothers. Going out there, he'd have to put up with being bumped and jostled. Maybe worst of all, they were selling French fries and cotton candy, and he wasn't so sure he could stand to smell French fries ever again.

Come on, Beeker, you love fries. You know you do.

"Not so. Not anymore," Beeker muttered. *"You* love fries."

A herd of kids plowed past him, nearly knocking him over. They dashed across the street without even looking. No. He was not walking out to the end of the pier, not with all those people. Besides, he still had Matt Redweather to deal with. He glanced at his watch. Half-past three. How long would it take to get to Altadena, wherever that was?

Plowing back through the crowd felt like swimming upstream, but he did make it to the parking garage in one piece. He slid onto the driver's seat of his SUV, locked Redweather's address into the navigation system, and studied the route that popped up on the car's computer screen.

He'd just pulled out onto the street when Deek launched into a whole set of instructions for how to finish off Redweather.

Well, he was not going to put up with that the whole way across L.A.

"Deek, I do not need your counsel. I'll take care of this one the same way we did the others. I need to—" Stop light. He leaned forward and fiddled the navigation screen to get more of the route: four blocks ahead, get on the freeway, 1.8 miles and change freeways to one that cut through downtown L.A., take another freeway through Pasadena, to Altadena. Pretty straightforward.

He joined the river of vehicles heading back through the city.

Traffic was slow enough to begin with. He had plenty of time to shift lanes in order to stay with U.S. 10. What wasn't so easy: as traffic went from slow, to a crawl, to barely creeping forward, Deek changed tactics. What started as moaning about the day, shifted to harping about the traffic, to complaints about the heat and Beeker's driving.

Deek was outright shouting. *Get off here, exitexitexit, next exit, go by city streets, here, turn, hereherehere.*

Eventually, there was nothing to do but wait where they were, in the intermittent shadow of L.A.'s downtown towers. For ten minutes they did not move at all. The late-afternoon sun kept bouncing off the Navigator's rear-view mirror and into his eyes.

And Deek changed his tune to *off ramp off ramp off ramp,* and Beeker finally shouted, "Shut Up!"

The shock of his voice cut like a slap in the air and he wasn't sure what that other part of him might do next. But miracle of miracles, the Deek part of him zipped it.

They moved ahead a car length. Then two.

He was still sweating, his hands were still slick on the leather steering wheel, and the sun was still beating in on him, but they moved three car lengths.

He should have used the alternate route that popped up on the driving directions back when they'd left Santa Monica, the one up to Sherman Oaks. It'd looked a lot farther. But it couldn't be this bad.

Traffic began to crawl in starts and fits. He was a millisecond slow moving forward and a flashy sportscar jammed in ahead of him. He barely stopped in time. Then, seconds later, the same jerk cut another guy off in the next lane over and ended up as a fender-bender.

Beeker pulled past them and, miracle of miracles, he was moving again, grinding his way uphill to the Arroyo-Seco exit.

Progress at last. But he was still miles from Redweather's house and time was ticking. He forced the Navigator over into an exit lane, abandoned the freeway, and pulled into a parking lot for a medical office where he fiddled with the navigation system.

From what he could make out, getting to Altadena from the far-south side of Pasadena actually seemed possible.

Wrong! Half the cross-streets he passed didn't show up on the navigation map, not all the streets on the map were two-way, and the freeway cut through the route to where he was going.

In spite of getting lost, in spite of the yammering voice of the GPS, in spite of stupid drivers, and missing street signs—in spite of it all, he finally made it to the Altadena address. Where he ended up cruising block after block, no parking anywhere. Finally, four houses down from Redweather's house, a dayglow orange delivery van pulled away from the curb. And he parked.

The house didn't fit in the neighborhood: white, not pastel for one thing, and not Spanish colonial for another. It was a Frankenstein house: part clapboard, part stucco, part something else. As if two or three houses had been joined together under an ugly dark roof.

His chest tightened and for a moment he felt dizzy, like the pressure in his head would explode. No... *Come on, Deek. If you're part of me, then step up and help!*

No response, no helpful suggestion now when he needed one. He climbed out of the Navigator anyway. His spine straightened. He took a deep breath. Then another. He felt taller, way taller, and stronger than his old self. He felt like he'd been born again. He retrieved a pair of syringes from the back of the Navigator, pocketed them, and headed up the sidewalk.

But as he stepped up on the porch, something didn't feel right. He forked a hand through his hair and peered deep into the house interior. The living room was empty, save a couple of bags of paper. Not a rug, a chair, a sofa, lamp, nothing.

He had busted his ass driving behind one stinking diesel after another to get across this miserable armpit of a town. And now that bastard has made a run for it?

Well, Matt Redweather was not getting away.

Chapter 29

Beeker kept staring in at the vacant interior. It didn't make sense. He'd shipped the Redweather package to this address. And Redweather must've received it because none of the packages had been returned to the Atlanta maildrop he'd used.

Well, it wasn't like Redweather could hide.

He could finish the guy off at a game if he had to. But that meant checking out the stadium, coming up with a uniform, and definitely more risk.

Beeker shut his eyes against the smoggy air. When he opened them, three women were standing at the end of the walkway, looking his direction. The skinniest woman stayed put; the other two said something to her then took off down the street.

White hair, eyebrows raised, she was older than he'd first thought. She started walking toward him. "If you're looking for the Redweathers, they've moved on," she said. "So, you can stop coming around here."

"Ma'am," he said. "I don't know who you think I am, but I've never been here before. I'm just trying to return some stuff that Matt left in my car."

Her eyes narrowed. If she saw him again, would she remember him? He went for the sympathy face. "Ma'am. If you've had trouble with these people, I'm sorry. I get it, sometimes your neighbors can drive you nuts. I don't really know Matt. I just worked a football game with him, that's all."

"Trouble?" The woman's eyebrows shot to the top of her forehead. "Cars all hours. Strange men you don't want in your neighborhood. We called and called the police. We begged and pleaded for action. And how did they deal with it? They told us to keep a log. We kept a log. It took months to get them to do anything."

Do the concerned face…

"That's terrible," he said. "And you think Matt was—"

"Not the *man*." She snapped. "That woman, India. And what kind of a name is that? She was a horror. You wouldn't believe the fights. Screaming, door slamming so loud it woke Ina and Ralph and they live four houses away. Twice, that woman smashed in the front window after he locked her out."

Beeker took a step to the side. The longer he stood there, the more likely she would remember something about him. But the more he sympathized and stepped aside, the more she ranted, following him down the sidewalk, going over the same events like a drumbeat that was getting him nowhere. Nothing he did seemed to give her an off ramp.

"I guess you don't know where they moved to then," he said. "Sorry, I was just hoping I could—"

She grimaced. "She's back living with her mother in Pasadena. Her name's India in case you're interested. The mother owns the house. She's on the board of the Los Angeles Opera, can you believe it?"

If he had to, that might be enough to track down *India,* but… "What about the man? Know where he went?"

She shrugged. "Movers emptied the house this

week. No idea."

"You remember which movers?"

That seemed to surprise her. Her lips parted, almost like she was whispering to herself. "Chico something," she said. "Chico. Same name as our daughter's cat."

Beeker settled in behind his steering wheel and thumbed a search into Google: Chico Moving Los Angeles. He called the first number that came up.

Chapter 30

Ben scanned Santa Monica's Ocean View Park for anything that looked wrong. The place was crisscrossed with paths, and old trees shaded a good half of the grounds but it looked okay. With plenty of open space for kids to play.

He refocused on the game of pass, catch and defense football that Mimi and Redweather's two boys had going. Harry, who looked maybe twelve, seemed serious. For sure, serious about sports, but from where Ben stood, the kid seemed skeptical. And why was that? The younger boy, Tad, seemed more ready to have a good time.

"We're new to Venice," Redweather said, his gaze never leaving his kids as they ran around. "The other day we saw a soccer game going here. So, when you called, I thought, why not meet at the park and give the kids something fun." Suddenly, his eyes went wide. "*All Right!*" he shouted as his little one pulled in a nice pass.

The pass itself was good, but not remarkable for a twelve-year-old. On the other hand, the little receiver, Tad, had snagged the ball out of the air like a pro. That kid was gonna be a player.

"You said new here?" Ben said.

Redweather's smile dropped away. "Moved over from Pasadena."

"You moved during football season?" Ben said.

"That must've been a grind."

Truth was, moving was probably a good idea. Providing Redweather hadn't let the world know his new address.

Fifty yards away, Harry came racing across the grass, chasing Mimi. As he made a grab to tag her, she did a complete cartwheel—really a flip, because she never put her hands down. As she landed, she kept running. Both boys stopped short and exploded with about a hundred questions that all boiled down to *how'd you do that?* She parked the football on the grass and demonstrated a couple of easy flips. When they wanted more, she helped them try their own cartwheels, then switched to doing them one-handed, which led to gymnastic moves that she said might help with snappy escapes.

It took Redweather a minute to recover from Mimi's trick. Even then, his eyes stayed tracking the boys.

Until Ben brought Redweather back. "You were talking about your move."

"We needed to get away from Pasadena. And I was running out of options," Redweather said. "Then we got offered this Venice house."

"Lucky."

"You can say that again."

"You said you needed to get away."

Redweather let out a sound like a steam radiator, then looked over. "You're thinking we moved because of that DVD I got. That was months ago. I've had two calls from Officiating here in L.A. And one from a guy from Texas. Now you. We didn't move because of a threatening letter."

So, Skip Jackson had called him.

"Okay," Ben said. "But it's probably good you moved, whatever the reason. The thing is, you are at risk. Seriously. You gotta know that."

Redweather shook his head. "I think I'm more at risk every time I get on the freeway. Look, this threat thing... You know the internet. You know the kind of stuff gets posted. If I took half the stuff I hear seriously, I couldn't do my job."

Ben nodded he understood. Still, there had to be something he could say. Before he came up with it, though, the younger boy, Tad, trotted up clutching the football.

"Did you see? Did you?" Tad kept jigging up and down, a gap-tooth grin splitting his face. "I got her, Dad, just like you showed me. And she fumbled!"

Mimi fumbled?

Ben swiveled his focus from Tad over to where Mimi was standing on the imaginary football field. She was already watching them—amazingly, beautifully, artfully, the innocent fumbler. At that distance, she looked like a teenage boy.

"Hey, Tad!" she yelled. "We're waiting over here. You playing or what?" A quick pat from his dad to the top of his football helmet and Tad raced back to his brother. The game resumed, and Redweather said, "If you saw what the DVD guy sent me, then you know he was right."

"You're saying he was right?" Ben said,

"Two years ago, it got so crazy with India and the police, I couldn't think. I screwed up a lot. But that was then. Once she... Anyway, I've turned it around. I'm the best man on our officiating crew this year. That's our review people talking. Look, the guy who wrote that letter has to know I'm good now. He has to if he follows football at all."

Seriously? Has to know?

"I guess I don't quite see that," Ben said.

Redweather stuffed his hands in his jacket pockets and glanced at where the kids were still playing. "We're doing fine. I cut my teaching hours so I'm around the boys more. It's a pay cut, but as long as I keep officiating, we get by."

Ben took a slow breath. "Just for the sake of looking at the threat from a different angle, how about I lay out where we are with this thing?"

Redweather gave him a nasty side-eye.

"First," Ben said. "You're one of five men who received DVDs and threats. There might be more, but so far, it's five we know of. The other four are all murdered. Second thing: you talk like if the killer was serious, he would've written you more than once; he didn't write any of the officials more than once. Third: from the order of their deaths, and their location, we believe the killer's been driving west on Route 66. The last man died two days ago, in Arizona. So, the killer is probably already in L.A."

Half the color in Redweather's face drained away. But his mouth stayed clamped into a tight narrow line. When it opened, it was like he was announcing the deciding penalty for a championship game. The guy was that determined.

"Nothing is going to happen," he said. "We've moved. Nobody knows where we are. Security has us covered. They've upped their protocols; they've added check points at the stadium entrances. They know what they're doing. I have to think I'm good. You've wasted your time coming here."

"Stadium security isn't the answer," Ben said. "None of the men died near a football stadium."

No reaction from Redweather.

Ben glanced over at Mimi. The kids were running out of steam. They'd be checking in with their dad in a couple of minutes. So, now or never…

"Matt? Matt? You have caller id on your phone?"

Redweather nodded.

"Any calls you didn't recognize?"

Redweather shrugged. The usual stuff; he ignored those.

"How about calls from Ohio?"

It took a second before Redweather exploded.

"What? You know this guy's from Ohio? If they have his phone, they must know who he is."

Good. He'd scared the guy.

"Well, they don't," Ben eyed him. "And the phone might be stolen. The one thing you've got going for you, you've moved. You change your address with officiating?"

"Not yet," Redweather croaked.

Redweather's eyes looked wild. "It doesn't make sense that ESPN or the blogs or…I don't know, the New York Times? Why hasn't there been anything in the papers? One of them would have a story about somebody killing football officials. They'd have to."

Ben licked his lip. Well, yeah, that made sense if you believed companies never sit on the kind of news that, if it got out, would make them look bad. "We didn't put the whole thing together until yesterday, when they found the man in Arizona."

"Look," Redweather said. "It's taken me two years

to get our lives back on track. And we're good now. If we survived my ex-wife, we can survive this. I can't quit officiating, that's the bottom line. We need the money."

Now he tells me.

"Nobody needs you to quit," Ben said. "It just needs to *look* like you quit."

Suddenly Redweather began gathering up the kids' stuff. And the boys must've spotted it, because they abandoned Mimi and took off for the car yelling *pizza.*

Redweather gave him a long look. "I'll think about it." But then booked it to catch up with his kids.

****

Ben held the car door open as Mimi climbed in. He couldn't shake the feeling he'd blown it. "Hotel or food?" he said.

"I'm a wreck," she said. "Shower first, then food. Meanwhile…" She pulled her phone out of her jacket. "Just checking a couple of things." And there was that crooked grin as she stared into the screen.

By the time they were closing in on their hotel, her grunts and *no ways* had morphed into *holy cats!* And she looked positively radiant.

"We got him." She grabbed his knee and squeezed it. "Winslow Beacham."

"Say that again."

"We heard back about the Ohio cellphone number. It's Winslow Beacham's cellphone. Check it out." She held her phone out so he could see.

"Just read it to me," he said and changed lanes.

"Ms. Fitzroy: The cellphone account mentioned in your inquiry belongs to our founder and former corporate president, Winslow Beacham. Mr. Beacham retired two years ago when Beacham Industries was

sold. Mr. Beacham retained his corporate phone number at that time. We are unable to provide you with his address or other personal information. However, should you desire that we forward to Mr. Beacham your request that he contact you, I am happy to do so. I hope this answers your questions."

"And about Beacham Industries," she said. "Apparently they were a specialty pharmaceutical company."

"Specialty pharmaceutical?" he said.

"They invent new kinds of anesthetics."

He hit the car's brakes a little too hard. "You're saying they invented stuff that puts people to sleep?"

"I have to think so...unnhhhh." She dropped the phone in her lap. "Phone's too slow."

She talked on—it sounded like more to herself than to him—outlining the databases she wanted to look at: the DMV, tax records, criminal records, patent records, anything she could pick up from court filings.

She had never explained how she was able to hack into high security sites, and truth was, he didn't want to know. But God, what a woman. She stopped talking. Which meant she was thinking, probably about which programs to run first and what she wanted to eat.

And he was right. The second they got into their suite, she launched the computer on some kind of government records search. Then, as she headed for the shower, she said, "Order me something, okay?"

He ordered dinner, then moved on to the phone calls he needed to make. His first, to Ally Lattimer in St. Louis, went to voicemail.

"Ally?" he said. "Ben Leit here. Following up on what we found in Savannah. Remember I said Ohio plates? Turns out there's an Ohio phone number on Pete Webber's call history—don't ask how we got that. It belongs to a guy named Winslow Beacham. His company invents new anesthetics."

Chapter 31

First things first. Beeker figured, catch Chico's
Moving the minute somebody was there answering the
phones, get what he needed, and take care of business.
Then he would actually enjoy his breakfast.

Naturally, the guy from Chico's Moving launched
into a long song and dance about why they couldn't give
out customer information. But no way that was going to
deter him.

Beeker waited 'til the guy stopped talking and
cleared his throat. Then heard himself say, "I sure
understand what you're sayin'. You can't be too careful
I s'pose. You think maybe I could talk with the fella in
charge?"

The phone at Chico's clunked down and it took the
better part of a minute for an older guy to say, "We don't
give out customer information. Sorry."

"Oh man." Beeker said. "I sure do understand. And
I sure don't mean to be giving you trouble. But I got
myself in a heck of situation here and I'd be real grateful
if you could help me out getting ol' Matt his stuff."

No response from the guy.

"Am I speaking to Mr. Chico?"

"No. Like I said—"

"See," Beeker drawled, "And I apologize for
interrupting. My trouble is... See, Matt and his ol' lady
split, you know? That's how come you guys did that

move for him. Matt left the stuff he didn't want his old lady getting hold of with me. Not that she knew about it but, you know. Anyhow, my wife is sick of it taking up half our garage. You know how women are. I was supposed to get it over there the day before he moved. But then things at my place got all fucked up— 'scuse me."

The moving guy snorted. "He's *your* friend and you don't have his phone number?"

"Oh man," Beeker agonized. "Matt's wife had his cell phone cut off. I figure he's got a new one but he hasn't called and… Help me out here man, can't you? Sure as God made little green apples, Matt won't tell nobody where I got his address, swear to God."

The dam broke. Beeker wrote down the street number, said, "I thank you, sir*,*" and entered the Venice, California address into Google.

In a nanosecond, Google came up with two photos of a bungalow. The overhead one answered a load of Beeker's questions about Matt Redweather's new digs. Almost all the houses on that block looked crammed together, side to side, but open to the street. He might as well hire search lights and invite the public if he took on Redweather from the front porch.

There was a narrow path running between Redweather's place and the one just to the north, with what looked like a tall hedge up both sides of the yard. Now that was the privacy he needed. Bonus points for the alley, more like a walking path, that ran across the back of the lot. Using those walkways, he could be in and out of there in no time and no one would see him. If he got on the road now, maybe he could take care of Redweather before the fool got away again.

Beeker stowed a packet of latex gloves and syringes in a little bag, stepped into the nearest elevator, and pushed the down button to the hotel's palm tree filled lobby. Passing the fourth floor, it felt like the elevator stumbled. A little electric charge ran through his whole body. But then everything seemed fine. Until he got to the lobby. The elevator stopped an inch or so below where it should've, and he tripped stepping out.

Nobody in the lobby? Not even the receptionist? What was going on? Finally, he spotted the hotel guy, standing outside on the guest turnaround alongside a couple dozen other people. The ones not talking were staring down the street. Either they were gawking at a wreck or a fight.

Well, he was not getting caught up in whatever it was. Rather than risk another elevator hiccup though, he took the stairs down to the parking garage.

Even before he pushed the stairwell door open, he could hear car alarms. The racket was bad enough when he'd stepped out onto the garage stairs. By the time he got to his Navigator, the chorus of beep-beep-beep felt like a dentist was drilling the side of his clenched jaw.

Redweather, that was the point.

He put the Navigator in reverse, backed out of his too-narrow parking spot, and followed the exit signs. There were three cars ahead of him, waiting for the garage gate to open. A couple of minutes crawled by during which time nobody moved.

He piled out of his car and walked up to where he could see what was going on. The big metal door to the garage had raised maybe two feet off the floor and stopped. Through the metal slats he could see a hotel guy, pacing the driveway, talking into a phone in

Spanish.

Beeker pivoted, marched back to his car, and managed to maneuver the Navigator into a disabled parking spot—it wasn't like anybody was going to be coming into the garage for a while. He grabbed the little bag he was going to need and took off up the stairs to the lobby.

Suddenly, it felt like the cement stairs he was on were going to drop out from under him. Blasts from a dozen car alarms pounded at his brain. He powered himself up to the landing and grabbed onto the door into the lobby just in time.

The stairs he'd just climbed, the landing he was standing on, the overhead pipes, all of it, shuddered and groaned. Plaster silted down on him. The railing he'd been holding popped loose from the wall. He crammed himself tight into the doorframe, braced himself, and waited.

Was this the Big One people in California talked about? Was he going to die here? Because the lurching and bucking seemed to go on and on. His chest pounded; his knees burned. It seemed like he was bathed in sweat. His life was coming apart.

Finally, the floor stopped rumbling and shaking and it seemed like he was okay. Like the building was okay.

He charged through the hotel lobby and out to the hotel's big circular turnaround where he spotted the hotel's front desk crew. It looked like every one of them was tied up fielding questions from dozens of people he assumed were guests at the hotel.

Do not let this sidetrack you.

With any luck, an earthquake would slow Redweather down too. He bypassed the throng and walked over to where he could see what was going on with the garage gate. If he could get his car out…

A pair of palm trees had uprooted and dropped across the driveway. Well, that took care of that. Removing that mess would likely take hours that he didn't have. He turned on his heel, joined the lineup in front of the hotel manager, and waited.

People are geese. "Was that an earthquake?" "Excuse me, but will there be more?" "Are we safe now?" "I have a flight…" Repeat. Repeat. Were they idiots?

He stepped up to the manager. "I need a rental car. Your website says you can make that happen."

The guy nodded, swallowed so hard his Adam's apple bounced, then made a half-footed attempt at an encouraging look. "We have an airporter van going—"

"Car," Beeker said.

Forty-eight minutes later, Enterprise dodged its way down the boulevard in front of the hotel, pulled in the turnaround, and handed off the keys to a Buick SUV. Beeker loaded his bag onto the passenger seat, parked his phone at an angle so he could access his driving directions, and headed for Venice.

There must've been hundreds of highway crews out checking the greater L.A. road system. Over and over, the three- and four-lane freeway narrowed to two lanes or even one. Emergency vehicles made the traffic even worse. And it seemed like every five minutes somebody's car overheated or some idiot had a rear-ender. Eventually it was just too much.

Beeker jettisoned freeway travel in favor of the city streets. It seemed like every stop light on the west side of Los Angeles was either blinking or out entirely. But at least he was inching along. The fact he'd skipped breakfast was now a nasty drumbeat he couldn't ignore. He was starving. And he needed a water.

When, finally, he spotted a café that looked like he wouldn't come away with ptomaine, he circled the block, parked, and grabbed a booth. He might as well eat. This time of day and with people milling around all over the place, he'd be better hitting Redweather after dark.

Including the time-out for his hot turkey sandwich and coffee, the drive to Venice took him almost seven hours. The sun would be setting in minutes, which made it less likely he'd be spotted, and more likely Redweather would be home.

He parked three blocks from the Redweather house. He opened the case with his syringes, readied two—if he'd learned anything from Arizona, it was he might need a backup—he capped them and stashed them in his jacket pocket. He pulled on a pair of latex gloves, locked the car, and strolled toward the house. The chilly ocean air left his skin tingling. Or maybe it was the excitement of meeting up with his target.

Redweather's house and yard had an Oriental theme going. And Google was right: a tall bamboo hedge lined the narrow walking path that led to the back of the property. Definitely a help. Especially because he hadn't considered the steady stream of people walking, biking, and skateboarding past the place.

On the other hand, how about a quick try.

He went through the front gate and knocked on the front door. Nobody home. For a millisecond, he considered looking inside. But no, he was not about to peer through the front window and alert some passing neighbor. Back through the front gate, he headed along the path leading to the back alley.

He barely noticed the alley's oleander. But the feel of the place overwhelmed him. The alley felt like the riverbank outside Purrysburg—close, a green tunnel, with Pete Webber staring out.

The sun must've gone below the horizon, because almost suddenly the light went, and he nearly missed it: right next to Redweather's garage, a weak place in the bamboo forest that screened the postage stamp yard behind the house.

Beeker squeezed through and scanned the space. A barbecue, a small patch of grass... Quiet except for the far-off sounds of the street out front. No lights on inside.

Redweather was using the enclosed back porch as a place to park his moving trash which had collapsed—probably the earthquake. At least that made it clear the man would be coming in the front door. All Beeker had to do was clear an exit path in case he needed a quick way out.

He squinted through the back door window. The porch door opened to a laundry room, then a kitchen. Farther in, he could make out the shadow shape of a sofa.

It took him three tries jimmying the lock before he was able to step inside. First impressions: the kitchen was too narrow and too far from the front door for him to lie in wait there.

The air was vibrating...his hand was shaking... water, he needed water.

Without thinking, he opened the refrigerator—a soda, a bottle of water. He grabbed a bottle, closed the heavy door, and one of the magnets came loose and fell to the floor along with a couple of pictures. Boys, one maybe twelve and the other younger.

The muscles at the back of Beeker's head seized like a vise. For a moment, he closed his eyes against the pain. When he opened them, a boy maybe six, maybe seven, was looking at him and laughing. And an older boy in a football helmet and uniform…was…

He couldn't breathe. He steadied himself against the counter. He couldn't see clearly. His penlight made a halo around the kid in the football uniform. The kid was younger than Deek, but just like him. Handsome. His dark eyes looked square into the camera the way Deek had always done. That right hand palming the football against his chest… And the younger boy…it was him. It was him and Deek was his big brother, together like they'd been back in Savannah.

The front gate clanged.

Redweather. Beeker stuffed the pictures in his pocket and pulled out a syringe. He shoved away its cover and stepped across into a little hallway. *Wait for him to get all the way inside, for the front door to close.* He would take Redweather down with half the load, park him on the sofa, and explain why he was going to die.

He took a deep breath.

The front door opened.

Beeker stepped out, syringe fisted, and ready. "No," he whispered.

The boy's mouth was wide open, a surprise. He was missing a front tooth. His eyes like black fists. "Daddy? Daddy!"

Wrong! All wrong. Not him. Not the boy.

Beeker stumbled back into the kitchen and was through the back door. In two strides he was off the porch and diving through the bamboo.

Chapter 32

Beeker untangled himself from the bamboo forest behind Redweather's house. A quick glance—nobody. He booked it down the long, dark alley. Glad for all the walled gardens, glad he'd worn his running shoes.

At the first cross street, he pulled up short. All he could hear was his breath.

Less than a block away, two women were standing at the corner that tied into Redweather's street. He stepped out from the alley and stopped. *Assume they see you.* He checked his watch and slowly headed toward them. He was a man on an evening stroll. It was pleasant enough outside after all.

By the time he was close to the corner, he could hear sirens. Obviously, the women could too. They turned one way and another, looking. They weren't moving on.

People are curious, he knew that.

He mimicked the women, turning and looking. He began walking toward them. Toward them, because the sirens were coming from that direction, because the sound was getting closer. And because, if he were an ordinary man out for a walk, he'd be curious. Like the women.

The blonde with her hair tied back checked him out. Her face said it all: he was dull, too old for her, and harmless. The other woman was different, older. She smiled at him. "You see anybody?" she called. He shook his head no. "Where is it?" he said. She walked out into the intersection and pointed up the street.

Beeker joined her and watched the commotion around a police car right in front of Redweather's house. Another cruiser blocked the intersection on the other end of Redweather's street. The sirens and the red/blue flashers brought people out of their houses, staring around.

Like all the others, Beeker and the women settled in to watch the excitement. Then a third car pulled up right beside them and stopped, blocking their view. The cop behind the wheel checked them out, then said they should go back inside, there was nothing for them there.

No point in arguing. They headed back to the sidewalk.

Be the gentleman.

"Let me walk you ladies home," Beeker said. "Just to be safe."

"Actually, I'm right here," the blonde said and motioned to the house on the corner behind them. The women confirmed some deal they had to meet the next day, and the blonde headed up her walk and disappeared behind her front door.

The older woman seemed happy to keep talking, so they continued to walk on west, toward the beach. Good for him—he was part of a couple and his car was that direction. His instinct was to hurry. But she wasn't in a hurry mood. He settled in to listen, and strolled. Sometimes he could hear her over the noise from a helicopter, sometimes not. But he nodded along, doing what he could to imply he was sympathetic or concerned or whatever.

Two and a half blocks later, he saw her to her door.

"Thank you," she said. "It was nice to be walked home."

He worked up a smile and stepped back off the porch. "See you around the neighborhood."

As if that was happening.

He waved at her from her gate and took off for his car. He was fine. Fine. He'd made it out. But Redweather was still breathing.

He dug out his car keys, tossed his jacket on the passenger seat, and slid behind the steering wheel. Had he dropped something? He opened his door wider and peered at the asphalt. The photos from the refrigerator, the boys.

He stepped back out of the car and fingered them off the pavement. The bottom one with the boy was wet. It looked like he was crying.

He hadn't cried in years. Not since that Saturday.

He'd been too scared to cry until after. When the police got there and the shooting was over.

He remembered that part. The peachy color of the pillar where the lady held onto his ankle. She held on so hard it hurt for a long time afterward. There was gunpowder and a terrible smell. And right in front of him, what was left of a little girl and her dad.

The drum of the helicopter overhead brought him back to California. And the street. And his rental car. He would not think about Savannah. He would not think about the fear on the Redweather boy's face, or how he'd screamed *Daddy*.

He would start the car. He would drive back to his Pasadena hotel. He would scrub himself down, though he had not earned it. Then and only then would he consider how he would fulfill his promise to Matthew

Redweather.

Back at his hotel, the body scrub did help clear his head. He used half a bottle of moisturizer bringing his neck and shoulders back. He stepped out onto the cold marble floor of the bathroom telling himself *forget everything else, the man is officiating.*

According to the Pac12 schedule, Redweather would be working this coming Saturday at the new Oceana Park Stadium.

He would need game tickets, a doctor's white coat, an identity tag that would pass muster at the stadium. He needed a local car not a rental. He needed to study the stadium's remodel plans. And, if he could arrange it, he needed a spot on this week's Stadium Executive Tour.

He had three days to manage it all.

Chapter 33

Ben glanced at his watch. It seemed like they'd been back at the hotel for hours. How long did it take the Redweather clan to eat a pizza? He pushed himself away from the hotel's sitting room desk, strolled over, and leaned against the doorway to the bedroom.

Mimi was still sitting cross-legged on their king bed, propped up by a heap of pillows. A couple of decorative ones served as a table for her laptop. She had the beginnings of a scowl going between her eyebrows. It disappeared as she looked up; her face one big question: *Any news?* She patted the bed next to her and waited.

As if he were summing up to a bunch of football students, he counted on his fingers.

Forefinger. "No word from Redweather."

Middle finger. "Pasadena PD can't do squat 'til there's a crime."

Ring finger. "Oceana Park Security says they'll keep an eye out but 'don't get your tail in a twist.' They didn't say the last part, but you could sure hear it."

Little finger. "And, there's been a coup at Officiating's head office, Skip Jackson's out on his ass. Other than that, no news. I sure hope you're having better luck." He stole two of her pillows and stretched out next to her.

"Okey dokey," she said and took a big breath. "As far as Ohio goes, there's just the one car registered to

Winslow Beacham. A white 2021 Lincoln Navigator, license AYY0120. Miss Martha did good, huh?"

Ben shifted his left hand away from her thigh and glanced at his watch. Less than two hours 'til the security people he'd hired were due at Redweather's house.

"Put it back," she said.

"Hmm?"

"Your hand. It was good there," she said. "Anyway, between Ohio's Bureau of Motor Vehicles and the hour I spent playing around in the old Beacham Pharmaceutical records—"

"You went after—"

"His social security number. Which got me into his tax records and his bank. His house is outside Cleveland, purchased twenty years ago for just under a million. Current tax valuation now is just about double. I can't find any record of other people living there. And that's the only real estate in his name."

"Married?" Ben said.

She shook her head, no. "His mother lived there with him. She died two years ago. And before you ask, heart attack. The interesting part came from his bank accounts."

Ben pinched the bridge of his nose. "Buddy, what happens when somebody discovers you've been rifling through their—"

"They won't find anything," she said.

Eeesh. "You said interesting."

"He's a long-time football fan. Season tickets since forever, and mega donations to the Number One Club. I'm guessing you know what that is."

"Their big donor fan club," he said. "Two of the officials worked for the Big Ten, remember?"

"Maybe something there got him going," she said.

His gaze drifted out the window to the night sky. He should be celebrating what she'd found. Beacham was their guy and they'd identified him. But he couldn't shake the thought of Redweather and his boys.

"That's not all," she said. "Over the past two months he's paid over a million dollars, always less than a hundred thousand dollars at a time, into Eleanor Holding. I haven't run Eleanor Holding to earth. I have to get the tax number. But what's that for?"

She shifted her computer over to the night table and curled up next to him. "And you're welcome."

He wrapped an arm around her. Was Beacham salting money away to make it harder to track him? Sounded like it. But the guy had driven his own car to Savannah. Did that make sense? "Lattimer know what you found?"

Mimi rolled onto her back. "Too late to call. I texted her."

He checked his phone. Still nothing from Redweather. Didn't the guy get it?

As his free arm slid away from her, Mimi vaulted off the bed and went to lacing up her shoes. "What if we drove over?" she said.

****

They were maybe seven blocks from Redweather's address when they heard sirens. "Keep your eye out for ambulances," he said.

Seconds later, a police car passed them. A couple of blocks more, they began seeing people out on the street, staring around. And right after, they heard the whump-whump-whump of a helicopter, another cruiser bulleted by.

"If it's like the others…" *Did he say that out loud?*

"It's another block," Mimi said. "And don't talk about the others."

At Redweather's street, Ben hung a right turn and pulled over to the curb. Ten yards ahead, a police cruiser was shutting down its flashers.

Ben's chest froze solid.

The cruiser was sitting right in front of the only house on the block with no lights on.

When his dad was murdered, he'd made a hash job of things with the cops and nearly gotten them, and himself, killed in the bargain. Well, he wasn't gonna let that happen this time. He piled out of the car and headed for the cruiser, hands up like he was no trouble.

The driver's window on the police car rolled down. A beam from a flashlight swung out and hit Ben full in the face. He blinked and the light shifted down onto his chest.

"It's all over, sir. Nothing to see here," the officer said. An older guy, thick neck, grizzled mustache. "Get back in your car and move on."

Ben rubbed at his eyes. He couldn't. Not without knowing. "What happened?" he said. "Please. We're working with Matt Redweather. The man who lives there."

The interior light in the cruiser came on and the flashlight went away.

"I don't mean to hold you up, Officer. But please." Jesus, had his voice cracked? "Something must've happened here, right? Can I just explain why we're here? Why we're worried?"

The cop glanced at the cruiser dashboard. "Make it quick."

And Ben laid it out: the threats, the four murders. He gave them the contact numbers for the St. Louis and Savannah cases. The cop glanced over to his partner, then back. "Your name?"

Ben offered his business card and said they were staying at Loews in Santa Monica. "Can you tell us what happened?"

A slow blink from the cop. "Home invasion," he said. "Nothing you can do here."

The lady cop leaned forward so he could see her. "Check out the news," she called, then said something Ben couldn't hear, and the cruiser slowly pulled away.

For a second or two, he stared at the house, and it hit him. Good news, maybe. He headed back to his car and climbed in. "Home invasion," he said. "But take a look at the house. See any crime scene tape?"

"Just invasion? Nobody hurt?" Her smile lit up the car. "You know where they are?"

That was the question. Where would Redweather go with the kids? They talked what to do next all the way back to the hotel.

As soon as they got into their suite, he made one manic pass at his phone: text, email, blog posts, LinkedIn, anything else he could think of. Nothing from Redweather. Nothing from Officiating in Texas. Nothing. It was like the air had gone out of the system.

He had a fleeting thought—maybe food would get his brain going. No. He didn't want food. Cold. He needed the cold. Needed something to hit him, knock him back. He unlocked the sliding door to the terrace and headed out.

For a while, he watched the play of traffic on the street below. He scrubbed a hand through his hair. Why couldn't he see the next move? There's always something you can do. You just have to see it.

Sometime later, the sliding door whooshed open and he heard her step out.

He couldn't look at her. Not just then. She came up behind him, slid her arms around his waist, and pulled him tight against her. A heartbeat. Another. She brought her hand up across his chest and pressed her head against his back.

For a moment, they just stood there, breathing together.

"I get it," she mumbled into his shirt. "Not hearing from Matt is driving you nuts. But right now, we can't do anything about Matt, can we? But we can give the police and Pac12 Security what they need to stop Winslow Beacham."

"You're right. It's on them now. I'll pull everything together tonight and put a call in to the police. Once we talk to Pac12 Security—"

She tapped the place over his heart again. "Before you do that. Can you take one more thing about Beacham? I don't know if it's good or bad but—don't turn around."

"What'd you find?" he said.

"It's what I didn't find. There's no evidence that Winslow Beacham was ever born," she said. "In fact, he doesn't show up anywhere until he's twelve years old."

He slipped her grip and turned so he could see her. "So, who is the guy?"

When she didn't say anything, he kept going with an idea. "Okay, spit-balling," he said. "The mother is dead."

"Two years ago," she said. "Heart attack. The census showed her living with him for twenty years."

"You find an obituary for her?" he said. "Because I'm thinking what's her—"

"Maiden name," Mimi said. "With that we can get a marriage record."

"And a last name."

Chapter 34

Los Angeles International Airport

Beeker locked his rental car and surveyed the airport's long-term parking lot. In spite of what happened in Venice, he felt better than he had in years. He could talk to people without ducking their eyes. He could say what he wanted. Now that Deek was helping him instead of yapping in his ear all the time, he could do anything. And he could see now, he was part of a long, long game to clean up football. Pete Webber, Brown, Mincey, Matsen, and soon enough, Redweather—they were just the beginning.

In the next phase, he'd take on the men *behind* the game: the ones who profited, the heads of the NCAA and Officiating, head coaches, and those clowns at the football website. Ben Leit and his bunch, they could've helped get officiating on track. They could've made a difference. So, what did they do? They did worse than nothing.

He could see it clearly now. Leit and the rest of his cronies didn't give a damn about football. If they had, they would have been beating the drum for making the game safe instead of claiming Officiating was doing their best.

Beeker stopped behind the trunk of a Lincoln Navigator some California driver had left in long-term parking—an exact twin of the Navigator he'd driven across half the country and that was still parked in his Pasadena hotel's garage.

In less than a minute, Beeker had the blue and gold plate off the California Navigator. He tucked it inside his jacket, wiped down anywhere he'd touched, and climbed back in his rental Buick. It was time for him to pick up his own Navigator, switch plates and disappear into the ocean of Californians cruising the freeways.

Back at his Pasadena hotel, the uprooted palm trees of the morning's earthquake were gone, in their place, a whole new planter of tropical greenery lined the driveway.

Beeker left his rental car in the hotel's guest parking, grabbed his black bag, and headed up to his room.

Fifteen minutes later he stepped up to the reception desk. "Checking out," he said, "And I've left the rental you got me out front. Can you take care of it?"

Done and done. He hauled his bags down to the parking garage and installed the stolen California plates on his own Navigator. Nothing to identify him as an Ohio man now. He climbed in behind the wheel and disappeared.

Chapter 35

Redweather's 6:30 a.m. text to Ben had said *meet with Det Marks. My place 8:00 am.*

No way was Ben gonna miss a chance to get the cops plugged in to what they'd uncovered. He flung himself out of bed and busted his butt getting to the house in Venice. He even magicked up a parking place.

But he was still five minutes late. And from where he was sitting in Redweather's overstuffed easy chair, Detective Marks was already clearly in command of the living room.

"You see what I mean?" Marks laid some papers on the coffee table and peered at Redweather. "Your back door's not secure. There's an alley back there. And your neighbors can't see into the back yard. Think about how long this house has stood empty." Marks raised his eyebrows and waited.

"I dunno." Redweather looked overwhelmed. His eyes darted between Ben and the detective. "You're right about the back door, but…"

Marks had one of those affable, pretty-boy faces and a serious suntan. At the moment, he was going with a way-too-patient, sympathetic but know-it-all expression that just might win Redweather over.

"Doesn't a junkie break-in make more sense than the idea that some crazy man is trying to kill you because you're a football official?" Marks cocked his head and peered at them like if they were reasonable men, of course they'd agree.

There had to be a police report from when he'd talked with the cops last night. Hadn't this guy read it? Ben cleared his throat. "I don't think you have the whole picture."

Marks's face kept going with that beach-boy-we're-all-cool-here thing, but the stone-gray eyes shifted to pure defense. "How is that, Mr. Leit?"

Ben kept his voice low and calm. He even leaned forward, mimicking Marks's body language. He told the whole story. Then pulled a printout of all the key names and phone numbers out of his jacket and slid it across the coffee table.

Marks fingered the page around so it was right side up. "Anything else, Mr. Leit?"

Ben took a deep breath. "We've made a connection between a guy named Winslow Beacham, a car that was seen at the Savannah victim's house, and a phone that made two calls there on the day Pete Webber disappeared. Somebody used that phone, traveling along Route 66, to post messages in the football website. That phone's gone dead now. We figure he may have changed cars or picked up a new phone or both."

Eventually, Marks stopped writing. "And this list you gave me has all that?"

Ben nodded.

Mark shifted his focus to Redweather. "Assuming for a second that this man with the needle isn't a junkie, any ideas how he found you?"

Redweather scrubbed his hair back. "No. We just moved. It was, would've been, our second night in the house. Nobody knew where we were. Not my boys' school—"

"And what about your boys?"

"I put them on a plane last night. They're with my sister in Arizona. My school principal is the only one who knows where we're living, he owns the house. And Ben."

Marks tapped his thumb against the little pad he'd been writing on. "Neighbors at your old house? DMV? Social media, or how about your boys?"

"I haven't changed anything yet. I don't do social media because of officiating. The boys didn't have the address. They just knew we'd be near the beach. And my last neighbors were probably glad to see the back of us."

"But whoever moved you has the address, don't they?" Ben interrupted.

Redweather's eyes went wide. He pulled out his cell phone, dialed and put the call on speaker.

"Chico's Moving."

"You guys helped me move a couple of days ago. My name's Redweather?"

"Hold on…" Noise of the phone being laid on a hard surface, paper shuffling, phone rattling. "Sorry, what's your name?"

Eye rolls all around the little living room. Redweather gave his name again, explained about his move again, and said, "And I'm wondering if you folks gave anybody my address? You know, maybe somebody called?"

"Oh, no. We don't do that. We don't give out customer information."

"Are you the one who dealt with Mr. Redweather?" Ben virtually shouted.

"No, but…just a minute."

And it took a minute, a real one. Finally, a woman came on the phone. Redweather explained what he was calling about, spelled his name this time, and… "Ah. No. We don't give out information. We don't even sell our mail lists."

Redweather glanced over to Ben, then leaned closer to the phone. "Would it be okay, could we talk with whoever was answering the phones yesterday and the day before? Maybe he remembers something."

"Hold on," she said.

Redweather was getting good at explaining what he needed. And even better at sounding worried and tired.

After getting the same *we don't do that* response from Chico himself, Redweather said, "See somebody showed up here and threatened my kids. You guys couldn't know that. But, uh, maybe somebody gave you a story about needing to get hold of me? It's really important. Can you remember anybody asking where I moved to?"

"Oh, man."

It felt like all the air got sucked out of Redweather's living room.

"Maybe it sounded so important you decided it'd be okay to give out the address?" Redweather said.

The phone crackled. "I talked to him. He said he was holding a bunch of your stuff for you so your ex wouldn't steal it. He was in a real lather."

"You get a name? You remember what day he called?" Ben said.

"No name. But it was the day after the move, because I still had the paperwork. So…day before yesterday? Or maybe yesterday morning?"

Marks pulled out his phone and headed for the

kitchen.

Ben turned to Redweather. The guy looked exhausted. "So, what happened? Last night, what'd you see?"

"Not much," Redweather said; his hands were shaking. "We got home about eight-thirty. I stopped to lock the front gate. Harry was going on about Mimi. Tad unlocked the front door, went in. Next thing I know, he's yelling *daddy*. He sounded terrified. That sound...I'll never...I never heard him that scared. By that time, Harry is yelling too. And I busted in there and...and..."

"And?"

"This guy was just staring at Tad. Kinda frozen." Redweather wiped his upper lip. "Harry said the guy had a needle. I didn't see it. But I believe him. Harry wouldn't make that up. He knows what a needle looks like and he wasn't more than six feet from the guy."

"And then?"

"The guy pivots. Just planted his foot like a player, you know? And he took off through the house. Out through the back door. I'm right after him, but by the time I got out there, he'd disappeared. And I figured it was better to stay with the boys, you know? I called the police."

"And that's it," Ben said.

"Right," Redweather said. "I talked with the police. Called my sister. Called for a substitute to fill in for me today." He looked bereft.

Marks reappeared and hovered beside Ben. "Can you be more specific about how the man looked?"

Redweather shook his head slowly. "Not really. My height, maybe in his forties or fifties. Short hair. Sandy or maybe gray."

"Scars? Facial hair? Tattoos?"

Redweather shook his head. "Nothing like that. Just so ordinary."

"Anything else?" Ben said.

"It's kinda weird." Redweather focused on Marks. "He stole two of the kids' pictures."

"Pictures?" Marks said.

"You know. School photos. It was the first thing the kids did when we moved in. Put them up on the fridge. One of Harry in his football uniform. And one of Tad."

Marks muttered that hadn't been in the report, then refocused on Ben. "Mr. Leit, maybe you know. Has your killer taken other trophies?"

Chapter 36

On the one hand, Ben couldn't help feeling like they were making progress. On the other, was it enough progress they'd be able to keep Matt Redweather alive? Let alone catch the guy.

What Mimi had pulled together was gonna go a long way toward answering that one… If she was able to do what she hoped.

As Ben opened the door to their hotel suite, he could see her, out on the terrace, on the phone. And nodding enthusiastically.

She raced back in and virtually tackled him in a bear-hug. "We've got him. And I know why." She unwrapped herself from around him and stepped back. "And I'm starving. Let's get some food and I'll tell you."

She steamed ahead of him, down the hallway and out onto the sidewalk. Talking with her hands, sometimes threading her fingers through her hair, sometimes pirouetting and walking backward.

"Okay, so One," she said, "Beacham was born in Savannah. He was John Sloane until he was twelve. So that's why, you know." Eyebrows up.

"And two: Beacham had one brother, eleven years older, named Declan. And I'm sure it's that brother that's the key to the murders."

"So, Karl was right. There's our other man."

She shook her head no. "Not exactly. And that's

three: the brother's dead."

No second man?

"The brother and the father were both gunshot deaths. I'll tell you about that in a minute. Four. A couple of months after Declan and the father died, his mother moved her surviving kid—that's our guy John Sloane—to Cleveland and changed their names to Mary and Winslow Beacham."

She did a little twist dance at the corner then headed off down the block. Going for the food trucks a couple of blocks away, he would put money on it.

"A name change, because somebody shot them?" he said.

She stopped for a red light. "The brother Declan is the key. But here's how it all ties together," she said and stepped off the curb. "Listen: Pete Webber officiated the opening football game this year at Ohio State. Beacham has season tickets to Ohio State games. A player died after being hurt in that game."

Walking backward...how was it she could walk backward almost as fast as he would walk forward?

He stopped to make her stop. "That's what got Beacham started."

"Exactly," she said. "Pete Webber was the manager for Declan Sloane's football team. That's what that football picture got me. And you won't believe this." She dug out her phone, pulled up that old team picture, and manipulated the image over to a dark-haired kid in the middle of the pack. "This is the brother, Declan Sloane. The guy at the paper said they called him Deek."

Ben bent closer. He scrubbed his hand across the top of his head. "Jesus," he said, "he looks like Redweather's older kid. Beacham must've seen it, too. This morning

Redweather said Beacham stole pictures of the kids off the refrigerator."

She turned, eyed him for a second, and headed down the block for the food cart.

As he caught up with her, he said, "You said Deek and the father are dead. From gunshots. How's that tie in?"

"I couldn't access the newspaper records—we are talking thirty years ago—so I called the Savannah Morning News. I talked with a sports guy who's worked there forever. He says Deek Sloane was a wild man, a huge football star in high school. He went to University of Georgia, was a big deal there, too. He played linebacker."

As they closed in on the flood truck lot, the aroma of Indian and Mexican and South Asian cooking hung thick in the air. Maybe he was hungry.

Mimi took a left turn into the Latin row and stepped in line at the sunburst truck they'd been to the day before. "Linebacker is one of those guys in defense, right?" she said, and looked very pleased with herself.

He did his best to suppress a smile. She said she was buying, that he should stake out a place. Halfway down the block he found a spot in the shade, sat on the cement ledge, and went back to watching Mimi's progress.

She fiddled with the bottom of her shirt, then stuffed her hands in her jeans. She shot him that perky smile and glanced around at the tourists with the kid, the guys ahead of her (even from where Ben sat, you could hear them arguing about a movie), the hotel dogwalker on the other side of the street. She rocked up on her toes, a knee shifted to the left, to the right…

It seemed like the people around her were all either

absorbed in their own conversations or plugged into their cellphones. For sure, they weren't paying any attention to the little brunette jigging from one foot to the other.

Finally, her turn. And a couple of minutes later, she showed up with enchiladas, fish tacos, and a little bag of churros.

He said, "You said you think the older brother is the key."

"Remember Karl said there was an initial trauma? Well, Brian... My sports guy? Said that Deek was a good kid and a good player. For a couple of years. But by halfway through high school, he'd turned into the local bad boy. The cops picked him up zillions of times drunk or for DUI but they always let him go."

She let him tell a little war story about how no sheriff in the south was gonna lock up the local football hero before she said, "Anyway: Deek goes to the NFL. He plays part of one year, keeps getting killed on the field, and finally they dump him midseason."

She was still talking, but somehow, he couldn't listen. He knew what it was like getting dropped from a roster. *He* had one bad hit to his head. One. Bad. Concussion. And his team of a decade dumped him.

A slow burn started right under his sternum.

"You're not listening, and you should." She licked her fingers and stuffed a taco wrapper in the sack. "Deek comes back to Savannah in 1988 and moves back in with his family. Apparently, he's not such a hero anymore because he keeps getting busted for drugs and DUIs. There were also a bunch of police calls to his folks' address."

"Drugs and alcohol, that's the thing for a lot of these guys," he said. "Self-medicating's one way you can tell who's in trouble."

She shot him a look, picked up a plastic fork, and went after her enchilada. "Okay if I finish?" she said.

He'd been mansplaining. He knew better.

"I get it; you're thinking CTE," she said. "Me too. But you're not this guy. You're not. Your folks didn't turn you into a god. Neither did your school. Or Seattle. And your family wasn't depending on you making it in the NFL. So, I repeat: this is not your story. I wouldn't be with you if it were."

Well, it could've been his story.

He had to work to swallow the bite he'd taken. "What about the gunshot?" he said.

"Just before Thanksgiving 1989, Deek took his little brother to the mall. He also took an AR-15 and a 44-automatic. Deek dragged the kid and a bag full of ammo up to the second level of the mall and started shooting. Eleven people died, some at the scene, some after. Bad enough, but Deek tried to kill his little brother, too. Some woman pulled the brother behind a pillar before Deek could finish him off. It ended with Deek shooting himself with the pistol. He died at the scene."

Ben dumped his half-eaten enchilada into the sack they were using for trash. "I guess that would qualify as the trauma Karl was talking about. Jesus."

Mimi eyed him and took a deep breath. "Brian says the news called it a massacre. Anyway, Savannah went nuts. All the stuff about the drinking and fighting came out. People blamed Deek's family. Said they should've done something about Deek, gone to the police, blah, blah, blah. Deek's father—well, Beacham's father—killed himself over it. And that was the last Brian heard of the family."

"No wonder she changed their name," Ben said.

"Three years later, Winslow Beacham graduates from high school. At fifteen. He wins every kind of chemistry prize they had at Ohio State. Then half-way through his PhD, he starts the company we know about. The rest you already know. Ready to take off?"

They headed back to the hotel. She said, "How'd it go with Redweather?" She was watching him, waiting for probably another CTE talk. Which he did not want to have.

"Okay," he said, "But, I need to think."

She stroked his arm. "Just as long as you remember: *this is not your story.*"

They walked the rest of the way back to their hotel not talking, and once they got inside, he motioned he'd be out on the terrace. It felt quiet out there.

He couldn't help running a comparison between Deek Sloane and how things had gone for him.

In the twenty years he'd played football, he'd had maybe five or six hits to the head. Probably Deek Sloane hadn't played more than ten years. Pretty likely, because he'd been playing linebacker, Deek Sloane had maybe seventy hits to the head. Linebackers and linemen, they took the most abuse.

A plane passed over. Too low, it seemed like. The sound made Ben's head go a little screwy for a second.

Back when Deek was playing, as long as a man could walk straight and said he was okay, back on the field he went.

Deek the wild man, grew up with everybody promising him a big career in the NFL. He went to the big show all right, but he doesn't make it even a full season. How much anger does that kick up in a drug-fueled twenty-two-year-old?

Beacham had put it all in those letters to the officials. Jesus…blaming these officials for head injuries that happened to his brother, thirty years ago.

Ben squinted into the sky: another plane, but higher this time.

Mimi just wasn't seeing it. Except for the fact he had ten years in the NFL where Deek had a few months, their stories weren't that different.

Not when you thought about it: starting with the day the great Ben Leit had been knocked cold and then carted off the field with a concussion. The Giants had dropped him just like Green Bay had dumped Deek.

He'd hit the booze hard after that. Not drugs—at least that was different than Deek.

That night in Seattle made the difference. The best thing happened to him was the cops rolling up in time to stop him killing that guy. That mandatory probation, that court order got him clean and sober. That made the difference: somebody stepped in.

The sliding door bumped open.

"You think he had CTE," Mimi said.

"I think," Ben said, "Winslow Beacham decided his big brother would never have had CTE if football officials had been doing their job."

She was waiting for him to say something more. When he didn't, she said, "What time's the game tomorrow?"

"Four o'clock," he said. "And Officiating's on board to keep Redweather safe. We'll work out the final details tomorrow morning. But they have a solid plan."

"How many people at the game?" she said. "Forty thousand? Sixty thousand?"

"I know it feels like we're looking for a needle in a haystack," he said. "But think. The police are looking for his car. We know why he's killing people. We know he's doing it with a needle. So, it's not hundreds of people at risk, it's one. And we can keep our man safe."

She was shaking her head. He wrapped an arm around her and pulled her over.

"Come on, Buddy. If this were Deek, you'd be right to worry about a gun. But Deek's dead. We're looking for a traumatized boy in a man's body. He's carried that scene at the mall for thirty years. He's just trying to fix what's broken."

"He's murdered four people," she said.

"Yes, he has. But we're ready for him. We'll be safe as houses."

Chapter 37

Game Day

Beeker headed for the new Oceana Park Stadium. He took the exact route he'd taken the day before when he'd done a two-thousand-dollar big donor tour of the facility. No surprise, game day traffic was a whole different animal from the Friday commute.

A good half-mile from the stadium, a parking cop motioned him *left here.* No problem. He had plenty of time; besides, the walk down the tree-lined streets would be pleasant enough and might help settle his nerves. He obediently swung left onto a winding side street.

Two and a half blocks later, he was finally able to shoehorn the Navigator against the curb into what looked like a legal parking place. He grabbed his binocular case and congratulated himself again for coming up with a plausible way to get the syringes past the stadium's security check. Nobody would see them packed beneath his binoculars. And Security would never question his lab coat. True, wearing it under his raincoat might be too many layers of clothing—once he was in the stadium, he could ditch the raincoat if he got too hot.

He fingered the lanyard holding the plastic name tag he'd made at the copy shop. It'd do if all he had to do was flash it at somebody, though he'd be better off with a medical badge from the stadium. Once he was past

Security, he'd drop by a medical services office. With luck, he be able to come up with an ID nobody would question. He climbed out of the Navigator, patted his pockets—tickets, binoculars, money—and joined the river of fans heading for the stadium.

He was used to ignoring people rushing by him, the jostling and shouting. That part was no different from Ohio, except here the shouts were mostly *Heigh-Ho Jack-o!* But the eucalyptus smell in the air wasn't so easy to get past. It seemed like he was breathing cough medicine. Hopefully, once he got inside, the stink of garlic fries and hot dogs would take over.

At the corner, he joined the hordes heading down the wide curving boulevard that sloped toward the stadium. Security had blocked off the traffic, so why not walk in the street? It was way less crowded. And once he could walk at his own pace, he began to relax, look around, and enjoy the day. If it was a little chilly, it wasn't raining. The houses along the boulevard had bushes he'd never seen before and they were still blooming, in October.

What really cheered him, though, he was about to wrap up this part of the campaign. Here's to you, Deek, couldn't have done it without you. Maybe the idiots behind Football Officiating would finally get the point.

Out of nowhere, something crashed into him. He pitched forward. His left foot caught and he was falling. He felt the asphalt scrape his left hand; his right knee crashed into the pavement. He closed his eyes for the face plant.

As sudden as whatever hit him, the front of his coat jerked up, catching him at his throat—he was face down in the trap of his coat. He couldn't breathe. Then he was being lifted.

"Gotcha," a big voice called.

It was like his whole body was suspended, inches above the street. He opened his eyes and saw a man's feet right in front of his face. The guy lifted him, enough he could get his own feet on the pavement.

Still out of balance, Beeker grabbed at the man's arm and straightened up. His head was spinning, his hand burned like hell, and his right knee felt like he must've landed on it. At least he was upright and getting steadier. He must've said thank you a dozen times to the man who caught him. The guy was big as a lineman but older.

Beeker finally realized a couple of other men were hanging behind the guy that helped him. They were saying a kid with a skateboard had hit him. "A kid?" Beeker said. Part of him still trying to make sense of what happened, another part wanting to get away and get on with things.

"Yeah, a kid," the big man said. "You okay now? Looks like your binoculars got the worst of it."

Binoculars. Beeker glanced down at the case. Still fastened but a huge scrape in the leather. What did that mean for his syringes?

"Well, yeah. Anyway, thank you," Beeker said.

Ten minutes later, the throng at the stadium was just like Ohio. The bag inspection man pronounced him safe to go in and motioned him through to the ticket people. Two steps forward and he flashed his game ticket at the girl with the card reader. And once he was through the turnstile, he took off through the crowd, his focus shifting left and right. Men's room or med station, whichever came first.

A med station came first but he bypassed it because two men in white coats were chatting right at the entry.

He'd keep that place in mind, but there had to be others. Meantime, he'd settle for a men's room. Finally, on the right. He pushed his way over and ducked in.

The dim light of a toilet wasn't the best for checking the syringes, but he needed privacy. He spotted an empty stall in a far corner, stepped in, and locked the door behind him. He leaned his back against the door, jammed the binoculars in his raincoat pocket, and, one by one, fingered the syringes free from the bottom of the case. He might need two to finish the job. And the top two looked undamaged. The bottom one had leaked, but it still held two milliliters. So... He had an extra.

He tucked the syringes in his lab coat, stuffed the binoculars back in their case and hung them on the door hook where he 'forgot' them. He flushed the toilet, stepped out to a washing station, and cleaned the blood and gravel off the place on his hand that took the worse of his fall. At last, he was ready.

People shuffled this way and that, stepped around one another, stared at TV monitors set high on the walls, and waited in line for nachos, tacos, hot pretzels and churros, hotdogs, hot and cold drinks. They clustered around tables of relish, mustard, and napkins and lifted their paper boxes to catch every drop. It was all so familiar, he found himself relaxing again and had to push himself to stay sharp.

Past the hawkers of memorial game books, past stands full of home team tee shirts, sweatshirts, plushy cuddle toys, and God knows what else. There had to be another med station. Where was it?

Finally. Nobody in sight, he made his way across the scrum, stepped inside, and pushed the door with the big red cross part-way closed. He tried one sticky drawer after another—nothing useful. He had an excuse for being there, of course. If somebody walked in, he was looking for a bandage.

But the issue was badges, dammit. Where the hell were they? Under lock and key?

He saw them just as he was about to give up and leave. In a basket on a top shelf. A quick shift of his photo to the stadium badge, he was official.

He dived back into the melee, checking faces, dodging kids. He kept expecting to spot some security, but not one cop in sight. He made it to the end of the public part of the stadium. *The Ledge,* the white wall said. Just yesterday he'd seen how this floor opened onto the big donor boxes and a few meeting rooms. By this time, Redweather had to be just one floor down in the officials' dressing rooms.

He was about to head down there when the door to the donor boxes opened and a big man backed out. The guy was still looking through the doorway at someone inside, still talking. The guy might have backed right into him. But at the last second, the man turned. "Excuse me," he said, keyed something in the phone he had out, then hurried away.

Beeker couldn't believe his luck. Ben Leit had just backed into him.

Ben Leit, he was certain it was Leit, headed up the public stairs. Beeker slipped past a handful of fans and followed him up. At the top of the stairs, easy enough to spot the man: Leit was nearly a head taller than most people. And he was heading for a door with a keycode next to it.

This was the part of the stadium with the coach's offices. The tour had gone through there just yesterday.

Beeker dragged out his phone and pushed past a blonde woman waving money at somebody.

He hit video record and panned the area like he was making a movie and angled himself closer and closer to the door. Fans ducked out of his way in time he was able to record Leit punching the keypad, opening the door, and heading inside.

Beeker bulleted forward, jammed his foot forward, and nudged the door open enough he could see. Leit had stopped in front of a little office, not fifteen feet away.

Beeker's heart nearly exploded. Bad angle, so he couldn't read the sign on the door.

But the sign was paper so it had to be temporary. And when Leit opened the door... TV screens, headphones. This had to be the official play review box. And the guy messing with a TV remote, Beeker knew that face. It was Matt Redweather.

Chapter 38

Phil Nichols, the guy from Pac12, followed Ben and Mimi into their box at Oceana Park Stadium. Nichols had the look of a man whose shorts were too tight. "Texas says we can't do it," he said.

Ben looked up from stuffing his binoculars under his chair. "Can't do what?"

"We can't reassign Mr. Redweather to reviewing plays."

Ben sucked in a breath. This felt exactly like one of those games that goes south right from the get-go: one screw-up after another until somebody gets hurt. "I thought we had an agreement with your head people that we could change Matt's assignment."

"We did, we did," Nichols said. "Yes. We did. But the guy who okayed it didn't have the authority. And last night, our head office called me and, unnh, Texas says we can't change how we do the official review."

"And that means?" Ben said.

"We can't assign Mr. Redweather to do it."

Ben licked his lip. "Jesus, Phil. Don't they know what's going on? What's the plan for Matt if he's not upstairs doing review?"

Nichols looked completely defeated. "Texas says, why can't he go on the field."

Ben glanced over at Mimi. She was hunched forward, watching the warm-up show below them on the football field, determinedly *not* part of the officiating talk. *So much for her input.*

Ben dug out his phone. "What's the number for your guy in Texas?"

In less than a minute, Ben had two Texas people on a conference call. "We are trying," he said, "to keep this man safe and to catch a man who has already killed four of your officials. You get that don't you? As I speak, we have Matt Redweather set up in a secure room, ready to do the play review on this game. Just like your man agreed to yesterday. Stadium security is set up, the local police are set up. And now, do I understand you're saying we can't do that? Has it slipped your mind that there's already been an attempt on Matt's life? His kids were there, too, did you know that? All three of them could be dead."

The Texas guys both started talking.

"I don't give a damn about your protocol," Ben said. "You people asked me to help you out, you asked me to keep these threats quiet and keep the media out of it, and now—" He scrubbed a finger across his upper lip.

Do not swear, do not name call.

"Tell you what," he interrupted another garbled, two-man response. "I'm scheduled to sit down for a network-wide interview on ESPN this afternoon. Either you're gonna agree right now that we work this out here in California the best way we can, or I'm gonna give ESPN the biggest story they've had all week. Do I make myself clear?"

Silence. And more silence.

"I figure, after due consideration, you're saying we should go for it the best way we can. Right? Because I'm hanging up now."

Nichols hovered by the door: wide-eyed, his mouth half open. Finally, he blinked. "Wow."

"To be safe," Ben said, "How about you make sure the play review crew in San Francisco is set to handle the game. I'll handle things with Mr. Redweather."

Mimi took out her ear buds. "I heard that," she said and suppressed a smirk.

"Be right back." He patted her shoulder and took off.

He headed through the Pacifica Club, out the guests-only door to the cavernous main concourse that ran almost the whole way around the stadium. From the concourse, he bolted up the stairs and through the key code door to the temporary review box they'd established on the coach's floor—a room so small it could barely hold the stuff Redweather needed to do his job.

Redweather was hovering over the shoulder of the techie who had set up the monitors that Redweather would use to review specific plays.

"Good to go," the techie said, squeezed past Ben, and stepped into the hallway.

Redweather glanced over at Ben. "What's going on? I heard there was a hang-up?"

Ben shot him a grin. For sure, the guy was way too stressed to be officiating anywhere. So maybe it was good to have San Francisco handle things today.

"Ready for one last practice session?" Ben said.

Redweather looked like a thousand-pound weight had shifted off his shoulders. "Seriously? Just practice? It's not all on me?"

"This time, yeah," Ben said. "Call it a dress rehearsal. You okay with that?"

"Absolutely." Redweather unfurled himself from

264

his chair and offered a hand to Ben. "Thank you. Thank you for my boys, for…everything. We owe you."

"No problem." Ben stepped back to the door. "Just have a good game."

"You're coming back for me, though."

Ben stopped partway into the corridor. "I have to do a quick interview at the end of the game. But then I'll be up to get you. Remember to keep the door locked."

The door was almost closed, when, *Had Redweather said something?*

Ben pulled the door open enough to check. "What, you want a secret door knock?"

Obviously chagrined, Redweather said no. But he nodded yes.

Ben gave a rat-a-tat-tat on the doorframe. "That work?"

Chapter 39

The third-floor concourse of Oceana Park Stadium echoed with a mish-mash of crowd noise, ESPN's pre-game sports broadcast, and the home team marching band's rah-rah version of "Louie, Louie." The few people who hadn't already headed to their seats were focused on grabbing a last plate of nachos and beer.

Beeker stepped behind a concourse food cart just in time for Ben Leit to step through that *no entry* door and disappear down the stairs.

As the national anthem dropped away, the entire building began trembling, the air rumbling louder and louder. The hairs on Beeker's arms stood away from his skin. Finally, the deafening sound shifted off, farther and farther away, to nothing.

You're right Deek. Not an earthquake. Why hadn't he thought? It was a fly-over. The Blue Angels or somebody like. Which meant if it was like Ohio State, in another five minutes, the game would be off and running and Redweather's attention wouldn't be on that door.

Beeker's heartbeat slowed and he took a long and careful look around. The only action on his end of the concourse was a drunk fan ranting away at a security guard.

That fan was gonna get himself thrown out of the game before it even started. Now wouldn't that be a shame—security on this end of the stadium, tied up showing Bubba Butt the door?

Beeker managed to ditch his raincoat in a waste can. He slid his hand down, inside his lab coat pocket. And there they were: three cool little cylinders. He palpated the plungers and stroked the familiar hairline seams in the plastic. *Show time.*

He shifted his medical badge to outside his lab jacket and headed for the keypad beside the door that would get him into the area where Ben Leit had stashed Matt Redweather.

Beeker fingered in the passcode, and heard what had to be the security guard.

"Scuse me, sir. You at the door. Scuse me!"

Beeker's entire nervous system did a reset. He pasted on a determined expression and turned to look. The guard had his hands on the fat drunk, but he was a hundred percent focused on Beeker. Beeker lifted his medical badge away from his chest and held it up. "Medical emergency," he said—curt, preoccupied, a true professional.

The guard's attitude evaporated. "Sorry, Doctor. You need help?"

Beeker turned back to the keypad. "A crew's already coming up the other way."

He entered the number code again and this time, as he pressed the last button, he heard the door click open. He stepped into the hallway and stopped just outside Redweather's room.

He closed the concourse door behind him, made sure it had locked, then scanned the empty hallway of the coaches' wing. He found the little rubber gizmo he'd spotted on his walk-through and wedged it under the door to the concourse. Then, quietly as he could, he tapped it with the toe of his shoe, forcing it tight, tighter.

Punch that keypad all you want, pal. That lock may give way, but that door ain't opening.

Satisfied he would not be interrupted, Beeker fingered a syringe out of his pocket. He slipped the cap off the needle, lightly pressed the plunger, and the first drop of his anesthetic glistened at the tip.

Ready? Absolutely.

He delivered Ben Leit's secret knock and waited.

Chapter 40

The last of the day's overcast burned away and Oceana Park Stadium gleamed under a wide blue California sky.

After the usual pre-game rock serenade, after the introduction of the Mayor of Los Angeles, a U.S. Senator, and the weekly winner of the Make-A-Wish Foundation, fifty shiny gold trumpets, fifty trombones, nearly a hundred drummers, an Oscar-winning actress, a men's chorus and the voices of 80,000 fans joined together to present, for its world premiere, a new and improved version of The Star-Spangled Banner.

As the last piercing notes of the anthem faded, fireworks exploded at the south end of the field behind the stadium's enormous American flag. Then, the ending everyone waited for: a squad of Blue Angels made an ear-splitting low pass over the stadium, turned skyward in a balletic path, and headed up and off over Los Angeles.

Ben slid into the seat beside Mimi.

"Okay?" she said.

Meaning he should relax. She was probably right, he should. He'd been telling her, and in a way telling himself, that once they got Redweather set up, once the local police and stadium security was in place, he could step back.

Only he couldn't.

For a moment, she studied his face. Then she scooted forward and without comment concentrated on the coin toss.

Before this officiating thing, anytime she leaned in with her elbows on her knees and focused like that, his heart lifted. But seeing her do it here, his heart went skidding on down to the pit of his stomach.

He abandoned his seat and squatted in front of her. "It's no good leaving him up there alone. You stay here. If I'm not back by the end of the first quarter, call Security."

Her eyes shot with fear, but he wasn't gonna discuss it. He booked it for the stairwell, took the steps two by two, and paused a second at the end of the concourse. Where the hell was Security? Redweather was working on the other side of that wall. Security was supposed to be by that door.

He stepped up to the keypad, entered the code, the lock clicked, and the door gave maybe a quarter-inch. Then nothing. Nothing? Jammed. *Jesus!* He put all he had into ramming the door with his shoulder and felt the security officer come up behind him. "Sorry sir. Authorized people—oh, Mr. Leit?"

"The killer's blocked the door," Ben said. "We need everybody here. Now."

Out came his phone, and the security officer went full tilt sending out the alert.

Meantime, Ben kept working at the door and it moved maybe another quarter of an inch. He was wasting time. "How do I get over there?" he yelled.

The guard shifted the two-way radio away from his face. "One flight down. Same door, same code."

Ben plunged down the staircase, shouting, "Not just

security. Send the police."

On the floor below, Ben punched in the entry code and dived into a darkened hallway. One second and a motion sensor turned the lights on. He spotted the stairway he figured led up to where Redweather was. He powered his way up to the third level and booked it back to the little office.

Talking. A man's voice, tight and higher pitched than Redweather's. It kept going louder then quieter, so Ben couldn't hear. He pressed his head against the door and got, "Did you pay any attention—" ... "—Arizona game, don't tell me—" ... "—hit that kid delivered. Straight—" ... "—dead or dying—" ... "—no penalty call—"

He wheeled around, staring. A weapon, a chair would work, even a wastebasket, anything to deflect a needle coming at him. Heart hammering, he raced from one office door to another: locked, locked.

But he'd seen a fire extinguisher, hadn't he?

In the stairwell. He thundered down to the stairwell landing, smashed the glass front open, and pried the cannister loose.

Back at Redweather's door, all he could hear was his own breathing. He primed the extinguisher, jerked open the door and aimed the icy spray into the middle of the room.

Beacham wheeled around, staring at him: his eyes wide, his mouth open, the needle flashing in his right hand. He charged straight at Ben, blindly slashing into the cold foamy spray.

Ben used the extinguisher like a shield and the canister caught the blow from the needle—a gritty skyttle sound against the metal. The needle slid away, and before Beacham could strike again, Ben swept the heavy cylinder up in an arc, aiming for the jaw.

Beacham went down like a stop sign on the wrong end of a car wreck. And Ben got his first look at the man they'd been chasing.

Beacham was wearing a medical coat. The fire extinguisher had smashed his jaw—the side of his face caved in, pieces of broken teeth, bone, and blood all over. Either he was out cold or...

Ben kicked the needle into a corner and shook off the thought he'd killed the man. "Hang on, Matt," he said, "I gotta do this first."

He used a bunch of electronics cords to hog-tie Beacham, then patted him down. He found two more syringes, picked up the one he'd kicked away and stashed all three in a cup next to the TV monitors.

His heart was still hammering. He dragged out his phone and fired off the crisis code.

Redweather... Had he blinked? Yes? No. But he was breathing.

"The ambulance is coming Matt, just hold on."

Redweather's face had marks where tears had been, and he had this unfocused stare going.

Ben squatted, so the two of them were nearly nose to nose. "Matt? It's over. We got him. You hang on. The ambulance is coming. We'll get you to a hospital."

Beacham moaned and the sound made Ben look. But clearly there was nothing more to be done on that score until the cops got there. The man had killed four officials and they'd stopped him.

Weird thing was, except for the blood and the wrecked jaw, Winslow Beacham looked like the most ordinary, middle-aged man he'd ever seen and forgotten.

Chapter 41

By the time he caught up with Mimi at the hospital cafe, he felt like he'd played a full game of football, had jogged five miles, and then a bus had run over him. She was still bright-eyed, her skin was glowing, and it looked like she was ready for another twelve hours' excitement.

"You got him," she said. "You scared the daylights out of me, but you did it."

"*We* did it," he said. "And I'm sorry. I didn't want to worry you. But I…you know."

"You okay now?" she said.

"Sorry it took so long to wrap things up with the cops. Any word on Matt Redweather?"

The ragged sound of chairs scraping across the floor ripped through his head. When he looked, a trio of hospital workers were getting ready to leave.

"I got hold of a nurse at ER and told her what we knew about the drug. The hospital's on top of how to treat it. Now we just wait. What about Beacham?"

"Police have him," he said. "But he's probably in the hospital."

He looked away at some people filing into the hot food area. The last thing he wanted was to tell her he'd nearly killed Beacham.

Mimi leaned closer. "You think he's crazy?"

"Cleveland thinks so," he said.

"Cleveland?"

He licked his lip. "The Cleveland P.D. is saying Beacham told his neighbors that his brother was living there."

"I didn't—"

"The police checked it out. There's no sign of anybody living in that house but Beacham." Ben leaned back against the flimsy chair. "Crazy or not, I think Winslow Beacham or John Sloane—whatever you want to call him—I think he's a victim too."

She scooted forward and leaned her elbows on the table.

For a long time, he just sat there, looking at her sweet face. They were done here. And it was time.

He wanted to think she'd go for his idea in a heartbeat, but what if she didn't? He cleared his throat and said, "What if we could do something about it?"

Her face was so serious. "Whadya mean? If you're thinking about CTE, about helping those guys, isn't there already help?"

"There's help for players when they leave the NFL," he said. "But there's nothing for their families. And I don't know of anybody following up on guys that leave football after college. By that time, they're self-medicating or violent—"

"Or both," she said.

"Exactly. Or both," he said. "By that time, it's too late. I get it, nobody knew about CTE when Beacham's family had to deal with it. But I keep thinking, what if somebody had intervened? What if that family had somebody they could trust that could have helped them with Deek? If they'd known the signs of trouble, maybe that mall shooting would never have happened. Maybe Beacham wouldn't have—"

"Okay. It would've made a real difference," she said. "But you're not saying… I'm sorry. What's your idea? Tell me."

He took a breath. "We've talked before about what I was gonna do with myself. I think what I'd like to do is put together something to help families like the Sloanes."

"At risk because of CTE," she said.

He nodded, and she said, "Not criticizing, but how would you find them?"

"I think we work that out," he said. "We put together a team. Coaches, doctors, maybe we partner with Boston Med, they sure know me. I know I could sell this idea to politicians and sports honchos, law enforcement…well, whoever. If we put it together right, we can build a network. Think what a difference something like that would've made to Beacham's family."

She leaned back in her chair, and for what seemed like hours, she looked at him with those chocolate-colored eyes. Was she going to say anything?

Finally, he went on with his idea. "Would it be enough for you? It doesn't have much to do with pure math." He flashed his best grin at her. "But you keep saying you want to do something good. I think this definitely is doing good. So, seriously, what do you think? You in?"

When the smile finally broke across her face, he stood and turned his back to her for a second. He dug the little packet out of the front pocket of his jeans. As he unfolded the paper, the main diamond caught the café's overhead light and shattered it onto his shirt.

When he turned back, people in the café were watching them. Didn't matter.

"Maybe we could seal the deal," he said and went

down on his knee. Her hand moved up and clamped across her mouth.

"You were right, before," he said. "I didn't do a very good job at this. I hope this time, I do a little better. Okay? I love you, Buddy. I love your courage, and kindness, and intelligence. I love the way you work to live the best life you can. I love that you want *us* to do good for people. I can't imagine I'll be much use to anybody if we're not together. Please. Marry me?"

His heart was going like a jackhammer and his left knee was going numb.

Her hand drifted away from her face; she had a wicked smile going, which she let drop away. "I know it's old-fashioned," she said, "but…is there a ring?"

He stood and held it out to her. "It was my mother's. We'll need to have it sized, I'm sure. Or if you would rather—"

"Oh. It's perfect," she said. "Perfect."

A word about the author…

Barbara fell in love with football watching games with her father. Her love of poetry and theatre came later. She wrote the book and lyrics to the musical comedy The Lady's Game, and subsequently spent several years acting and working as a producer/director. To support her theatre life, she worked in law. During those "legal" years (where she did both technical writing and designed and built databases to support complex litigation), she began writing poetry. She published numerous poems in literary journals, as well as one book of poetry, Millennial Spring. *Trap Play*, her first suspense novel, was published by Wild Rose Press in 2020. *Revenge Hit* is her second suspense novel in the Ben Leit series.

http://www.bdaviskroon.com

Thank you for purchasing
this publication of The Wild Rose Press, Inc.

Other Wild Rose Press Titles by B. Davis Kroon

Trap Play
(Book One, the Ben Leit Series)

For questions or more information
contact us at
info@thewildrosepress.com.

The Wild Rose Press, Inc.
www.thewildrosepress.com

www.ingramcontent.com/pod-product-compliance
Lightning Source LLC
Chambersburg PA
CBHW050450070726
47506CB00018B/539

* 9 7 8 1 5 0 9 2 4 9 5 6 5 *